The Chosen

Relics Series, Volume 3

K. A. Moore

Published by K. A. Moore, 2024.

This is a work of fiction. Names, characters, businesses, places, events, locales, and incidents are either the products of the author's imagination or used in a fictitious manner. Any resemblance to actual persons, living or dead, or actual events is purely coincidental.

Book cover design by Betibup33 design

Edited by Ginny and Judith at bookhelpline

ISBN 9781957223063 (ebook)

ISBN 9781957223155 (paperback)

Also by K. A. Moore

Relics Series

Relics

The Key

The Chosen

Standalone

Watching Her Sleep

Sentinel

Weeping Widow's Heirloom

One

Clint had been gone for three days.

A rumble vibrated through the floor under Casey. She picked herself up and brushed off her hands. Her knees ached after being on them for days, her hands clasped tight enough in desperation to make her fingertips white. Her anguish was more than she could handle. Her legs wobbled as she took her first steps in hours. Casey thought back to when Clint first went through the sphere, leaving her destitute. Her prayers still echoed in her mind.

She had to call someone. To tell Chloe what happened.

She swept everything on top of the desk to the side. Where was the phone? She checked each object on the surface she moved, making sure she didn't miss anything, looking for the lifeline to help her contact her friend. She almost yanked the drawers completely out of their slots as she ransacked the insides.

"No, no no no." Casey ran upstairs. "This is not happening right now."

By the time she was done going through her room, it looked like a tornado struck. She even ripped the comforter off the bed. The phone was nowhere to be seen. Clint's room was next. It didn't fare any better than hers by the time she finished.

She skipped several steps as she bounded down to the kitchen. The phone wasn't there. The last time she remembered seeing it was in the office. Clint palmed it, saying he needed to make a call later that morning after he got up for the day and slid it into the back pocket of his jeans when the sphere came back to life.

"Oh no. The phone was on Clint when he went through the shimmer." Casey collapsed in the chair.

She was truly alone. No one to help her and no way to call anyone for backup. It would only be a matter of time before the Monarchs came after her again and she would have to take them on with simply the relics as her support and hope they hadn't come up with better sedatives to disable her powers.

"God, I can't do this," Casey cried out.

She got up long enough to eat something, and then she was back seeking God's advice on what to do. The sphere was in tattered ruins after Clint transported back for Ben and Amanda.

At least the shield was intact, so the house was still in one piece.

She staggered to the back door and yanked on the handle so hard, it surprised her the door still hung on its hinges.

Several Monarchs populated the fields on several sides of the shield. Tents were set up and several fires dotted the scene as they grilled meat over the flames. Dirt and grime discolored their clothes to the point you couldn't tell the true color of the material. Greasy, unwashed hair hung limply from their scalps.

If only the coming winter would deter them from pursuing her. Imagining a foot of snow blanketing the landscape gave her hope that they wouldn't be stubborn enough to camp out in the glacial temps and go home.

They started to trickle in two days ago. More than there were yesterday, at least fifty by her guess; they waved their arms in the air to catch her attention.

Not in the mood to deal with them, she made the shield opaque and marched back toward the house. Casey checked to see if anything was added to the parchment to let her know why the shield hadn't retracted. She was the key of the chosen four. It was their legacy to fight in God's armies and help protect His followers and fight for the ones who couldn't fight for themselves. Her ability to activate the healing relic unlocking the other three cemented her place as one of the chosen. One of, shouldn't that mean there should be more? She shook her head coming back to the problem at hand.

She didn't get overheated from its use. Not wanting to jinx herself, she tried to keep her mind from wandering to when she used the shield before and how her core temperature would skyrocket. Another thunderous rumble shook the ground. She turned toward the men on the far side of the shield past the barn and focused the shield to translucent. There was a crater in the ground about the size of a car. She almost chuckled that they thought they would be able to blow a hole deep enough to tunnel under.

The ground shook again as another explosion ripped through the air behind her. She whirled to look at a bigger crater. When did more Monarchs join the party on this side?

Monarchs stood several deep outside the shield while mantises skittered across the dome. Their metal barbed legs clicked along the surface while their shiny eyes followed her every movement.

This time, arcs of electricity crawled up the shield, making their way to the top. What did they detonate to affect her protective bubble? The shield flickered and dimmed.

"You have got to be kidding!" Casey gulped in a large breath as her eyes widened when it blinked again.

She wasn't strong enough to fend off the Monarchs. Twenty or thirty men glared at her. Her hand sizzled and electric shocks tingled up and down her arm with the colors of Clint's weapon and Ben's weaponized ring. Red and yellow lights danced, illuminating the symbols.

Her eyes met who she thought may be the leader since he stood back from the main group in an expensive, custom-tailored suit. He pulled at the cuffs of the shirt, straightening them out. The smirk on his face would haunt her dreams. The shield flickered and shrank several feet. Chills swept over her body; palpitations fluttered through her heart. Casey concentrated on solidifying the shield to its former strength. The man cocked his head and jutted out his chin. The shield collapsed, launching dust and grass in the air, to be blown away in the humid breeze, marking a perfect ring in the soil where the shield had once been.

Men raced forward; their guns trained on her. The first bullet tore through her shoulder when a second whizzed past, and she swore she felt the wind from it as it zipped past her ear. That was too close for comfort.

Casey's legs trembled and not because she lay on the floor for countless hours. This level of fear she never dealt with before. "Father." She cast up her hands sending the shield into place, ignoring the pain rippling through her arm, locking the Monarchs out. They emptied full clips into the mass without denting it.

If she couldn't keep the shield up, she was as good as dead.

She couldn't believe so many had accumulated along the exterior. How long had it taken them to draft so many for their cause? Those gathered overnight were about the size of a small squadron; more ran up over the hill they'd hid behind, adding to the Monarchs total. The twenty or so she numbered before paled in comparison to now. She couldn't count them all.

Another blast at the back of the house made her flinch. On the far side, the Monarchs held up a device and smiled at her, some had the audacity to wave.

A large mantis stood on the other side of the shield next to the Monarchs. Its beady red eyes tracked her like the smaller ones, but this one was different. It tilted its head to the side like humans do as it studied her.

"Casey? If you surrender, we won't harm you. You can help us purge this filth from the face of the planet." A man's voice sounded off in the shadows to the right. The man in the suit.

"Help you? You say you won't harm me yet your men shot me." Casey snorted. "You murder people, my friend, the man that I loved. So why on earth would I ever help you? There's not a single reason in this entire world why I'd ever help you."

Casey stitched the torn flesh from the bullet, blue flooding her vision.

"They were nothing but a scourge and must be done away with."

"Scourge?" Casey narrowed her eyes. "You mean believers?"

He smiled. "If that's what they call themselves."

"They are human beings who choose to believe in one true God. Just because you don't believe in Jesus and God the Father doesn't mean He doesn't exist."

"Imagine the wealth at your disposal if you come over to our side." He had to be crazy if he thought wealth in this world was worth selling her soul for.

"It's not worth giving up what waits for me in Heaven. You do realize you can't take it with you when you die." Casey wasted her words.

"That has yet to be seen if you believe anything exists after death. Your choice, but this may sting a little." The man raised his hand; she noticed he held a flat disc in his palm like the other one. Several Monarchs, evenly spaced around the shield, also held up their hands. They carried the same round devices.

As they placed the objects against the shield, electric impulses flashed through her mind. A charge equivalent to what she imagined a Taser would feel like zapped her entire body. A scream lodged in her throat as the shield dissolved.

Bullets ripped into her torso. The impact stole her breath. Casey curled onto her side and tried to make herself as small as possible.

Symbols along her skin glowed blue instead of the normal amber color as before when they first etched themselves into her. She raised her palm to defend herself.

A pistol discharged as her shoulder knit itself back together after a bullet tore through the muscles that attached her arm to her body.

Five men collapsed while another two tripped over the bodies in front of them. Another bullet lodged in her back as she rolled, sending a wave in their direction. They were coming from both sides.

Casey cried out as a slug pierced her thigh. They were hitting her faster than she healed. If she took too much more, she'd pass out before she eradicated them. She flung a wave with her left hand to the group behind her as she rose and hurled a pulse to a second set of Monarchs on the right.

Men screamed as their bodies came in contact with the relics' powers before silencing them for good. In a few short moments, it quieted as she took in the carnage. Her hands shook from an adrenaline dump. Her body ached. She would have to see the aftermath but marked at least six impacts from bullets, if her count of blood seeping through holes in her clothes was correct.

Her knees banged against the ground when she tried to stand. She sunk to the dry, cracked earth where sprouts of grass tried to grow, but because of the lasting effects of a hot dry summer, wouldn't be able to until the spring rains kicked in in several months.

A shadow fell over her. She missed someone!

"If you only listened to us, you wouldn't be in so much agony." The leader ran his finger down her cheek before grabbing her chin so tight she'd bruise.

Her healing ability went into overdrive as she tried to push the man away from her; he was a lot taller than her. It was hard to tell for sure while laying down. He sported dark, slicked-back hair, while his gray eyes seemed to shimmer like the mantises.

"Ah, you saw my eyes change, didn't you? See, since you go through our men so easily because the human body is so fragile and easily prone to fail, they decided to create me. If they built a man like my little pets here, it'd be harder to destroy. I can finally finish the work the leader has requested of me." His teeth were obscenely white behind his crooked-lipped smile.

"You're not human?" Casey realized why his hands were so cold and unforgiving when he gripped her face.

"No, I am not, my dear. My programming is to make sure you survive today to be broken down for our leader and teach you that you can't go into battle against us." He sat next to her, his motions fluid as if he poured himself into the seated position. He wasn't wearing a suit at all, but it was part of him being a machine, the sun glinting off the microfibers of the smallest components she had ever seen making up the fabric of his armor.

Casey gritted her teeth as another hole closed. A tremor ran through her body.

He probed with his finger the injury to her shoulder, making her cry out. "This is interesting. I don't understand this word pain. You humans have so many flaws."

"You speak as if you can think on your own. Computer components are unable to think or be inclined to have feelings or believe something is *interesting*, so how do you do that?" Casey tried to tug her legs up, but the bullet, yet to be expelled from her thigh, kept her from doing so. Ribbons of spasms through her damaged muscles would make a Charlie horse seem insignificant in comparison. Biting the inside of her cheek was the only thing keeping her screams silent.

"You are from the past, yes?" his synthetic voice asked.

Casey refused to answer, not sure what information they'd been able to gather about her, and she didn't want to give them more ammunition than they already had.

"Ah, not going to answer me? This does not matter. Emotional responses are easy enough to write into my synapses and I can mimic what movements the body makes to blend into any environment. It does not mean I actually feel or empathize with a human. I am made to complete my mission and cannot be swayed one way or the other. I follow my programming. Does this make sense to you?" If he hadn't explained he mimicked body responses to appear more human, she would believe he genuinely cared whether she understood him from watching his facial expressions.

She nodded and knew she would have to melt this machine like the mantises. If she could keep him from realizing she healed, maybe she could take a moment and think through how to retreat long enough to see if her weapons still functioned or if they were made inert like the shield.

"Your pulse is back to normal. You are good to travel, yes?" His eyes glowed.

"No. I'm not." The familiar tingles in Casey's hands as she flexed her fingers called to Ben and Clint's weapons.

The machine gripped her by the arm. She was on her feet before she gave the smallest bit of resistance. She didn't think it was possible how he smoothly moved the way he did. Shouldn't artificial life have jerky movements, not this fluid ability?

"Burn it down!" he bellowed.

Two men stepped forward from the back of the squadron that lay in shambles, aiming large weapons at the house. She thought they were the same as the rocket launchers they used on them when they were at the motel, six or so months ago, but wasn't sure. It's not like she was well-versed on what every firearm, launcher, or bomb could do. The shield repelled them last time. The searing heat would be imprinted on her mind forever.

"No!" Casey yanked on her arm, but the android held on without causing her any discomfort. His fingers locked in an unforgiving manacle, so they circled her arm but didn't squeeze.

Clint's uncle's house headed to becoming a box of tinder, and there was nothing to stop it if she couldn't deflect their weapons. Prickling in the tips of her fingers was a welcome feeling. She screamed as she put up her hand, and yellow and red mixed together, forming a pulse around herself that shoved the Monarchs back as it electrified the shield covering her and the house as it sprang forth.

The Monarchs weren't fast enough. The rockets were no match to the relics' powers. Mantises fell one by one to the side as their electronic systems melted. The android looked at her as the yellow static seemed to rush to him, liquifying his hand around her arm and sending him back with the men outside the shield.

The last two ran as their mighty synthetic commander fell by the side, soon only a puddle of melted alloy.

Casey took in the destruction of the creatures and their attempts at creating a man. Her eyes drifted down, taking in her appearance. Blood drenched her clothes.

Nothing to do now except let her body heal and rest.

"Father, please give me rest on all sides for a few hours." Her eyelids began to droop as if weighing a ton.

She stumbled on her feet and up the steps to the house. She only made it to the couch before she sagged down and rested her head on the arm of the sofa. She checked the placement of the shield before her lips parted and her breaths evened out. She slipped into a deep slumber.

By the time she woke and showered, a light rainstorm blew in and the pitter-patter of raindrops sounded against the thin, single-paned glass windows. The shield let in the moisture to water the earth. Her stomach rumbled throughout her shower. She made a quick lunch since she slept through the morning and went out to the covered wrap-a-round porch.

How long did she have before the Monarchs came back? Did they have more machines that mimicked man? Casey longed to connect with another human being so she wouldn't be the sole survivor of their group. First Amanda, then Ben—the man she loved more than life itself—and lastly there was Clint. He hadn't died but she lost him all the same the day he went through the shield for Ben and Amanda, to reunite the four chosen ones.

"You are not alone. I am with you always."

"But Father, I'm not strong enough to take this on by myself."

"Child, did you not hear me? You are not alone. My Spirit is in your heart; all you have to do is open your ears to hear, open your eyes to see, and open your mind to do my commandments. I will provide everything you need."

"Thank you, Father. Please give me the wisdom to know what you need me to do, and I'll do it with love in my heart." Casey let the tears fall. For now, she grieved for the friends she'd grown to love but didn't count it as a loss since they were in Heaven, waiting for her when she joined them. From when they had been in the warehouse to now had been over two years. Her life was inexplicably changed forever when Ben kidnapped her, brought her to the future, and marked her place in the prophecy when she released the healing relic from its prison in the black rock. Now her place had been permanently etched as one of the chosen ones to battle evil bent on destruction of believers all over the world.

Clint was well aware of where she lived. Why hadn't they come to join her unless they were gone? Tracking through normal time, they should at least have shown up by now.

An hour later, she dried her face, hauled herself to her feet, and squared her shoulders. She allowed herself a moment of weakness to purge all of her grief and fear so she could move forward with her new life and a clean slate. Like the food she ate earlier nourished her body, now she would nourish her mind and heart in God's word.

She read Clint's family Bible, spread out in front of her on the desk in the den, while she figured out her next move. She nodded off as she read, her mind at peace for the time being. The shield stood as a vigilant sentry, keeping its watch over her world that endured through her solitary existence.

The setting sun took the light from the earth as it lowered into a dark burnt orange before it dipped below the horizon. Taunting everything of its ability to prevail and rise again, no matter what happened below on the barren wasteland of earth. Humans were so bent on destruction that they were forgetting if they destroyed everything on the planet, they would die with no resources and aid from fellow man.

Oh, to go back and tell your younger self what to expect and how to avoid it. Wishes were a child's dream when it came to real life, and how naive she had been when she started into adulthood. If she possessed the capability to go back and tell herself everything she witnessed, she hoped she'd believe herself.

Look how long it took for her to believe in time travel's existence after Ben brought her to the future. Evil was more than stories and silly tales about monsters under kids' beds that parents told to con their offspring into behaving so the creatures wouldn't pull them under the bed while they slept.

Two

A shrill whistle startled Casey as she rinsed off the last dinner plate. She hadn't been able to sleep so she'd gotten up in the middle of the night to wash the pathetic pile of leftover dishes from her last meal.

She made her way with a hand on the faded chair rail, guided by the moon shining in the windows, toward the front door. She didn't turn on a light, hoping to mask her movements in the house. As she edged the curtain to the side, a second loud whistle pierced the night, making her jump. Her hand flew to her chest as she tried to slow her breathing.

A rush of air left her lungs; they were burning before she reminded herself to inhale again. She saw shadows moving behind large vehicles with their headlamps brightly lighting up the farmhouse she adored. The hieroglyphs glowed on her arms. The shapes were lit in an array of different levels of brightness. Her left arm repeated a pattern showing Clint's relic weapon, a necessity to thwart evil. Her right swirled with a mass of symbols illuminating Ben's after God changed the ring into a powerful instrument of its own.

Heartbeats too many to count thrummed out a steady rhythm from the Monarchs that permeated her head with her amplified hearing. She focused to see if she could read the situation before she charged outside. They all remained silent, their subdued show of force enough, for now.

"Oh, Miss Casey. If you would please join us." Goosebumps rose on her skin at the familiar voice that should not exist.

She couldn't ghost him, hoping he'd go away. So, she decided to meet them head-on since they developed the technology to reduce the shield to nothing if they wanted to. The fact they hadn't yet told her they were trying to lure her into a false sense of security. Clint would know what to do if he were here. He'd use all the stealthy moves he learned in his military training.

The only sound was the clomping from her boots hitting the boards on the front porch. The crickets seemed to have taken a break from the monotonous chirping of their nightly songs to see what conclusion she would come to.

"There she is. I told you men she's incapable of staying away. Anxious to see what proposition I have for her this time around. We are alike, her and I. Although I have to say, knowing how the last time we met ended, I wasn't too keen on rushing back out here." He spoke so politely, yet incapable of having any sort of humanity in his entire being.

Casey crossed her arms and widened her stance.

"So obstinate. A good quality to have, although I must say inadequate since you won't survive if you keep denying the leader what he wishes." He strolled across the grass, which had needed to be mowed several weeks ago.

The emerald green blades swayed in the wind as the tops bloomed full of seeds, ready to be released in the following spring to grow and join the rest of their brothers and sisters lining the twisting pathway from the drive down to and around the porch.

Casey held up her hand to stop him from getting any closer.

He obeyed and tucked his hands into his pockets. "My counterpart communicated with me before his untimely demise you were less than cooperative. The leader doesn't understand the draw of celebrating a God who would let you suffer through loss the way you have."

"He didn't do this to me. A bunch of terrorists did. They believe they should rule the world and are so full of themselves, they can't help but terrorize anyone who doesn't get in line with their rules and hierarchy. You are no better than a gang of grown-up school bullies." Casey couldn't believe she tried reasoning with a machine.

"The offer is still on the table if you want to rethink your stance. I think it's the least you owe me for killing my brother."

"He doesn't count as your brother, and you're incapable of knowing what the loss of family is about." Casey suffered loss on a deep, personal level.

His eyes flashed silver. "He was my brother and I felt what he did when you ended his life."

"So, you're linked through a server?" This type of technology, only a futuristic threat in movies back in her time, gave her a clueless hint about their capabilities.

"Server?" His eyes turned black, becoming a motionless statue.

"It's what several computers communicate with." Why was she trying to explain what she meant? She wanted to smack her hand against her forehead for her dumb move.

"Yes, server, an outdated system that hasn't been used in decades. This confirms our earlier intelligence that you are not from here. I had not heard of that term, but this server as you say is the brain linking all of us." He swept his arm wide to include all the mantises.

"So, you don't have individual thought processes but share one mind?" Casey didn't like that as soon as something happened, all of them knew about it instantly. How were people supposed to combat that system?

"We prefer to call it our soul."

Casey couldn't help the snort of laughter that escaped. "A soul is a single entity in each human life, and it implies you have feelings and are capable of reasoning on your own as individuals. You aren't a living breathing being, so you don't have a soul. God created people and they are the only living things on this planet with souls."

"Deny this so-called God as you call it, and join the winning side."

"I will never deny my God. To do so would be to blaspheme against everything I am and have faith in." Casey gritted her teeth.

"No one has ever seen this God so why do so many rely on Him?" he asked.

"That's why it's called faith." She stood taller.

"Now!" the android in front of her yelled.

She recoiled and put her hands up, strengthening the shield. Dozens of mantises rained down on her as they took flight from behind the line of Monarchs. She swiped to the left with her right hand and cleared away that side of the shield only for them to be replaced in seconds. Casey couldn't see anything, but the small spindly creatures dug into the shield by their legs.

Energy drawn from her fed the shield. Fast, erratic, unsteady beats fluttered in her chest as she realized it was draining her strength. It extracted the power from her; she didn't discharge it. Their eyes flickered from silver to red and then to yellow, the same colors as the relics' weapons she used as she tried to disperse them from her safety net. As soon as one group was immobilized, the next set took their place. An endless stream of them. The fields beyond them slithered—in the same movement a river flowed—with their kind. She couldn't keep track of how many she wiped away.

Ribbons of yellow and red static coursed from her to them as they siphoned everything from her. She couldn't stop the flow to the shield. They were drawing it from her without her permission. She tried to retract the relics, but pulses surged and flew out. Dark clouds roiled in the sky. Soon, streaks of lightning zigzagged through the air.

Churning in her chest spread through her arms and legs into her hands and feet. Pins and needles started at her fingertips and trickled through her limbs until her whole body hummed with a low, prickling sensation. She screamed out in frustration.

Casey sank onto the dew-laden ground. The red and yellow flowed up and down her arms, lighting up the veins and arteries from the inside. She watched as they became as fluid as her own blood, the power leaving her body through her fingers.

Her eyes glowed as her powers swirled around her faster and faster until they were a blur. Heart racing, her anger took over and she let it build until it filled every inch of the shield on the inside. Rumbling thunder sounded continuously.

Casey shook her head and extended the shield. It expanded to the distance of the farthest field, taking with it the creatures and the men who she heard screaming as they were tossed aside. The more she projected the shield, the more intense her pain became.

The shield increased as more creatures appeared and covered its surface. Her heart slowed down as yellow and red flecks of static coursed over her before it abandoned her and passed to the power-hungry insects as they devoured everything. They vibrated, beating their wings as they held on, gorging themselves with the pent-up energy surging through their circuits. She hoped they choked on it.

The cyborg watched her, smiling, as though it were proud of its children tearing the relics from her a little at a time. He placed his hand on the shield and filtered some of the force through his body. His chest expanded as he grew taller; his shoulders broadened. She couldn't fight like this. They would kill her before they got the shield down. Was this how they would get their greedy hands on the relics? Before, they hadn't dared to kill her or lose the relics' powers along with her life. It looked like they'd come up with an alternative solution of seeing if it passed down through her offspring as they suggested before when she, Ben, and Clint were captured and tortured by the Monarchs.

"Delicious." He licked his lips, smacking them together. His voice broke through her amplified hearing. His eyes glowed a faintly familiar blue of the healing relic before switching to coal voids devouring the light.

He tapped into the relics' powers from the insects, storing them inside him. Could the Monarchs extract everything from her and toss her aside like an empty husk? Her life slipped more and more with each minute of energy draining from her life force.

She couldn't keep doing this. She covered her eyes with her clasped fists. "Father, I'm not strong enough."

Gusts of wind blew through the trees as rumbling grew louder. Lightning crisscrossed overhead before slamming down into the shield. Energy poured through her, amping up her powers and regenerating her depleted levels.

The shield flew out farther than before, carrying away in a mass of multicolored static pulses not only bugs, but also the men as it pushed past the boundaries and shoved against the ground like a bulldozer, clearing away everything in its path except nature.

She didn't know what happened, but the deafening quiet rocked her. She couldn't see the outline of the shield. How far did it travel? Were any innocents lost in the surge of power she expended?

Casey wouldn't be able to live with herself if she killed families.

"Rest, my darling daughter. I am proud of you. I am not yet done writing your story; there is still more to come. Rest now. You will know when it is time."

"Time? For what?" Casey waited for an answer.

And waited.

When dawn started to soften the darkness from the edges of the fields, she knew she wouldn't get any further information.

Casey tried to drag the shield to her. She didn't feel it. She held her palms up and willed the relics to do something. Anything. The weapon, the last relic she absorbed when Clint went through the sphere, didn't respond to her. They were disconnected from her consciousness.

A cold shiver worked its way down her spine, depositing goosebumps all over her skin. Did she exterminate every living being? No breeze blew to stir the air. Calmness blanketed the earth.

She scanned the horizon before she heard it. She closed her eyes and said a prayer of thanks.

Casey smiled as she secured the door behind her. Birds chirped as the sun warmed the horizon. The shield hadn't exterminated all life on the planet. Soon enough she would rise again from some crucial sleep. Her mind tackled what may have taken place while she tried to defend herself and believers from total annihilation. Her legs were stiff and her muscles taut, but she felt her life stores full again after the mantises drained so much from her.

She fell back on the bed without removing her boots, already asleep before her head sank into the soft cushion of the mattress beneath her cradling her whole body.

Sometime later, she rolled out of bed and realized she slept longer than she planned to. The sun peeked on the horizon, through the slats of the blinds, not all the way fastened, dawning a new day. How many days passed her by?

Casey flexed her fingers and couldn't feel the familiar power of the relics. She was defenseless for when the Monarchs charged her way again. Piqued by how many she wiped out, including their little toys. What type of retribution would they seek against her for her actions? It wouldn't be long before they admitted she was a bigger threat and stopped trying to steal her powers or capture her. Would they simply kill her like they did Ben? Off from a distance, taking out their prey with no thought about the life they ended, as long as it remained part of their agenda?

Her first course of action was to take stock of any injuries and see what the rest of the world looked like. She cataloged everything she needed for the coming season. Without having a phone to schedule food pick-ups, would they have someone check on her when Clint didn't arrange another trip? Did they know Clint was no longer in this time? She hadn't gone on the one and only pick-up Clint took before he...nope, not going to go there again.

Animals announced their existence with their morning calls, breaking the stillness in the atmosphere. The tops of the trees rustled with the gentle wind, but she felt nothing around her. She expected to see some sort of debris left behind from the events of the other day. It appeared as if the Monarchs were never there. She closed her eyes and tilted up her face to meet the sun's warmth. There was nothing else for her to do so she headed in to figure out her future.

Casey pulled down Clint's aunt's books for homesteading and living off the grid. Time to move ahead and make a life for herself here. She turned on the radio to check for any news broadcast, but silence met her. She twisted the dial up and down the tuner, but there was no one, no signal, nothing.

The radio must have been affected by the shield. She rotated on her heels and marched through the back door out to the solar panels. She hadn't been on this side of the property before. They looked like a crazy science experiment. A large, welded steel cage encased the panels. The sun shone through the bars on the grid-like sections of glass. A lit display gave her a glaring green light. Green meant good, right?

She hadn't noticed anything not working in the house, but she'd slept for the past unknown number of days. She didn't have a calendar to check the date.

Casey spent the next few minutes running around flipping light switches. Everything functioned properly.

The horizon brightened as Casey sat in the chair and nibbled on the last store-bought breakfast bar. Maybe she should venture out and find some place with food. No, that wouldn't work. She couldn't pay for anything. She was in worse trouble than she thought. Some canned goods Clint stocked up on weren't the healthiest in the world, but eating canned peaches for breakfast for the next uncountable days was better than nothing.

Smoke billowed off in the distance. It looked to be several miles over the land to the east. She had to keep an eye on it. The last thing she needed was for a large wildfire to sweep through and scorch everything.

Stomping her way to the barn, Casey gawked at the bulky tractor. How did you get one of those large pieces started much less not mow down everything to plant crops?

She trudged past the corner to the gardening supplies. She smiled as she shook the dust off an overly floppy straw hat.

She settled it on her head. The brim overshadowed her face by several inches on all sides, slipping down and covering her eyes. Laughing, she took it off and tied a bandanna around her head. She then tried the hat again, and the loose feeling around the band disappeared. It fit snugly.

Several tools adorned the wall. She pulled down a hoe, rake, and shovel. Casey thought of the stacks of plant seeds she retrieved in the cellar Clint suggested they hide in when the tornado came. She didn't hold onto her optimism when she'd seen the expiration dates on the packets—at least ten years ago. The percentage rate of getting them to sprout lowered for every year they sat unused. If they germinated, she would be in luck.

The bucket she found quickly packed with her pilfered items. Seeds, trays with water pans under them, and vegetable markers to note what she planted where. She took her bounty in the house. Next, she mapped out the best location for the garden. Her grandparents had a small plot when she was a child, and she would help her Mamaw start the seeds for Papaw to plant when they were big enough. The books in the den helped direct her on how to prepare the land, becoming her nightly reading.

The midday sun was hot even though a cool breeze took it down a few degrees. Winter would be here before she knew it. Too late to try and germinate the seeds now, she'd wait until spring. Casey took a stake and hammered it into the ground to mark the start of the fields.

She counted off twenty paces, and the next stake went in. She turned and counted forty before she punched through the soil with the third marker. The final twenty gave her a nice size rectangle to start with.

The shovel cut through the ground as she broke up the luscious rich black soil. This was promising. By the time she finished, sweat dampened her clothes as if she had run a marathon. If she hadn't found the hat, she would have burned to a crisp.

The hoe easily tilled the soil she unearthed. Casey laughed as she took a bale hook and dragged straw to the dirt section she cordoned off. She used another bandanna and tied it around her nose and mouth as she broke open the mildewed and rotting straw. Despite her pink fabric mask, she still coughed and sneezed until she raked the offending bale into the ground.

Casey wiped her forehead with the back of her arm to keep the stinging sweat from dripping into her eyes. Imaginary crops popped up in her mind, and she pictured walking down the rows as they sprang to life with new growth.

The coming frigid temperatures would help break down the nutrients in the decomposing compost and help prepare for spring planting.

Casey perused the bookshelves and pulled out more with the promise of how to start providing for a family, and she stacked them in a pile.

She pulled the first one and sat sideways on the couch, her legs stretched out in front of her. The back of her thighs were sore from putting in a good day's work.

She glanced at the chair Clint sat in their first night, her sigh the only sound. The calls of the wild things didn't penetrate the walls. The radio against the wall mocked her to try it again.

The dial spun all the way to the end when she turned the knob. Slowly she scanned through to the other end. Still nothing but dead air. No static sounded through the antique speaker on the other side of the fabric secured behind an ornate design carved in the wood.

She'd try again another day. It wasn't like her social calendar was full with anything else to do besides trying to survive the coming chilly months.

Three

Casey let the ax fall again, hitting the wood at an odd angle, kicking the log off the stump but not splitting it. How did Clint make this look so easy? Drenched from head to toe from her attempts to stock up more firewood amounted to nothing but a failure of colossal proportions. Several inches of white fluffy flakes on the ground heralded in wintry weather. The freak blustery winds and snow pummeled the region, coating the fall foliage and turning it white.

She counted the days since Clint left, and by her calculations, there were still a couple of weeks before winter. Fifty-seven tally marks on a page now marked her time. Not knowing what month or even the day of the week it was left her feeling forlorn.

She bowed her head and prayed for God to help her figure this out and give her the strength to carry out providing for herself.

She stretched her neck from side to side. She hooted as she imagined herself spitting on her hands before gripping the handle again and taking her first swing like they did in old movies.

She put the chunk of wood back up on the stump and swung. The axe came down in a perfect arch, hitting the log and sending pieces flying to either side as it split in two. She whooped and did a small happy dance before throwing her head back and letting the sun warm her damp skin as she thanked her Heavenly Father for helping her yet again. Her cheeks would be chapped by the time she got through the small pile she tried to split.

Casey labored on creating a heap of firewood for several hours before her muscles were screaming at her. She forced herself to take a break. She added what she finished to the stack she and Clint cleaned up after the storm blew through when they first moved into his uncle's. Without any knowledge of how much wood to burn through to keep the house warm, she wanted to error on the side of caution and have more than enough rather than not enough firewood.

She put her hands on her hips and bent back to stretch out the taut muscles along her spine. She held her hand out over her eyes to shade them from the setting sun as it glared off the pristine snow. A blur of movement snagged her attention at the edge of the wooded area up in the trees. A large, black bird perched on the smallest of the highest branches. Something gripped in one of its taloned feet.

Casey recognized it as a raven; it watched her before taking flight. The flapping of the wings took it high before swooping down low enough that she ducked, thinking it wanted to peck her. She stumbled to the shelter of a tree. Wetness splattered against her ankles, that peeked out between her low socks and the bottom hem of her pants.

Her eyes widened in wonder as she took in the almost blood-red massacre.

Several overripe tomatoes clung to a vine; one burst open when they landed on the overgrown weeds under a tree sheltered from the fallen snow. A gurgling croak sounded above her before a half-eaten cucumber thumped against the ground next to the tomatoes. Her mouth watered at the thought of a huge salad. She wouldn't have all the unhealthy additives such as croutons, tortilla strips, sunflower seeds, fattening dressings, but even then it sounded wonderful.

She made fresh bread weekly for a few slices of toast in the mornings and beans or noodles for an evening meal, but her taste buds yearned for fresh foods grown on a vine. The flour reserves were dwindling; soon, even that tasty treat would be gone.

She ran as fast as her legs could carry her through the snow back toward her house to grab a bowl to put everything in. If she was correct, God used the ravens to feed her, like He did for Elijah during a famine.

A deep chuffing sound directed Casey to look to the skies. She knew that sound, a helicopter. When did the Monarchs nab themselves one of those? Already halfway back to the house, she skidded to a stop, her feet kicking up white flakes, and ran back for the tomatoes. She couldn't in good conscious leave the bounty God gave her behind to hide only to have some nefarious critters steal it or for the bright red to contrast with the snow as a beacon for whoever loomed on the horizon. The fragile skin of the produce wanted to burst as she nimbly plucked them up.

The back door thumped against the frame as she slammed the door. She darted around like a crazy woman, closing all the blinds and curtains. She didn't know what kind of technology the helicopter might be armed with to see inside.

Her pulse raced as the rotor wash grew louder. They were overhead.

"Father, please keep the enemy from me." She tried to sharpen her hearing, but the blades thrumming through the air were too loud to pick up the chatter in the cabin of the machine hovering over her.

She slipped up to the side of the front window. Her finger inched the fabric over. Not wanting an ambush, she made sure no one repelled out to rush inside. It banked a hard right and zoomed off.

On wobbly legs, she stayed still until she no longer heard anything.

Back at the kitchen door, she lifted the latch she'd flipped in place and took stock of the damage.

An ear of corn, clumps of garlic, and a potato with sprouted eyes and growing roots added to the donations to her being self-sufficient. She wanted to cry and could already taste the fried potatoes in the next year. She searched the skies and the tops of the trees, looking for her new pets, but they were nowhere to be found, scared off by the machinery. She placed everything in a large bowl she brought out with her for her additional bounty.

Hope sprung up at the thought of the seeds taking root and having fresh plants and vegetables. Winter would still be touch and go, but having fresh seeds to go with the old seed packets she salvaged from the cellar would go a long way.

Harvesting seeds was a new experience for her. She hadn't gone through the entire stack of books in the den about gardening yet. They were in the pile she intended to read through after she prepared the plot of land she wanted to use for growing produce. If they were no help, she'd wing it. How hard could it be; put a seed in the ground, and it grew, right?

The ravens pilfered the items from somewhere. The rationing wouldn't look so bleak if she added to her storehouse. She slipped on her gardening pouch she had the privilege of finding hanging on a hook in the pantry. Made of jean material, it expanded out to carry several pounds of produce.

Casey daydreamed and didn't watch where she headed, distracted by all the thoughts of vegetables. She came to a clearing. Several bushes with a few ripe pieces of ruby red fruit hung from its branches.

On closer inspection, she recognized the plump red fruit. Raspberries about the size of her thumb adorned the bushes. She looked around to check her surroundings and tracked the landscape. Several acres away, the roof of the house peeked through the foliage. Casey tied the scarf from around her neck to a branch as high as she could reach. A few of the almost overripe fruit burst as she plucked the delicious berries from the small bushes they still clung to, taking care to not grab onto a thorn. The freeze and surprise fall snowstorm would kill off any of the fruit that was left.

Littered over several feet were more morsels of vegetation deposited by the ravens. Casey spun in a circle, taking in the yield.

She quickly reached the house and deposited her haul on the table. Standing on the back porch, she happily spotted the bright pink fabric off in the distance. A beacon for her to follow to her crop. Next year she'd harvest the delicious juicy fruit before wildlife devoured it.

Tears tracked down her cheeks. God in all His infinite wisdom took the time to provide for her, one insignificant person. She bowed her head. "Thank you, Father."

She still had a long way to go to make it through the season. There wasn't nearly enough to keep her fed and healthy. She tugged up the waistband of her loose pants. Her stomach growled but there was nothing to do about it. She already ate two meals that day, her self-imposed limit. Until she saw the pantry holding more food, she couldn't risk running out in the middle of a snowstorm in the months to come.

Hours after the sun set, she got up from the table and took in the kitchen. She couldn't help the snicker that bubbled up and out of her. Seeds strewn all over the place to dry. Tomatoes took up residence on the counter by the stove, while cucumber seeds were next to the sink. Ears of corn strung with string draped across a doorway. It looked like a mass vegetable slaughter.

If half of everything in front of her grew, she wouldn't complain.

Some of the small crop was edible. She separated the flesh of the produce from the seeds, taking in the promise of the first bright spot in the year to come.

Casey used a pen and paper to jot down how much food she stored. Dividing her food into the number of days until the crop's yield the next summer deflated the small, pleasant outlook and shredded it into such tiny pieces, she would never be able to pick them up and piece them together. She was several weeks if not a couple months shy of feeding herself. She rationed and rationed but the numbers didn't add up.

It would help if she doubled her groceries with a delivery. She mentally scolded herself for going down that road, pun intended.

"Well Casey, looks like we're on a diet." She didn't like how much weight she lost over the last couple of weeks. Defeat sat at the edge of her mind, ready to tug her down into its depths.

CASEY SAT UP WITH A start, the sun peeking through the slats in the blinds. She didn't remember falling asleep. Something woke her but she didn't hear anything. A memory tugged at her consciousness. Maybe from a dream, then it hit her. She remembered a crossbow hanging in the shed along with a large target tossed in the corner. Did God remind her of the one contraption that could make or break her cold weather survival?

Mumbling filled the hushed morning as she heaved a large rectangular bale, flopping it end over end. Her boots slipped on the dew-soaked grass. After the first couple of times she fell; her legs were coated in a thick layer of mud halfway down her shins from the now-melted snow.

Next, she lifted one end of another bale on top of the bottom one, jumped to the other side, and lifted it so it stacked two high. The first attempt was appalling when the end flipped back off, almost taking her with it. The second try, no better than the first.

By the eighth attempt, she laughed so hard she was unable to lift any part. She walked away to calm down before she took a jab at it again. This time she shoved it as far back as she could and then lifted the other end. It gave her the leverage to inch it back, running from end to end centering it.

Casey sprayed yellow, red, and blue paint to decorate the front of the target into a bullseye to practice with. She gave the red center a smiley face and stood back to enjoy her handiwork.

The crossbow goaded her from the ground, daring her to pick it up. The consensus was it operated like a regular bow and arrow. The string pulled back to launch the arrows through the air when the trigger was pulled. Casey developed halfway decent mechanical skills since buying her house. She learned the right way through trial and error and several wrong ways of doing some of the repairs herself, including a sink trap that disintegrated when she tried to loosen the nut underneath just to fish her earring out that she dropped down the drain.

She used both hands to position the string. Lifting the bow, she held it like the manual said and depressed the trigger. She flinched when it flung forward. She tried a couple of times more to familiarize herself with the feel of the string slinging forward, and she readied an arrow.

The first arrow flew well over the target. She searched for a while before she found it lodged in the dirt. It went farther than she thought. This was going to be a big waste of time if she kept having to find the arrows every time she missed. She should have set it up against the panels of the outbuilding. That would damage the old wood with a ton of holes, but at least she wouldn't be running around like a chicken with its head cut off. If she had more than four arrows, it wouldn't have mattered.

Yum, chicken. Now, if she could wrangle her some of those!

Shaking her head, she concentrated and lowered the bow, trying to aim it properly this time.

The trigger released and the arrow flew straight, and hit the side of the target.

Casey yelled, excited she didn't have to go hunting for this round.

Hours later, her fingers were blistered from setting the string. She ought to soak and wrap them so they wouldn't break in the middle of the night and rip open.

Learning to shoot arrows jam-packed her day from early light to dusk. Now drained, she hadn't yet accomplished anything with her day wasted on training to hit a target.

Casey brought down the comforter and pillow from her room and crashed on the couch and slept peacefully. She figured if the Monarchs came back, she wouldn't be trapped upstairs, unable to find a safe way out. Cornered, she'd end up hurting herself either from jumping or being taken.

The next morning, the pale colors in the sky woke her. Normally, she was up and out on the porch watching the sunrise, but today it didn't wait for her.

Not bothering to eat since already low on rations, she wanted to practice again with the bow. With this being a farm, somewhere in the trees hid a deer blind. She put a double layer of socks on to deter blisters on her heels. The boots she found were a size too big so if she doubled up, she got around pretty well.

Her calves would be burning later from climbing up and down to grab the arrows she planned to shoot. Hitting a bullseye on level ground was one thing but another to take out her intended target hoisted high in the trees.

Casey kept the peaks of the roof in her sights as she looked for what she wanted to call a treehouse for grownups. Men wanted to be all macho but to her, hammering boards together to sit in a tree made it a big person's escape from adulthood. What would Clint say about her analogy of a deer blind? Giggling, she gasped when she finally spotted it. She glanced back and still saw the house. Some of the boards screwed into the bark and trunk didn't look like they were very sturdy, but she slung the bow across her back and started up.

She let go when her blistered fingers scraped against the rough boards. Times like now were when she missed her healing abilities the most. She shook out her hands, flexing her fingers, and tried again.

She blew out a sigh through her nose because she didn't trust herself not to cry out in exasperation when she stopped halfway up. Finally at the top, she rested with her legs swinging over the side as she refused to let her small injuries stop her from attempting to bag a deer.

The gauze she taped around her fingers this morning protected them to an extent, but sometimes they throbbed no matter what she did.

The sun lit the sky to the east. It hadn't peeked over the landscape yet, but it was close. The fields were steaming as the heat of the morning burned off any dew from the night before.

She blew on her hands and waited.

And waited.

How could this be more boring than fishing?

Something moved under her. She tensed and tried to keep her movements to a minimum. An arrow nestled in the groove as she peeked over the edge of the railing. An opossum waddled by with several babies clinging to its back.

Casey sat hard as her hands shook; she was hungry but not enough to kill a mama with young that depended on her to survive.

Clint probably would have three deer already cleaned and in the freezer, along with twenty rabbits if he were here. She scolded herself to stop thinking that way. She only had herself to rely on. With God's help of course.

Crunching leaves shook her from her daydreams. Whatever it was definitely didn't have ninja skills to stay quiet. She saw what she waited for all morning. Four deer pushed through to the clearing below her. She didn't move for several minutes. Realizing she should be aiming, she fumbled with the crossbow and almost dropped it.

Their huge brown eyes alert, their ears flickered every which way. She couldn't do it. Stomach cramps almost gave away her position. She had to or she wouldn't survive.

She said a prayer and concentrated on the feel of the stock against her shoulder. Her finger caressed the trigger.

On the next exhale, she squeezed, releasing the arrow. It struck the ground near the second deer.

Their white tails flipped up, and they bounded away before she tried to reload. Casey fell back against the treehouse. Her hands shook from the adrenaline. No meat for her today.

She never butchered an animal before, but if she didn't, only her skeletal remains would be found before spring.

Not sure how long she lay there, she started to sweat as the sun bathed her in its warm rays. Yep, she should get up, but she appreciated the calm she got from playing in a treehouse as an adult. It was cathartic as nature continued around her as if she didn't exist.

The too-big shoes slipped on the first rung as she swung herself over the side, her foot searching for the wood board attached to the side of the tree. The last thing she needed to be bothered with was falling. It wasn't as if she could rush down to the local clinic to reset a dislocation, a minor injury, if she wounded herself. What if it were something worse?

If the healing relic worked, it would change things. Lured into a false sense of security, she thought she would always have them to fall back on. Now she felt exposed after relying on them for so long only to have them taken away.

Casey peeled the gauze and tape from her fingers. She sucked in air as the blisters tore and bled. Something would have to be done, or she wouldn't be able to do anything with her hands. Maybe the first aid kit stored with the weather radio under the stairs would have something to use.

"Medipac. What a weird name." Casey read the stamped word on the front of the bright red box. She found a transfusion kit like the one Clint used back in the cabin after their escape from the Monarchs. He had to pump his blood into her veins in an attempt to save her. She thumbed through several sleeves of products.

"Restorative skin. So, Band-Aids?" Casey gripped the corner with her teeth and tore into the sealed pouch since her fingers weren't useful.

A small bottle fell out along with a wand with a red lens on the end. "Instructions would be good. Ahh, here they are. Uncap the bottle. Easy enough. Place enough drops of solution on damaged dermal area to cover the exposed dermis layer. Use laser heating implement to sear and seal the solution."

That concerned her. Would it burn her skin? In the next second, she touched the case with a damaged finger; hissing in a gulp of air, she made up her mind to go with it. It couldn't hurt worse than they already did.

She let several drops fall on the first finger. The wand lit up when she pressed the end. She aimed it over the edge of the wet area in contact with her untorn skin. It sizzled and bubbled but didn't burn. It soon dried. She tapped the table with her finger. No pain. The new skin overlay didn't have any feeling, but it didn't hurt.

"This is my new best friend." Casey continued until all of the spots were taken care of.

Worn out, she hopped into the shower and scrubbed the dirt and grime from her body she accumulated over the last several hours. A nap sounded like the best idea she had in a long while. Afterward, she would work more on tilling the soil, preparing it for spring planting.

Four

Casey groaned when her stomach rumbled again. It had been two weeks since she rationed herself down to one meal a day. She became a prolific failure at deer hunting. She'd missed more times than she could count.

A black-and-red checkered scarf wrapped twice around her lower face and neck, a thick red knitted hat on her head, and a down coat with knitted mittens matching the hat kept her warm enough to try to supplement her waning pantry.

She looked sickly thin, her cheeks sunken in as her eyes looked huge in her declining body. Things couldn't keep going the way they were, or she wouldn't survive her first winter. A book on wilderness survival that was her nighttime reading the last evening reminded her that there were other options.

As she passed the hallway mirror, she couldn't stop the giggle that burst forth. She looked like a little kid going out to play in the snow when parents stuffed them in snowsuits to keep them warm, leaving them barely able to move their arms and legs. Her situation wasn't quite so dire, or she wouldn't be able to trudge through the woods.

Her handy dandy little field guide of edible wild plants to be foraged in cold weather was tucked in her pocket. She needed something, anything to give her a second meal, or she wouldn't last the coldest part of the season. Her new food goal, foraging. She trudged through snow up to her calves. The winds were brutal.

Casey stumbled over her feet as a wave of dizziness swamped her. She clung to the closest tree and rested her forehead against the bark. She was armed with a bookmarked list of what she was going to look for, and hopefully, she would have a halfway full belly by the end of the day.

The detailed pictures in the book of rose hips, black walnuts, cranberries, wild garlic, and onions cleared up some of the confusion about which plants were toxic. If lucky, she would be able to find some pine nuts and wild rye grass. Salivating over the thoughts of fresh bread made from the fresh ground rye seeds mixed in with the dwindling flour on hand had her shaking off the dizzy spell and lumbering off into the wooded area. The pine trees called to her with the promise of pine nuts. She wanted to take a crack at roasting some. As she made her way under the canopy of trees, the snow didn't pass her ankles, even though the leaves had fallen months ago, giving the snow no resistance in plummeting to earth.

Casey stopped herself from putting her boot down and shuffled back. She tried not to get her hopes up, but the prominent curled leaves that looked like green onion stalks stood in front of her. Garlic. She found garlic.

The spade dug into the soft soil around each clump easily. She thanked God the temperatures hadn't dipped too far below freezing, or she wouldn't be able to dig in the dirt around the plants. Casey dusted the mud off and wanted to cry. Twelve bundles later and happy with her first find, she already sat in a better position than she did that morning.

Wheezing, she couldn't give up. Tired and exhausted, her body revolted from lack of food. Casey forced her feet to move one at a time until she came to a boundary of pine trees and spruce. With her fading energy, this wasn't the first time she wondered if she would make it out of this fiasco. She took for granted all the food trips she'd relied on everyone else to cover and bring back their stocks for the next few months.

The only good thing about being out in the middle of nowhere farmland? Clint stockpiled so many staples she wouldn't need anything for a while, but you couldn't cut up a stick of butter for a meal. Well, she guessed some may, and she did love her butter, but a little bread or potatoes to go with it would be so much better.

"Oh my gosh!" Casey fumbled for her book and tried to flip the pages but failed with her gloved hands.

She bit into the first finger of her left glove and yanked her hand out so she could thumb to the mushroom section. If she was right about what she discovered, she was about to have a feast tonight.

"Oh, come on." Casey flipped three more pages and found it.

She did a small happy dance before kneeling in the pine needles.

"This is so much better than pine nuts, although looking under these trees, I'll also have plenty of those. Chanterelle mushrooms will be a great meal or addition to what I already have."

The yellow funnel-shaped fungus demanded to be eaten.

Casey blinked rapidly. "Father. I have no words. Thank You for this."

They weren't as fresh as they would have been when they first grew, but she would have to watch this area and come back next year. With her bag overflowing, she tromped her way home. A snuffling sound stopped her in her tracks. What animal would be out in the snow?

It made the noise again, and she sidestepped to the closest tree and tried to keep her footfalls quiet, so she didn't startle whatever lurked on the other side of the spruce. Her quick inhale also gathered the moisture in her mouth and had her coughing as spit went down the wrong pipe. She didn't have to worry about startling the creature because a very large buck lolled on the ground, steam trailing out of its nostrils with every exhale. There were no injuries on the old, scarred hide. One of the books talked about the stress of a rut being enough to kill an older buck. Could that be what happened to this magnificent animal?

Galloping hooves took off in the opposite direction. His herd was so quick she never got a glimpse of them. God gifted her with a deer that would feed her for months. A glance over her shoulder and she spotted the tip of the tallest peak of the roof. She would have a long way to travel to try and dress the buck back at the house. Moving the large creature wasn't a possibility.

She pulled out a small ball of twine and tied it off on a branch, picked up her foraged food, and started toward the house. The string trailed off long before she thought it would, but when she came to the end and tied it off, she knew her way home from there. She jogged as fast as possible to the house in the deep snow for the butchering kit she put together and the wagon she also decided would make a great way to bring back large hauls. She lined the metal wagon with plastic and started toward the large beast.

Casey worked tirelessly for the next hour hanging and butchering the animal, who expired by the time she got back to it. She was surprised she did as well as she did and only threw up twice. Well, they were dry heaves since she didn't have anything in her stomach to revolt.

She left the rest of the carcass for the other wildlife to enjoy after she took everything the book instructed her how to cut and prepare. The wagon overflowing with huge slabs of meat made her mouth water at the possibility of having a ground deer burger. She would have to wait for a few days because meat had to be hung first to process it before freezing it.

Two large coolers packed with snow around them would hold a consistent temperature and do the same job as hanging it in a commercial cooler like meat packing plants did. Large rocks she could barely lift piled on top of them would keep out any critters from getting to her hard work.

An hour later, she propped her feet up and thought of how the mushrooms would taste fried in butter. She rested her eyes for a minute before she got started. It drained her to dispense with the large buck.

Taking in her rations, she decided she would splurge tonight with brown rice with mushrooms. She would see what other staples to toss together. Her body wasn't accustomed to eating so much so she would have to pace herself and not overindulge so she didn't make herself sick, which would only be wasting food.

The stocked coolers gave her the freedom to loosen up the rationing. Tomorrow, she would still head out and see if she could find more foraged foods. She couldn't wait for spring so she could milk maple trees for their sap and make her own syrup. It took her several days to correctly identify the maples around the property, and she marked them to tap in spires and drain their delicious nectar.

Casey prayed thanking God for providing her with more than she deserved. He never let her down.

Five

Casey flinched as another mosquito buzzed around her ear. Over a year had passed since Ben's death. Clint traveling through the sphere to bring Amanda and Ben back left her serving an involuntary solitary confinement sentence when the sphere collapsed.

One of the radio stations she tuned in when she and Clint first moved into his uncle's house came back on the air about a month after the shield defended her, announcing why they were missing in action for so long. The magnitude of what the shield did during the last attempted Monarch incursion still rocked her to her core. Every piece of electronics, from components to the smallest circuit fried. It extended several states away. After they came back on the air, she realized she should be tracking the date they announced every day for her to create her own calendar marking system. She counted back and hadn't seen anyone for over seven months.

She figured the Monarchs had their hands busy bullying the states and cities that still reeled from the aftermath of the EM pulse.

Cell towers were rendered useless, total abandonment of the now inoperable power plants due to cascade failures. Old classic cars dominated the highways as the elderly, who kept vehicles that were easy to work on without all the upgraded computer systems, dusted them off and loaded them up with their earthly possessions. Gridlock led to carjackings and murders of the owners, who drove those precious works of art trying to leave the devastation behind.

States were still in emergency-level status. The broadcast employees brought in a portable system until they replaced everything ruined in the aftermath.

Casey figured out the metal cage housed around the solar panels protected them from EM attacks of that magnitude, since her electricity never faltered. It seemed to reason the cage could have been put in originally for lightning strikes. She'd seen several storms with lightning being the main element.

Looting and riots filtered down from the larger cities to the small suburbs. The DJ on the radio hinted at apocalyptic conditions. Burned-out shells of cars and buildings emptied of anything of value were notably reported on. Without seeing the damage the pulse caused, her imagination was running wild to all the crazy things going on. It didn't do her heart any good knowing she caused it. Her only saving grace was all the vehicles rendered inoperable because of the pulse clogged the roadways, so she didn't really have to worry about unwanted visitors unless they walked miles away from the cities with nothing to carry away their haul in.

Casey straightened from where she'd been working in the garden hoping for a yield as good as the previous harvest. She held her hand up to shade her eyes as smoke rose in the east again. It was too far from the vicinity around her to be worried about it as long as it stayed away. The news told of buildings being torched for entertainment since the businesses didn't operate anymore.

Most of the people who survived the initial pulse closed up shop once the criminals took over and moved across the country to be with family or friends. Now, those small cities were overrun with Monarchs, who killed indiscriminately. Since the beginning, the Monarchs behaved that way, yet people were now having a problem with it. They didn't think it was their place to get involved until the Monarchs strolled into their backyard and helped themselves to whatever they wanted.

Casey considered all the negative issues caused by her powers. She felt responsible.

She shook off her morose thoughts and smiled as she surveyed the rows of corn, tomatoes, cucumbers, and other vegetables God provided for her. His promise rang true. She did have rest. She hadn't seen a single Monarch or mantis since the last incursion.

Loneliness tapped at Casey's mind. She wondered what happened to Clint when he went back. Was his other self there also? Were both alive and still fighting the cause? Two Clints? Heaven help the Monarchs if they fought side by side to take them out.

The relics no longer held power. Did that mean the other three didn't make it? Had the relics gone dormant waiting for the chosen to come forward again?

What astonished her were the hieroglyphs still on her skin. They faded so much, on certain days she almost couldn't see them, yet on other days they seemed to darken and rejuvenate.

She still didn't have a way to contact anyone from her previous group, and she wasn't brave enough to use Clint's truck to try and find somebody. She wouldn't have a clue which direction to head. They'd withheld their location to keep them safe, even from each other in their group.

Chloe and her uncle knew but they hadn't tried to get in touch or send someone to check on her. Casey was sure they had their hands full with the fallout of the latest attacks. At least Chloe was out of the line of fire since she went to join her uncle to fight, not on the front lines. It still gave Casey a gut punch thinking they'd written her and Clint off.

Days like today were especially hard. Nothing much to do other than tending to her garden every day to fill the time. She occasionally stocked up on firewood, so it cured before she burned it. She now considered herself an expert log splitter, and her toned arms and shoulder blades backed up her belief.

The heat affected her vision on days like today when it made the fields shimmer. She found it hard to focus on objects. Halfway done with work, she added a piece of fabric to drape over the rim of the hat to shade her eyes more. It had to be hysterical looking, but Casey didn't mind; it got the job done. Who was she going to impress?

A single dog bark broke her concentration. She froze, waiting to see if she heard what she thought or if it was a hallucination from overheating in the sun's rays.

Bark.

Casey flattened her hand above her eyes to give her added shading as she took in the span of horizon beyond the unkempt fields.

Bark.

A black, tan, and white, long-haired dog loped toward her.

It stopped halfway down the row of corn and sat. Wary of the strange person he didn't know, the dog barked once and then dropped to its belly.

"Where did you come from?" Casey hadn't seen a dog since Mason, her Rottweiler back home, and remembered Ben once telling her dogs were extinct.

She looked around but couldn't see anyone who the mutt ran away from. She hadn't heard any sounds to hint at neighbors in the area. How far did this poor pooch travel to reach her?

The dog crawled on its belly until he sat at the edge of the row where the dirt met the grass.

"I won't hurt you." Casey squatted and held out her hand.

He backed up and tilted his head to the side, taking her in.

Casey moved to the next row of tomatoes, checking for suckers to pluck from the plants so nutrients would flow to the fruit instead of the extra shoots, making them juicier and tastier. She continued to talk quietly to the dog as she went about her day.

He leisurely inched along only a few feet from her.

"Come on. It's okay. You're such a cute little boy." She didn't move.

The last thing she wanted to do was startle the poor thing, that was skin and bones.

He stretched his neck as far as he could, sniffing the air. She still didn't budge or breathe.

He trotted off and sat down several feet from her, not making it easy for her to win him over. When she started for the house, he trotted along with her but never shortened the distance between them.

She filled a bowl with leftovers and slid it out the door. The dog sprinted around the side of the house. "Oh well, it'll be here for you tonight. I hope to see you in the morning."

Casey went about securing the house and settled in for the evening.

She didn't remember falling asleep, but her dreams were of her previous life and her dog Mason. Casey stumbled down the hall to peek out. The bowl sat empty. She couldn't stop the smile as she saw the dog curled up on one of the chairs.

She stepped out and the dog lifted its head. "Morning."

He recoiled with his tail tucked between his legs and angled back away from her.

It could take some time before he learned she would never hurt him.

A WEEK LATER, THE DOG still was around, and it kept Casey company while she toiled in the garden and around the yard. She employed a soft calm voice as she regaled the dog with stories of her Mason and how much she missed him when she came to the future.

Sweat poured from her with the exceptionally sunny day. Movement caught her eye and she turned to see the dog only a couple of steps from her. She held out her hand.

His cold nose skimmed the back of her hand.

Progress!

Another touch.

He licked her before rolling to his back.

"Oh, good boy. Uh okay, girl. Sorry pretty lady for calling you a gross stinky boy. With all the matted fur it was hard to tell, and I'm used to male dogs. Yep, my Mason was the bestest thing ever." Casey stood and the dog scurried several feet back. "Do you want to eat?"

Casey propped the screen open as she pulled a large metal bowl out of the pantry.

She hummed as she put green beans, potatoes, and some of the dwindling venison she had left, topped with gravy. She added in some corn. Sniffing noises sounded at the door. Casey put the bowl on the floor and backed up to lean against the pantry door and observed how the dog would handle the bowl being inside. It kept its distance, never getting close.

A raven's caw spooked the dog, but she steadied herself quickly and approached the bowl. She kept her eyes on Casey as she licked the food; a small pathetic growl left her lips. There were no holds barred as she nosedived into the slop.

The bowl scooted across the linoleum floor, the metal ringing out, as she licked it clean.

"What is your name? Do you have an owner somewhere nearby?" Because of the state the animal was in, Casey didn't think anyone looked out for her. In the week she started feeding her, she already noticed a change in the dog's weight and energy.

"Do you have a name? What would someone call you? Daisy needs a good washing, doesn't she?" The dog's body wiggled as she shimmied up to Casey, knocking into her legs.

Casey laughed. "Daisy it is. Come on."

Casey turned on the faucet in the tub and pulled several bottles out of the cabinet when she spied bubble bath in the back. "Oh, you owe me one, pretty little lady. I could have been living in the lap of luxury, and here I am giving *you* a bubble bath."

She patted the side of the tub. Overgrown nails clicked against the porcelain surface as she peered into the water.

Daisy backpedaled. Not wanting to have to lure her into the bathroom again, Casey ran her hand down her back. The dog stopped retreating, which gave Casey time to latch the door before she bolted.

"It's okay, pretty girl. We are going to clean you up a bit." With a little coaxing, Daisy rested her paws on the side of the porcelain.

A few more pets and she waggled her lower body in the same rhythm as her tail.

Without further prompting, the dog plopped into the suds for a spa day. Casey heard some dogs, once they trusted you, were known to do a complete turnaround.

Bubbles floated through the air, and splashes landed on the floor around her as Casey rinsed Daisy for the second time.

She wrapped two towels around her before carrying her to the back porch and letting her loose to shake out her fur, slinging water every which direction. Daisy ran full tilt in circles around the house lap after lap. Casey's laugh built up from her stomach; she couldn't remember the last time she felt so free to let herself feel. The wind soon dried Daisy's double-thick layer of fur. She sagged to the porch, groaning in appreciation of a full belly and clean fur. Soon her eyes drifted shut.

Casey left the screen door open for Daisy to come and go while she ran through the prophecy and translated the newest section on the parchment to figure out what her next steps would be.

Was there a way to get her friends back? If so, she needed to start working on it. She found it necessary, for her mental health, to come to terms with the fact that she may never see them again, but they were all she had left. Her family was long gone. Had being separated changed them, and did they miss her as much as she did them?

Casey rubbed her temples to stave off the headache from concentrating so hard. She wondered where Daisy disappeared to or if she slept all afternoon soaking up the rays of the sun.

"Daisy?" The vacant porch glared at her.

Casey tried not to worry, but it wasn't in her nature to let something suffer. Would she go hungry again if Casey didn't feed her? The selfish side of her wanted the dog to stay. They were great companions, and she wouldn't feel so lonely.

With reluctance she locked the door for the night after the sun set, knowing she might never see Daisy again.

Cackling and crowing broke through her dream. What in the world? Ready for it to be a setup, she snuck out, bypassing the sections of the boards that rubbed against nails.

It probably looked like she played hopscotch.

A bark sent her sprinting for the backyard.

Daisy!

Casey opened the door before the dog issued another demand for Casey to show herself.

Six chickens ruffled their feathers as Daisy ran in circles herding them toward her. Every so often she would squat down, but as soon as one of the birds moved, she circled them again.

"Daisy, where am I going to put them? If someone comes looking for their flock, I'm blaming you."

Casey shook her head as she jogged to gather up supplies. She didn't know the first thing about chickens, what they ate or the care they required.

Boards and metal fencing leaned against one stall of the barn. With everything laid out, she visualized a quick design for a temporary coop. Soon, she nailed the boards together to make a large enclosure she could stand in. An old wooden screen door fit perfectly on one end.

Her neighbors raised chickens back in her lifetime, but she remembered only a little about them. A snake made it into the coop and swallowed eggs, sending her neighbor screeching down the street, wanting someone to save her babies. As she put it.

Casey stacked milk crates on their sides two high and three wide. They looked like shoe racks. Now thankful for the leftover grass she cut from the next field over when it grew taller than she wanted, she lined the inside of the crates. She didn't want to imagine the wildlife that would encroach on her little paradise if she left the grasses to grow as tall as they wanted. Her first foray into using a scythe, she almost nicked her shin on the first swipe. Now months later, she had to say it was her favorite mind-clearing chore.

This would work until she came up with something better. An old milking pail would keep water available for them. Casey held open the door she secured wire fencing over to help cover the holes in the screens. Knowing she couldn't tell them to go inside, she pondered. What next?

As if Daisy knew what she wanted, she herded them to the opening, and they flew in perching on the tops of their beds, clucking away in protest. Casey shut the door before they made a getaway.

So, she had chickens.

"Come on, you deserve a big meal after that." Casey didn't need to say anything further as Daisy yipped and danced around her feet.

Not waiting for the bowl to touch the floor, Daisy buried her snout in the mess.

"Worked up an appetite, did ya? I don't doubt it. How far did you have to go to find a chicken dinner?" Casey cracked up at her joke as she pulled the tea kettle off the stove and made her morning cup. The stoneware warmed her chilly hands.

Her thoughts ran rampant about the supplies she would need to feed the chickens. They ate store feed but other than that, she didn't know bupkes. She shuffled through the books on livestock and pulled out a small manual on how to keep chickens. The date on the copyright page was decades before her birth.

Casey, with a better understanding of what it took to keep hens, wasn't kidding herself into thinking she knew enough to try it. One of the manuals stated free-range chickens would eat their weight in insects and seeds from the ground. It suggested to put them in a coop to roost at night.

Daisy was a pro at herding already. She wondered if someone trained her to herd chickens. She'd heard of dogs herding sheep and cattle but never birds. A secure place to come to at night would keep predators from dining on her newfound flock.

God put the chickens in her life, so she only saw them as a gift. Planning to work in the garden, she opened the door to her haphazardly put together coop. Today she would try to keep them comfortable with being out during the day and inside at bedtime.

The sun beat down on her back. Her bandanna was wrapped around her forehead to keep the sweat from dripping into her eyes and the sun hat kept the rays from burning her face. Casey leaned against the hoe she used to keep the weeds at bay and turned to look at the already wilted pile she pulled from the garden and burst out laughing at the chickens enjoying the feast. Dandelion leaves were quickly gobbled up.

She would have to keep an eye on them if she wanted her plants to survive. They clucked and preened while she finished. Now done for the day, how did she get them back in their enclosure? The foxes and coyotes would pick them off one by one if she left them out.

"Come on, Daisy. These ladies need to go in their shelter." Casey swept her arms out to her sides as she made a shooing motion with her hands.

With no further instruction, Daisy yipped and darted back and forth, gathering the flock and guiding them to the coop.

Casey crossed her arms and smiled. She gazed at heaven. "Thank you, Father."

She was astonished at the small delights He sent her way. She shouldn't be, He always blessed her with the simplest pleasures to make life better.

Large branches secured through the wire several inches off the ground supported the birds as they shook out their feathers. They were all so different. One a reddish brown, another solid white, two tan, with another sporting white patterns on black feathers.

"Goodnight, ladies. I'll see you bright and early in the morning." Casey started to turn but stopped. On the end perched a larger chicken with a couple of large, curved tail feathers. "What do we have here? Are you a rooster? This is going to be fun. I won't have to worry about sleeping late."

The larger and brighter comb and waddle defined this majestic creature as male.

"Let's grab some sleep before Rufus starts crowing." Casey patted her leg for Daisy to follow and almost skipped back to the house.

Excitement was not a common theme in her life, but this was such a blessing. The thrill was short-lived as she heard the all too familiar chuffing of a helicopter swooping through the air.

In the last two years, they flew through the area about sixteen times. In every instance, she was close enough to the house to hide. This time she stayed out as the darkness cloaked her since she hadn't turned on any lights inside. They performed a sweeping pattern from one field to the next. Other farms were around but why were the Monarchs flying like they followed a grid pattern?

They never came this way like the first flight. It's not like the Monarchs didn't know where she lived. Maybe this whole time it wasn't the Monarchs. Could it be someone who could help? Or someone worse than the terrorists who haunted her dreams?

She backed up and secured the door, keeping her eyes on the object using a spotlight to search for something or someone. She didn't bother turning on the lights as she headed to bed. Was it worth her discovery to find out if they were friend or foe? This was her home now and she wanted to defend it.

"Come on, Daisy. You can crash next to me." Casey ran her hand through the slick soft fur down her back. She had a hard time getting her to stand still earlier while she brushed her after her bath.

The poor dog was the wriggliest thing she ever tried to restrain. With each reprimand to stop, it flipped a switch. It turned into a game, and she tried harder to run only to stop, spin around, and lunge back toward Casey to stop again far enough away she couldn't reach her.

It took longer than she intended when she first grabbed the brush. Now, her shiny coat would only look better with more meat on her bones. It would take a month or more to fatten her up. A little bit of food aggression in her made dinner interesting, but she corrected Mason when she first got him. This little girl should be a piece of cake.

Casey ran her hand from Daisy's mid-back to her tail while she inhaled her food earlier. With each caress, the growling and snarling became less and less.

An old pillow, now the dog's bed, lay by the foot of the couch. Daisy dug with her front paws and nipped it with her teeth, pulling and shifting the pillow until it fluffed how she wanted it before she circled about fifteen times. She crashed and then released a groan.

Casey smiled at the ceiling and nodded off, knowing for the first time she let go of the need to listen for any unwanted guests. Daisy would be on guard.

Six

"Ben, come on. Let's go. Clint expected us ten minutes ago." Amanda intentionally whined, knowing how much her brother hated it.

"Coming!" Ben growled.

Amanda chuckled and leaned against the wall. She couldn't believe when Clint had appeared in her room as she talked to Ben a few months ago. He wasn't their Clint if that made sense.

He talked about her dying, which she didn't like to hear, and to follow him back to Casey when the sphere winked out and the portal dissolved.

Senior Clint meeting junior Clint was interesting and disturbing. They were different, though. The senior Clint, as she referred to him, though they were the same person, was stoic and reticent. Or quieter than junior Clint. He looked at her differently; the only word she could associate with it was longing. He didn't joke with Ben as much as his other self did. The absorbed relic from his timeline he defended them with launched itself back to the relics box, so they only had one weapon.

It would have given them a good edge over the Monarchs if they owned two, as it would allow them to cripple their fleet of vehicles. It would definitely put a dent in their ambitions to take over America if the Monarchs had to do it on foot. The military lingo Ben and Clint reverted to since they knew what the other meant left her on the outs as if they spoke a different language.

She recalled that the first time she saw Clint in uniform, after he joined the military, stopped her in her tracks when she came home from school years ago. Without a doubt the best-looking man she had ever laid eyes on. Her innocent crush only deepened as she saw the man he would be and all the potential to be a hero. He was her superman when he looked out for her keeping jerks away who only wanted to use her.

She never told him how much it meant to her. At the time, it annoyed her, and she wanted to prove she could look after herself. She didn't need another big brother telling her what she should or shouldn't do. Technically not related by blood but being Ben's best friend relegated him to the brother category. Rebellion during her senior year got her in trouble with the law when the kids she hung out with decided to joyride in one of their parents' cars.

Amanda didn't find out until they were all sitting on the curb in a neighborhood, he in fact didn't have permission to take his dad's car. Their parents were called to come pick up anyone underage. Ben happened to answer the phone when the officer called. Clint arrived on leave from training and spent a couple of days with them.

Ben and Clint, in uniform, showed up to take her home. A small conversation with the officer, who they came to find out later went to high school with them, kept her from trouble. The look the officer gave her as Ben and Clint directed her into the backseat of the truck made her stomach drop. He almost looked sorry for her. Oh boy, was she going to be in trouble.

"Amanda?" Ben stopped her with a tug on her elbow.

"Yeah?"

"I called your name three times." Ben slung his arm over her and kissed her head.

"I want to go to Casey, but I don't know how with the sphere broken, and if what Clint said is true she won't be at the farm for another year and a half or so." Amanda was confused about the turn of events when senior Clint popped up saying he used the sphere. Theirs lay in pieces.

Ben pulled her into an alcove. "Why do you think she disappeared, yet there are two of Clint?"

"That's what I'm saying. Do you think she ran away and maybe the Monarchs got their hands on her with all the crazy surrounding Clint?" Amanda didn't want to believe Casey would abandon them and take the key with her.

"No. No way did she leave of her own free will. I think someone took her. Remember Clint talking about them...us...ah! I can't keep up with who's where and when. That's it. I'm calling them senior and junior, otherwise I'll give myself an aneurism." Amanda waved her hands in front of her face. "James is a Monarch, and he brings them here, according to Clint senior. What if the Monarchs are already here and took her?"

"Our sentries would have alerted us to their movements. You know they would be storming our lovely castle here if he told them our location. Clint senior and junior are taking James out tonight so we can stay off their radar. He hasn't come close to getting near the exterior. We've had a man on him since Clint senior told us about him." Ben looked around as scuffing sounded at the end of the hall.

"Come on, let's go. Mom called again asking us to move to the west coast again so we are close and away from the fighting." Amanda tugged on his arm as if to move him by sheer force.

Ben grunted but followed her as they made their way to the lab. He didn't usually have much to say about their parents urging them to move. She thought of how Clint senior told them the Monarchs fatally shot Ben in the head while burying a mother and daughter who were a part of their group. Casey was out there by herself. The priority was to figure out an arrangement to jump to her time and rejoin the chosen ones with the key.

Amanda and Chloe scoured the parchment, looking for anything showing a reunion of the four later. The parchment didn't show any evidence of additional text having been added to the original. Nothing hinted the prophecy still wrote its story as the chosen ones evolved like Clint said. He reported they took constant image sequences to track the new passages. How could one in essence have a version of the parchment that in the future read so differently than the one that lay in front of them?

The amazing part, no blank sections currently existed to add additional script. Clint senior agreed that the length right now was at least a foot shorter than the last time he and Casey looked at it.

Clint senior rubbed his hand against the side of his head and squinted.

"Headache?" Amanda didn't like seeing his discomfort since joining them.

She wondered if it had something to do with two Clints occupying the same time. Would it have any ill effects on them? What harm would befall either of them? Junior didn't have any problems, only Clint senior from the future.

"I'm fine. Nothing to worry about." Senior moved closer and leaned in.

The scent of his soap made her realize they were still the same person yet occupied two bodies. He smelled like himself. Senior made her nervous and unsure of herself. Her heart ached knowing he lived through both hers and Ben's deaths. Since they were still there years after they left the warehouse in the first timeline, she prayed she changed the series of events leading to her death. She shivered as a chill raced down her spine.

"You okay?" Senior's hand rested on her shoulder.

"Thinking about when you told me I died."

"What about it?" Senior stiffened next to her.

"Did I suffer?" She wanted it to have been quick and painless, but how do you ask how you handled dying?

Senior shifted away from her, not answering as Junior joined them.

"Anything on the changes Clint told us about?" Junior sat on the stool next to her, pointing to the parchment.

Senior squinted at the bright lights. "We didn't notice that happened until several major events ensued, so I couldn't tell you when anything shifted."

She shook her head. "No, nothing. This parchment isn't as long as the other one you described. What happened to trigger it to start rewriting itself? And just so we can keep things clear—because my brain is going to melt trying to call you both Clint. Future Clint is now Senior and current Clint is Junior. Does either of you have a problem just so we know who we are talking to?"

Both shook their heads as Junior winked at her.

Seven

"Come on, guys." Senior Clint tapped his foot on the floor as he studied a map he laid out.

It was unnerving to see himself sitting across from, well, himself. They communicated without needing to say a word. He did the same with his team while in the military, but this took it to a whole new level.

It was tough keeping everyone in the dark about the two Clints. Doc and Chloe were the only two not a part of the chosen ones, who had seen them both at the same time. Amanda's suggesting going by senior and junior made it easy to know who to answer.

Tonight, they were taking James out of the building to neutralize the threat to the men and women who lived with them. Clint had the insight of living through one botched attempt to separate themselves from this spy, and the cost was Amanda's life, so he wasn't taking any chances by keeping him around.

Clint senior had a horrible feeling in his gut. Casey went missing and he wanted to interrogate James and see what he knew about it. They couldn't do that here because it would only put the others at risk. The urge to leave them and go to the farm almost became a physical ache. They didn't have a working sphere to use so it would be years for them before she showed up.

Ben came in and placed a syringe on the table next to him. "Doc said this should do the trick."

Clint fashioned his vest over his long-sleeved shirt and motioned Junior to take the hypodermic. "We're ready to go. I expect us to be back in a couple of hours. Pray everything goes as planned. If we aren't back in three hours, we're either dead or the Monarchs took us. I won't expose your location. Our military training will help deal with torture enough so they will give up or outright kill us. If it passes the three-hour mark, move to the next location. Don't wait or try and rescue me. Get everyone moved to the basements in the houses Chloe's uncle has ready."

It was easier if they sedated James. He couldn't defend himself or injure Junior. Sheesh, talk about thinking of yourself in the third person. This took that to a whole new level.

"Are you sure you don't want us to come along?" Amanda studied the map on the table.

"The fewer people out there, the better it will be," Clint senior explained.

"Plus, we have a spare. If something happens to me, my replacement is right here." Junior nudged her.

He remembered being carefree and joking more. Watching the deaths of your two best friends who were in the room dulled your ability to laugh and make light of the situation.

"Don't joke!" Amanda turned her back.

"Two for the price of one." Ben tossed his head back as he laughed with Junior.

"That isn't funny at all. You can't joke like that." Junior pulled Amanda into a hug.

"It's a little funny." His chuckle rumbled in his chest where she rested her cheek.

She smacked his arm. "No, it's not!"

Senior stood. "I think we should go. We'll try to check in when we arrive."

Junior tapped his ear. "They will have front-row seats for the festivities."

Ben gave each of them a quick clap on the back. "Don't take any risks. We need to know Casey's location so we can go to her. Leave him by the side of the road and be done with it."

"When did you become big brother?" Senior tagged Ben in a quick one-armed hug. When Amanda gave both of them hugs, Senior admitted when she gave Junior a lengthier hug, his jealousy spiked.

Yep, he seriously lost it to be jealous of himself. "No unnecessary risks. If we get a line on Casey and are on their doorstep, we'll recon the area. We'll come back here to work out a plan to pull her out."

Clint held Amanda's hand, who then clutched Junior's. Ben joined their circle last. "Heavenly Father, be with us as we remove the threat from the innocent. Let our journey be quick and without any obstacles to turn the tides of this endeavor in the Monarchs' favor. Amen."

The other three repeated his Amen.

"Take care, brothers." Ben tugged his sister into a hug.

Junior slipped the syringe into his right hand and nodded at Ben to head to James' room to distract him enough so Junior could knock him out.

If it wasn't such a serious time, it would almost be comical to see the panic on James' face when Senior stood by Junior and soon overpowered him. James was out like a light. Now thrown over Senior's shoulder, they double-timed it through the tunnels and up the stairs to the garage they utilized for their trips. Senior's steps almost faltered as they ran to the same car Amanda died in. He kept telling himself she was still alive, and he would do everything in his power to make sure she stayed that way this time around.

Dumping James in the trunk before sliding behind the wheel, Clint's gut still told him they were missing something. They were going to leave James in an old baseball field after a short conversation. The sooner they got this done, the sooner they'd be back with his friends.

Clint senior's head pounded all the time, and he hadn't informed his friends or Doc about it, although Amanda might have caught on. He thought two of him in the same place put something off balance. Junior didn't suffer from the same problems. Because he invaded into the other's time?

"You're squinting. Did you need me to drive?"

"No, I'll be alright. A headache, nothing I can't handle." No reason to keep the truth from himself since he was a human lie detector.

"What happened?" Junior didn't pull any punches and dove right in.

"Ever since I ported here, a constant buildup of pressure behind my eyes has been affecting me." He turned down the last street to their destination.

Junior angled in his seat. "I'm not having headaches. Do you think only one of us can be in a timeline at once?"

"I'm the wrong person to ask, but that would be my guess." He shifted the car into park in the deserted lot.

Concern etched on Junior's face as he met Senior around at the trunk when pounding under the latch broke the moment.

They sidestepped and popped the trunk. James hurtled himself out ready for battle but struck nothing except air and landed hard on the ground, knocking the wind from him. They each took an arm and twisted it around his back and secured him to a light pole.

"Where is Casey?" Clint's head pounded worse.

James kicked out with his feet trying to make contact with their legs. A quick move back and they were out of his range.

Junior pulled an electro-shock wand. The jolt made James rethink his volatile reaction.

"You going to answer us? Where is Casey?" Clint senior asked again.

"Why are you asking me? You hid her as soon as the Monarchs got wind of what she can do." James jerked back when Junior tapped the wand against him again.

"She disappeared after you became a member of our little group. Kinda paints you as the culprit. We are asking only one more time. Where is she?" Senior was having a hard time staying conscious from the pressure building up in his head.

"I had nothing to do with that. They keep asking me where she is, and I'm making excuses why I can't find her. Maybe she left and decided it was safer to be on her own than stay with the bunch of losers you are." James' laugh changed to a gurgle with the next press of the shock stick.

Shots embedded in the ground at their feet. The Clints pulled their guns and found themselves staring down a legion of Monarchs. A man in front raised his rifle a few inches and released another round, making Clint senior flinch.

Senior cast a glance at James to find a perfect hole in his forehead. How long before they pulled the trigger again on each of them left standing? Even with Casey's healing abilities, if she were there, wouldn't be enough against a headshot.

A sharp pain pierced his head, and the world went dark.

Eight

Casey dragged the rake over the farmland, evening out the tilled clumps. She prepared the fertile soil for seed for the third spring since she started. Last year's crops were the most bountiful. She'd amused herself with her first stint at farming; she had no clue what to do but lucked out with some books on farm-steading and canning. Reusing the jars she emptied when she and Clint arrived helped her through the tough seasons.

She plucked the seeds from the pockets of the gardening apron she proudly made. If men wore tool belts, she could have a seed pocket apron with elastic bands to hold her tools on the side of her hip for working in the garden.

The sun beat down on her as she adjusted her sun hat so it covered more of her neck. She flipped the rake over and plunged the handle into the ground to the perfect depth of the seeds she planted. She let go of the first one and smiled as she took in the vast area she strived so hard with God's help to develop into a producing crop.

This summer would be a scorcher if these early temperatures were anything to go by. She lost track of time long ago and quit tracking it, only knowing of the season by the broadcasts she listened to on the vintage stereo. She followed the seasons when the temperatures changed, watching the plants and trees spring to life when the weather turned for the next season. Clint left in the fall three years ago. This would be her third year without her friends.

She wiped her brow as she planted the next seed. The Monarchs hadn't been around. Her heart yearned for the life she thought she would live with Ben. She still longed to be with him but knew everyone's time had run its course. No one had been by to see what was going on with them. Granted, very few knew where they were, but Clint told Chloe and her uncle their location.

The first couple of months she watched the road for hours on end, hoping and praying for a car to come along to check on her and Clint; of course, Clint left but they didn't know that. She would sit on the porch in the old rickety chair she dragged out the door and placed under the overhang. Every morning that first winter she would make tea and drink it out there wrapped in a quilt, her eyes never leaving the gravel drive, watching as far as she could see. In the afternoon when her stomach would start rumbling, she would check her food supplies and make sure her rations would make it through the harsh wind chill the radio predicted. Waiting to see a familiar face arrive, she never left the porch for very long, scared she would miss them if someone drove by.

No one ever came. She wondered if her friends assumed they died when they never heard from them again. Her heart was overwhelmed with sadness they didn't bother to try and reach out. What was going on in the rest of the world? Did the Monarchs give up? Were they taken out?

A raven flew overhead, calling out with its gurgling caw that differentiated its kind from crows. The fanned-out tail feathers confirmed her suspicions. A raven. It landed in a large oak that sat between the field and the house.

She went back to her planting. She couldn't wait for the fresh produce to sprout up and grow delicious vegetables again. Tomatoes, green beans, cucumbers, the list grew every year.

She managed to collect enough sap to make about a gallon of syrup from the maple trees and perfected the system to process it. The final resulting liquid was so delicious nothing in the stores could compete.

Soon a second raven flew in. On her way to finishing the fourth row, a roar sounded off in the distance. It almost sounded like a freight train. She glanced at the bright blue sky without a cloud in sight. At least it wasn't a tornado again like when she and Clint first moved in.

She hadn't seen the shield since it frizzled out after her last solo battle with the Monarchs. She ended up taking six bullets that day. She also found the healing ability hadn't fully healed her scars, so several puckered indentions along her torso told of the battles she fought. She won them all but only because God went before her and led the way to her victories.

The low, constant roar continued. Train tracks weren't anywhere near the area. Were the Monarchs finally making another stand to try and take her? At first when the shield permanently safeguarded her, they taunted her with all the ways they were going to slowly cut her open to see how she ticked and let her bleed out. They said they couldn't wait to see how much her healing could handle before they'd put a bullet in her head. The amount of time between the two attacks led to their downfall. They announced their first arrival by using a bullhorn, making threats before they made their move only after their leader's permission. They got their answers when she took them out, eradicating them like vermin.

Casey shook her head as the rumble drew closer, and she spotted smoke approaching at her back. Acrid soot caused her to cough as it burned the back of her throat and her eyes. She tossed the rake and ran as fast as she could to the house. The seeds tumbled to the table and spilled everywhere where she tossed her apron. She grabbed the relics bag and bolted through the front door, yelling for Daisy. The chickens would be lost; she couldn't put them on a leash and take them with her.

With no way to stop the roaring flames from heading toward the house, her only option was to leave and hope the wind didn't pick up and help the inferno overtake her. She made it across the street when the wind shifted and cut off her escape route.

She was thrown several feet in the air as the quick rush of heat seared her back. The shield kept her from slamming into the ground.

A celebratory holler escaped from her at the fact that the shield was back. Casey turned and saw flames eating up the trees and farmlands.

"No!" Fire raced across the dry timber and grass, consuming everything in its path.

The road would be no match to keep the flames from spreading. Clint's uncle's house wouldn't survive this.

She darted from the trees and back across the road, trying to judge the distance on the prairie fire through all the thick smoke. There was no outrunning the monster eating everything in its path. It was time for her to try to fight. A couple of trees dotted the yard, but none were detrimentally close to the house.

She cranked the knob on the faucet to turn on the water as she yelled for Daisy again. It gushed from the hose. If she drenched the grass and house, maybe it would be enough to keep the fire at bay while she tried to use the shield to circle everything. Right now, the shield only wrapped around her, and she couldn't project it further than that.

Water splashed everywhere. Pretty soon she stood in mud squished up over the bottom of her shoes. The blaze danced across the road in a decade's worth of overgrown brush.

The inferno surrounded her as she kept the shield up and battled the heat. She looked up and realized what happened, but it may be too late to win this battle. The dry timber on the backside of the property sparked the fueled fire into burning faster and hotter than before. It surrounded her on several sides.

"Father, I messed up and didn't move fast enough. I didn't anticipate the winds would force the flames to cut off my escape. If it is Your will for me to live through this, please help me. If it's time for me to come home, let me go quick." She shivered at the thought of burning alive as the reason she would leave this world, but when she glanced up, the fire ignited the tall, overgrown prairie grass and surrounded her, converging on one side of the house.

The oppressive heat seared the wood siding. Soon it started smoking. She quickly sprayed water, but it heated up too fast even with the shield as a buffer between the flames and the dry siding. The heat alone would be enough to turn the house into kindling. Sweat poured from her pores, soaking her clothes and making the fabric hang limp from her.

"Clint, I'm sorry I didn't preserve your uncle's house." Casey ignored the wetness streaking through the soot accumulating on her face.

Wind kicked the flames up higher. Soon, she used her hand to protect her eyes from the dust and smoke that made its way through the shield. The shield was once an impenetrable force used to keep the inside pristine. Not anymore.

A bright flash behind her cast her shadow against the front of the house. She whirled around and her jaw dropped. She shook her head, unable to stop the waterworks.

In the center of the road a portal wavered. Three people walked through. The wind came from them. The woman in the middle looked like she lifted weights every day of her life. The sparkle in her eyes stole Casey's breath.

Amanda.

A nasty scar ran from her hairline to the middle of her left cheek.

The man on the right bulked up so much that it seemed like he took up so much more space than the last time she saw him. He winked at her and directed the relic's weapon to dig a trench in the ground that separated the fire from the unscathed areas.

Clint.

The man on the left smiled as yellow winds from his ring extinguished the flames enough so they could walk through the wall of heat straight to her. He hooted as if the fire was a small nuisance for his enjoyment.

Ben.

Casey stumbled a couple of steps toward him, but they aimed their weapons at her. Her feet skidded against the gravel, and she held up her hands as she stopped. His piercing blue eyes studied her as her pulse raced. She took another step, ignoring the weapons that could end her life. These were her friends and the man she loved. "Ben?"

How could he be here? Did they repair the sphere after Clint stepped through to bring him and Amanda back to them?

"Sorry, don't know you, sweetheart, but I'm sure my friend appreciates you saving his house. Are you a neighbor from around here?" Ben pushed past her when she froze, mouth gaping.

"Clint?" She touched his arm when he tried to move around her.

Amanda sucked in a breath. "Lady, he don't like anyone touching him. I'd let go if I were you."

Casey peered into Clint's lifeless eyes. Burn scars ran up the side of his neck. He didn't move, towering over her as his eyes raked up and down her, judging why she stood in his way. She swore he puffed his chest out more.

"You don't remember me." Casey didn't pose it as a question.

How were the relics active if she hadn't been the key and turned them on?

"Never seen you before. As my friend said, much appreciate you keeping the fire at bay, but you can git now. I'm home and don't need no stray thinking I should be obligated to let them stay." Clint brushed past her, almost shoving her over.

Casey backed up, clinging to the strap of the satchel with both of her hands. Defeated, she started walking in the opposite direction of the fire. The plants in the garden swayed in the breeze, as she walked away from all of her hard work. One step forward, twenty back. That's what she felt happened ever since they came into her life. A lone bark sounded on the other side of the farm. Daisy!

"What's in the bag?" Casey yelped at Clint's hardened voice.

"It's mine." Casey kept her voice steady as she pulled the bag closer to her body.

"You seemed to have helped yourself to my house and my land. It's not too far off to think you helped yourself to anything you wanted. I'm going to have to ask you to empty the contents before you go." Clint reached for the strap as Ben lunged at her.

She narrowed her eyes and threw her hands up on instinct to stop them. It did. When she looked again, all three were suspended in their own personal sphere, holding them back from grabbing her. How did she stop them? Was this like when she operated the sphere to move them around before, once for Ben in the tunnels fighting the mantis and once for an injured Clint when she couldn't reach him fast enough, so she sent out a shield with the healing stone?

"Who are you and how did you do that?" Ben kicked out, not able to break free.

"Where did you find the ability to do this?" Amanda sneered.

"I know you won't believe me, but we have all met before. Ben took me from my house and pulled me through time to thirty-five years in the future. We have fought side by side against the Monarchs." Clint's roaring laughter interrupted her.

Clint finally got himself under control. "Sorry sweetheart, but we've never seen you before and the Monarchs won. This is our prison. We can never leave this horrible place. I should have let you burn with the house, but I'm not in the mood to sleep on the ground for the foreseeable future."

Rattling in her bag got their attention. She pressed her palm against it to quiet it down.

"I'm tired of this boring conversation. Clint, take her out. I want to sleep for the next week before I drag myself back out of bed. I'm exhausted and smell. I need a soak in a hot bubble bath, and a pedicure does sound delightful." Amanda studied her fingernails. "Ooh and maybe a manicure."

"How did you activate the relics?" It couldn't be done without the key.

Several shots rang out, making Casey duck her head as she bent at the waist trying to make herself as small as possible without curling up in a ball on the ground.

"These are pretty durable." Clint tapped the barrel of his Glock against the inside of his shell.

"Come on, let us out, and we'll let you walk away." Ben gave her a chin lift.

"You seem to have forgotten I'm the one in charge here. If I want to walk away as you say, I can and I will. I don't need your permission or promises to not come after me. I'm trying to understand how things changed from when I fought alongside you to now. How did your paths change so much since the last time we met?" Casey looked down when the sphere vibrated again. It acted the same way it did when it pieced itself together.

She let it rest in her right palm and waited to see what it wanted to do.

Clint patted his tactical pants pockets and pulled out his own sphere.

"How did you find the fourth to God's chosen? The key needs to wake up the other relics. Without it, they were as dormant as if they were never unearthed." Some answers might help her get back to her friends.

"Honey, God hasn't had anything to do with this world in a really long time. Now, why don't you let us down, or do we need to use this?" Clint's hand hovered over the sphere to open a portal inside his bubble.

"Ben, what's she talking about a key for? We don't need one to get in the house. This here belongs to Clint. We stay out of the Monarchs' way, and they leave us be." Amanda ran her hand along the surface of hers, testing the solidness of it.

"How did you find the relics?" Casey's inquisitive side couldn't let it lie.

Something about this version of her friends told her they were nothing like hers, and her missing from their timeline altered the relics' abilities and their fight for freedom.

"They were lying around in some old factory. Three of them and three of us, so finders keepers." Clint acted like it was no big deal.

"Three?" That didn't make sense. They were kept in airtight rooms in secret tunnels.

"This girl dense or something? Like I said, three. Now, how's about you tell us how you know about them and what they do?"

Amanda gave up waiting to be let out and sat down, leaned against the side, and crossed her ankles.

Ben's ring never influenced the elements. How did he master the wind?

"Can you all manipulate the elements?" Casey stalked up the stairs to the porch and gave a little hop to sit on the porch railing and let her legs dangle over the side.

"That's what they are for, so the answer is yes." Clint shrugged.

Casey drummed her fingers on the railing where her hands were propped on either side of her. These were different relics, and those three were not her friends. "When I met you, there were four relics, and the prophecy stated the key activated the remaining three relics once the four chosen were united."

"Yeah well, I don't know what you are talking about with a key. Mandy, did you read anything about a key?" Clint rolled the sphere around in his palm.

"Ain't no key." Amanda scoffed.

"I beg to differ. I'm the key and before I met my friends, the relics lay dormant in their crystal treasure chest boxes." Clint never called Amanda Mandy; she hated that name. Amanda told Casey when they spent time together talking about their families, one summer when they were still in grade school, Ben called her Mandy. She socked him and he never called her that again.

"All you gotta do is press on the glyphs on the top two corners on the inside of the boxes." Ben tossed out as he gave a nod to Clint.

"Don't tell her the secrets of the relics. She apparently works for the other side." Clint's voice boomed.

"I don't work for the Monarchs." Casey wasn't sure what they meant. She pictured the boxes in her mind but never remembered seeing glyphs on them. Curious, she almost removed one from the satchel to look but held herself back.

Clint coughed and caught her attention when he finally opened a portal in the shield and walked out. He was on her in seconds, before she could react. Ben and Amanda cheered him on.

The first swing caught her off guard and snapped her head back. She landed on her back, the rough boards of the porch scratching her skin. While she was trying to sort out what happened, he sat on her chest within seconds with his hands around her neck. She concentrated on keeping the other two in their shields.

Black dots danced in front of her eyes as he applied more pressure. She mentally called for the yellow and red relics. Static pulsed out from her palms, tossing Clint to the side. She quickly transported him in a shield back to his friends.

He opened the sphere again when glowing light engulfed the inside. It pulled the other two to him and merged so they were all in the same balloon.

Their screams intermingled as they disappeared only to reappear again. Something went wrong. They didn't look quite right. Amanda clutched her arms to her body while Ben's back hunched over at an awkward angle. Clint barely held himself up.

Casey didn't think. She opened a portal before hitting them with the wall of the shield, propelling them backward through the opening.

Still coughing, she rubbed her throat and winced at the soreness. Those people were not her chosen. Were there different outcomes if they didn't find her and transport her to their time? What other versions of them did she have to look forward to? The shield protected her from them, so they weren't the chosen, were they? Dealing with staying alive and growing her food and whatnot was more than she could handle some days, and now, to add to it terminator-style versions of her best friends. No, thank you.

Not today or any day.

If Satan wanted to play his little games, he was in for a rude awakening. God was on her side. She read Revelations, so, spoiler alert: she knew how it all turned out in the end.

God won.

Daisy yipped and bounded around the side of the house. Soot clung to the charred grass and trees that still smoldered slightly. She would hose down the area to make sure everything was extinguished.

"Where were you? Thought you were my partner, and here you abandon me on the first true test of friendship. Fail, my little fuzzy girl. Fail." Casey rubbed her hand up and down her back.

The chickens waddled around, chasing after Daisy. Casey had added a pull rope attached to a lever to the pen's door so Daisy could let them out in the mornings. It saved Casey a trip across the yard until after breakfast.

"I see where I rank. Chickens first, Casey second." Casey made a shooing motion with her arms, and the chickens took off to search for something to peck and dig into.

"Come on, I need a shower and then a nap." She locked out the world, exhausted from her encounter with the evil adaptations of Amanda, Ben, and Clint.

Nine

"Where is he?" Ben struggled to stay calm, but it had been several hours since Junior and Senior were scheduled back.

"Do we need to move? Clint said if they hadn't returned in three hours to expect the worst and get out of here." Amanda pinched her lips together.

Seven hours passed. Everyone else slept. It didn't feel right to abandon Clint and leave. What if they came back after everyone left and they didn't have a way to them? Ben couldn't leave his best friend. They'd always been there for each other.

"I think we need to stay. I'm not leaving without them." Ben straightened.

"Oh, thank goodness!" Amanda rested her head on her folded arms on the table.

"Maybe we should have everyone else go on and the two of us wait for both Clints to return." Ben, the next one in charge, didn't want to be the cause of so many of their friends losing their lives.

Amanda shook her head. "I say we put it to a vote. We can't keep making decisions for everyone. Tell them what's going on so we don't keep anything from them, and if they want to leave, they can. Takes the pressure off us so we can concentrate on finding them and bringing them home."

Ben saw tears collect in his sister's eyes. He didn't think he would be able to handle it if she broke down. Her true feelings were written on her face. She could never hide what she thought of Clint. Ever since Ben read her diary and told Clint she had a crush on him, Ben had been able to read her whenever Clint was in the room. She thought she covered it so well, but he knew his baby sister better than she thought.

"Great idea. Do you want to gather everyone in the cafeteria, and I'll meet you?" Ben gave her something to do instead of sitting around imagining the worst.

Amanda hopped off the stool and disappeared through the door.

He slumped onto the stool she vacated and pressed his forehead against the cool surface of the table. "Father, I'm not sure I can handle losing my best friend. I know he went through the horrific loss of both me and my sister. Keep him safe and help us to find him so we can bring him back into our fold. Until that time, let him know You are with him and will never leave him, but carry him through this. In Jesus' name, Amen."

"Amen."

Ben jerked his head up to see Doc leaning heavily on his cane. Most days he got by without needing the implement, but other days his leg gave him fits.

"Talk to me, son." Doc's concern almost broke Ben.

"They left seven hours ago to take James and question him. They didn't come back, and I can't hear them on our communicators. We want to discuss our options with everyone all together and decide if they should leave for their safety. Amanda and I will be staying until our friend is home."

Doc patted him on the back. "Come on, let's join the group and get a rescue mission started."

Hushed voices filtered through the cracked door to the cafeteria. It sounded like Amanda gathered everyone in record time. Sure enough, as Ben followed Doc through, everyone stood or sat in the chairs around the tables where they ate their meals.

Everyone grew somber as he stood in front of them for the first time as their leader. "Clint is missing. It's possible the Monarchs have captured him."

Frantic no's echoed in the room.

"Amanda and I are staying until either option, to one, rescue him, or two, he rescues himself and comes back here, is completed." Ben almost slipped and mentioned Junior and Senior.

"I'm staying." Mark spoke up first.

"Me too." Chloe was the sweetest shy girl he ever met, but she never hesitated to be frank about what she believed in.

Soon, the entire room agreed they were not leaving until they liberated his best friend. The back of his eyes tingled with the outpouring of love in the room.

"I can't thank you enough for wanting to stay. They knocked James out when they left. He shouldn't be able to leak our location to the Monarchs. I say we pack a go bag and be ready to move at a moment's notice. We need to double our sentry schedules for the foreseeable future. If you can help out anywhere, let me know, and we will work out a schedule that suits each of you." Ben was beyond blessed to stand in front of so many amazing men and women.

"I'll organize a roster so you can concentrate on Clint. If everyone can give me preferred shifts, I'll set up the first watch this afternoon." Mark clapped him on the shoulder.

"I agree, if anything major needs to be addressed, still bring it to me and we'll see how to handle the issue. Other than that, our main focus is our missing brother in Christ." Ben bowed his head to pray, but his voice stuck in his throat.

Doc's voice echoed in the room. "Father, keep Your son safe and help bring him home. We know the Monarchs are capable of unspeakable horrors against fellow believers and want to wipe us off the planet. Keep Clint in Your hands, and send Your warriors to protect him in these trying times. In Jesus Christ's name, Amen."

Ben kept his head lowered as everyone whispered their support on the way out. They had to get Clint back. No other option or outcome was acceptable to Ben.

"I can't hear them, can you?" Amanda leaned into his side.

"Me either." He guided them to the lab to work up some sort of rescue attempt.

THE COUPLE OF MONTHS since Clint's disappearance crushed Amanda. There were no signs of the Monarchs in the area, which suggested they didn't know where they were. Clint's military friends transmitted locations for them to check, but they were either too late or received incorrect intel.

After two weeks, they went back to their normal sentry details and lucked out with no unwanted visitors. She would feel if Clint wasn't alive, but with each passing day the Monarchs didn't breach their shelter, she knew he didn't spill his secrets under torture or he...nope, not going there. Ben hardly slept and Amanda worried about him. She hadn't slept much either. They were no closer to finding the Clints than the first day. Senior informed them of a few things that happened when he came to retrieve her and Ben to take them to his uncle's where Casey waited, but so far, nothing played out the same.

Amanda and Ben wore scars from their time away from Casey's healing ability as they searched for Senior and Junior. Without the healing relic, they barely made it out of a skirmish alive. Amanda now sported a deep scar across her arm. Ben bore lash marks along his back when one of the soldiers got him down and whipped him with a metal bar he picked up.

The days they found nothing were almost better than the ones when they weren't sure they would make it back.

Doc kept them alive, but they healed so much slower without the key. The best tip Clint's friend gave them led to their last trip out. He couldn't go himself to recover Clint, so he relayed the details to Ben.

They walked into an ambush. The friend had the right intel, but Clint had fought his way out and escaped before Amanda and Ben arrived. They were still outnumbered five to one with most of the squadron out looking for Senior and Junior. The shield functioned enough for them to escape before it failed through a tool the Monarchs had and knocked Amanda unconscious. Ben hiked back with her over his shoulder in a fireman's carry, Amanda didn't remember the trip. It was a secret they would never tell Junior. Crazy protective of her, Junior wouldn't like her putting herself in danger to try and rescue him when he already rescued himself.

Casey'd vanished with no hint as to where she ended up and no rumors or sightings. Chloe's uncle couldn't find any trace to show she ever existed here. Amanda wanted to rail against the Monarchs and tell them to quit harassing everyone and go back to where they came from. Why couldn't they live in peace? They were always in some dire situation or another. She tired of always wondering when the next shoe was going to drop because it always did.

First the infections. Then the deaths from the bogus vaccines. This ultimately ended in the invasion and turning good old boys into traitors, killing their own neighbors to further their rank. It sickened her. Never a moment's peace to sit back and relax for one calm day.

Static buzzed in her ear through her communicator. She scrunched her eyes and tried to turn it off. Their nonstop hum for the first time since the Clints were taken filtered something through besides her or her brother's voices.

Running feet pounded down the hall, and Ben skated around the doorframe. "Did you hear that?"

"The static? I think my eardrums are bleeding." She pressed her hands against her ears.

"No, the voice. It's Clint." Ben's haunted eyes widened in disbelief.

"Hello?" Amanda yelped at Clint's voice.

"I'm here, Clint. Where are you?" Ben grabbed his weapon.

Amanda ran to keep up.

"I'm coming in from the north. Let the sentries know it'll be me."

Amanda unclipped her radio and alerted their friends. Moisture cascaded down her cheeks.

"Clint, is it bad?" She couldn't keep her voice steady.

"You could say that." He didn't sound like the Clint she knew.

"Wait, is there only one of you?" Ben stopped by the hidden tunnel they took to the parking garages they stored their vehicles in.

"I'll fill you in as soon as I'm inside. No one followed me, but let everyone know to be on alert. Wait, I thought you left. I didn't expect to find anyone here. Your orders were to leave so the Monarchs couldn't find you if they broke me. Why are you here?" Clint's voice quieted.

The wall scooted out of the way to access the ladder to bring Clint the last few feet into their fold. Clint grabbed Ben's outstretched hand as he helped him up the last few rungs. Ben pulled him into a hug and clapped him on the back.

"I wasn't leaving you, brother." Ben secured the tunnel and turned to catch Clint senior limping away, dragging his footsteps.

Senior, shoulders slumped in defeat, favored his left leg. Half of his head had been shaved at one point since one side was an inch shorter than the rest of his hair. The noticeable weight loss was shocking. Amanda gasped before running to him and throwing herself into his arms. Clint, always the fit, muscled one, staggered back. Ben steadied both of them. Now Clint's clothes seemed to be two sizes too big and sagged from his frame.

"Come on, let's go." Clint pushed Amanda away from him.

Amanda's gut churned at the rejection.

"Doc will want to see you first. Afterward, we'll get some food in you, and you can catch us up with what happened and where you were." Ben secured the latch behind them.

"No, we need to find Casey now. She isn't who you think she is. That woman is evil incarnate." Clint wouldn't make eye contact.

Amanda raised her eyebrows to Ben. What happened to the friend who left a few months ago? What had the Monarchs done to him? "Doc first, no arguments."

Clint headed toward the infirmary. Several people they passed talked in hushed whispers and gawked. Ben didn't say anything, but she wanted to rail against them for the blatant open shock they didn't have the decency to hide as they passed.

"Clint!" Doc bustled over and immediately went to work checking his vitals and doing a complete work-up.

"I'll meet you guys in a bit." Clint gave Ben a quick head jerk toward the hall and then at Amanda.

He was right, She didn't want to see any of his injuries.

"Come on, sis." Ben guided her out by her elbow.

"He doesn't look good." Amanda choked. "And where is Junior?"

"I don't think he made it." Ben draped his arm around her and pulled her to him as her first sob tore free.

No one would understand since Senior was technically still with them, yet they lost their Clint. This broken version survived, while theirs didn't.

Several minutes went by as they waited for him to join them. Amanda's face was a red blotchy mess. She went to rinse her face off and made it back before Clint stood in the doorway.

"Ben." Clint stumbled.

Ben gripped him by the arm and guided him to sit. "What happened?"

"I'm not sure. We were getting ready to question James. A sharp pain and a white-hot light incapacitated us. Then I woke up strapped to a chair. It was the same building they held Casey in. My other half screamed incessantly next door. They came in and were talking to me, but I couldn't comprehend what they were saying because I worried about him. His screams cut off and that is all I remember after they pushed a medical cart with squeaky wheels into my room. I woke up several times, and they fed me and let me shower, and I made my escape. There are holes in time and gaps in my mind." Clint's chin tremored.

"So, you never saw him again?" Amanda asked from the door, scared to step into the same room with this man. He was her hero in more ways than she could count.

"No. They filmed a vidcast. Casey was there."

"We have to go back for her." Ben leaped to his feet.

Clint shook his head. "No, as in: working with them. The vidcast played showing her killing the other me. She didn't hesitate; she pulled the trigger and walked out of the room as if she were bored."

"Not Casey." Ben lowered into a squat.

"She did and we have to stop her before she kills anyone else. Did you hear about the pulse taking out all the central states? All the riots and lawlessness? She's responsible. The relics have gone to her head. Our priority is to take her out before she can do more damage than she already has. I think she's still at my uncle's where I left her. If we can get the sphere to work, we need to jump to finish her off. Otherwise, we'll need to wait a couple of years for her to be there in the future where I came from. Right now, she's in Monarchs' headquarters, living in the lap of luxury, so we'll never touch her there. It's our only option to put an end to her reign." Clint tore through the storeroom and retrieved the sphere.

The pieces were as lifeless as when they'd stowed them in the box years ago.

"She would never do that!" Amanda ranted after getting herself under control enough to respond.

Ten

"Casey would never, and I mean never, murder someone, much less one of us." Ben's blood boiled at Clint's accusation.

"Are you calling me, your oldest friend, a liar? I know what I saw." Clint gripped the edge of the table and leaned toward Ben. It was an intimidation tactic Clint frequently used when he wasn't happy.

Amanda put her hand on Clint's arm. "We aren't saying that, but even you have to admit when you ported to us, you wanted us to follow you to Casey to unite the chosen. Why would you want that if you didn't trust her?"

Clint shoved away from the countertop and punched the wall by the door. "I was wrong. There is a side of Casey you haven't been introduced to yet."

"And the fact that she is the key, and you are sworn to protect her?" Ben rubbed at the tightness in his chest.

Clint clutched his head with both hands.

A phased-out field appeared in front of them, and Amanda yelped, jumping behind Ben. He couldn't believe who he saw, as Casey—no, not their Casey but another version—sprang through with an active sphere in her hand.

Ben couldn't move. Knockout gorgeous. He couldn't look away. Her mechanical arm gripped the sphere. She glared at them and started to raise her hand to aim at them.

Clint vaulted over the desk. He kicked up with his foot, and the sphere launched into the air.

Ben dove and caught it as Clint delivered another jolting kick, and Casey screamed as she flew toward the phased-out field and disappeared. Amanda slammed her hand down on the sphere and turned it off.

"What happened?" Chloe stood in the doorway.

"Casey works for the Monarchs. She tried to kill us." Clint plucked the sphere out of Ben's hand. "We need to make a few jumps before we go after her."

Ben nodded in agreement. That Casey was not the sweet woman he fell in love with.

"Ben?" Amanda's eyes brimmed with moisture. "What did the Monarchs do to her? Her arm—"

Blood flowed from Clint's nose; he gripped the sides of his head before he slumped to the floor.

AMANDA AND BEN WERE talking over each other, but all he heard were their murmurings as if they were in a tunnel. He heard their voices but couldn't make out the individual words they were saying.

"Give him another jolt." A guy laughed.

Clint screamed as electricity flowed over and through him. In all of his years in the military, nothing hurt like this. His other self in the room next to him screamed.

He wasn't sure if his suffering or the other one's made it worse. The longer they were together the closer they became, so when something happened to one, the other felt it. Like the twin theory where when one twin cried, the other was sad.

He never believed until now. But he felt everything that happened to his own self because they were the same person. There were two of him living in the same time.

"By the time we are done with him, he'll dispatch his own mother, believing anything we tell him." Who said that?

Clint tried to turn his head, but the shock seized his muscles again, so they were locked in spastic clenches.

"This guy is strong. Anyone would have given in by now and denounced his friends, believing they are the monsters we portray them to be. Crank it up."

"No, you idiot. You will fry his brain." Another guy's voice sounded within reach.

"So what? We have another one in the other room. I've never seen twins look so much alike, though. It's downright creep factor one hundred on the creep-o-meter." His chuckles made bumps break out along Clint's arms.

The next set of charges drove his head back as a silent scream opened his mouth without releasing a sound. How much more of this could he handle?

Casey's face flashed up on the screen in front of him, and they gave another jolt. Every time a picture appeared, the charge increased in potency.

He started to hate seeing her in front of him, because of what followed.

Junior gurgled out a scream but was suddenly silent.

Clint's head popped up when the door opened, and a woman stood in front of him holding a firearm. Blood splatter covered her. Her hair, like Casey's, stood at about the same height and weight.

Casey's face flashed in his mind as another surge went through him. He screamed when this one continued without giving him a break. He was ready to die when a voice came from his left, so close to his ear that if he turned his head, their noses would probably bump into each other.

"I'm going to kill you like I did your brother next door. Pathetic, the way he begged for his life. Never mentioned you, though. I'm also going to come for Amanda and Ben." Casey's face flashed across the screen when the electrical surge increased to such a level he fell into darkness.

Clint shivered as the memory assaulted him.

He struggled to get out of bed as Doc walked in but didn't have the strength.

"I see he's awake." Doc shuffled over to the edge of the bed next to Amanda. "It probably would have been a good idea for me to fully check you out the first time you were here instead of being pigheaded and refusing to let me complete my blood panels. Don't see nothing to be concerned about. He needs to have a few good meals to gain his weight back, but other than that, he's healthy."

"Thanks, Doc. Not sure what we would do without you." Ben followed him to the door.

"You want to tell us anything you can about your capture?" Amanda shifted uncomfortably.

"Is there more than one of her like more than one of me?" Clint fought against the tears his body, for unknown reasons, wanted to shed. He didn't cry. It must be the other one locked in his head pounding on an imaginary door to get out.

"Maybe, but are you sure you saw what you did? Casey? She's been gone for a long time. I didn't think the Monarchs had her. Can we find a way to rescue her? What she must be going through." Ben flipped the chair around and rested his arms over the back of it.

"Were you listening? Casey is working with them! She killed me. Clint or Junior...oh, you know what I mean." Clint ran his hands over his face.

"They must have made her do it. She's no match against them. You saw what they did to her when they held her only for a few hours. Imagine months and months of being at their mercy. We have to go in." Ben jumped back up antsy.

"Ben, she's not who we thought. She is now part of the enemy. We have to take her out, or she won't hesitate to do to us what she did to him." Clint stumbled, not waiting for them to follow. The veins in his temple pulsed violently.

"What about the Casey who came through the portal? She wore a bionic arm. Did the one in the vidcast have a mechanical arm?" Ben caught up to him.

"No, she didn't." Clint's hands shook as he palmed the sphere. "Now we evened the playing field having a working sphere."

"What do we do with the broken one?" Amanda carried the case from the storage room.

When she opened the lid, the pieces were gone.

Clint placed the sphere he pilfered from the other Casey into the molded cloth. "Disappeared like the weapon did when I came."

"Does that mean there can only be one relic or sphere in each timeline?" Amanda lowered the lid.

"I wouldn't doubt it, or someone would be able to collect as many as they wanted to arm an army. Although it wouldn't be a bad idea to test that theory." Clint squinted; a grimace crossed his face.

"Are you okay?" Amanda touched his arm.

"Yeah, need to eat something and rest. I'll catch up with you guys later. Let me know if there are any new developments." He didn't wait for them to acknowledge him.

The more he thought about Casey, the more intense the jolt through his head. He didn't want to scare them on how bad he felt. It would be his little secret right now until he figured out how to reverse what the Monarchs did to him. He could contact his friends from his team in the military and see if they had any insight into what he was dealing with.

He lay back on his bed and sighed. He stretched out flat for the first time in months; he hummed out a satisfied groan. He swore his muscles sighed along with him.

Having an operational sphere was a game changer. Now, how did he convince the others Casey threatened their very existence? Ben would follow his heart. He didn't have enough time to convince him otherwise. It would take a lot to get Ben on his side. Amanda would be easier.

Would he be better off starting with Amanda? She did have feelings for him; maybe he could use it to his advantage. Once Casey was out of the way, things would be better.

Another charge barreled through his temple. He turned over and muffled his scream with his pillow. How much more could he take? Footsteps sounded outside his and Ben's room. He evened out his breathing and faced the wall. He was not in the mood for the questions Ben would ask.

"Clint, are you awake?" He at least asked it in a quiet voice.

Clint didn't move and soon Ben left the room, leaving him to work on a strategy for them to get out of this alive. All except Casey. His mind filtered to when he first awakened in Doc's infirmary.

A hand on his forehead woke him, stirring him from a nightmare he hadn't been able to escape.

"Clint?" Amanda sounded to his right. "Ben, he's waking up."

"Water."

Ben appeared with a cup and helped him sit up. He drained it in one go. Still thirsty, he handed it back to be refilled. His voice didn't sound like his with the stress on the larynx from his screams. One particular rough patch was when he started coughing after an extended session and spit out blood from tearing the thin tender lining of his throat.

Clint drifted away into nothingness as the other side took over. The side the Monarchs controlled. "We have to kill Casey."

Clint struggled to stay in the present as the other lumbered just on the other side of the unconsciousness of sleep. Ben and Amanda needed to know what the Monarchs did. What he was capable of. They shouldn't trust him. Clint realized the chip was recording what happened around him and fed it directly to their headquarters. They were implanting thoughts and orders for him to carry out. The Monarchs had front-row seats to the relics and their powers.

He needed to leave a message the Monarchs wouldn't hear or see so Ben and Amanda could continue acting normal and help find a way to get this stupid thing out of his head. Casey, she wasn't the monster the Monarchs twisted her to be.

A white-hot jolt pierced through his left temple as everything went dark.

Eleven

The hair raised on the back of Casey's neck, coinciding with Daisy's growl. Metallic clicks reminded her of the mantises. The rush of fluttering wings drowned out Daisy's protests.

"Daisy, hide!" Casey wasn't sure if the dog would know what she meant, but she took off for the barn.

The noise grew louder until she was tempted to plug her ears. A layer of mantises crested over the trees and headed toward her. The shield acted on its own through her fear and popped open.

Her stomach hardened to the point of being painful as her ribs tightened around her heart. No Monarchs joined the creatures. Did they have anyone left who would fight for them?

A figure stood on the back of a large mantis as it settled in front of her.

"Where are all of your little minions you brainwashed into fighting against their own country?" Casey was more worried this time without the Monarchs.

"No comment about my entrance? I thought it was very benevolent, fitting of someone such as myself." It landed with a thud, bending one knee and then rising to tower over her.

"Kinda slow on the learning, aren't you? You are not benevolent, nor do you have a soul. You're a machine that some *man* made. You wouldn't exist without us humans to build you." Casey kept her grin to a minimum.

"I'll let you in on a little secret. I'm the leader. My synapses are firing faster than any human brain can even imagine. We build ourselves. I no longer need fragile mankind to endure, although their numbers give us an advantage on the battlefield. Since my large friend here is the only one we have rebuilt and because of the destruction of most motorized contraptions of travel, we put off bringing my soldiers."

"There has to be a creator out there somewhere. You didn't just blink into existence." Casey was steaming with the pride this machine demonstrated.

"Oh, he is no longer needed for us to function."

"Then why worry about me being out here? What makes me such a threat to something like you?" Casey listened as the mantises surrounded the shield and concentrated on the ones congregating behind her.

"You have powers the leader was interested in passing down through his lineage. His obsession with obtaining those gifts was written into our intelligence. Once he was discarded, we realized that incorporating the powers into our circuits would make us the top predator on the food chain, so to speak." His eyes flicked between black and silver.

"Just one problem with your take-over-the-world scheme. Humans don't give up, they fight. For their freedoms, for their God, for their loved ones." Casey was done with this thing's psychotic ramblings.

"You can't stop us." He gave a nod as the mantises covered her dome, blocking out the android.

"And you forgot what happened the last time your group came up against me." Casey swirled the red pulse across her fingers, tumbling it over and over as her left hand readied the yellow laser.

She felt the familiar pull of the relics as the mantises sucked the power from her through the shield. Not hesitating, she combined the powers and sent all she had into the shield, electrifying everything that touched the outer shell.

"Heal the shield."

Casey smiled so wide her cheeks hurt. Blue flew from her chest to the shield and reinforced it, knocking the creatures to the ground as yellow and red static melted the metal it touched. The cyborg screamed as his babies were crushed under the weight of the relics' powers.

"Your turn." Casey sent all that she had to the android, who turned to run but failed to get more than ten steps away before he was a pile of ash like his small minions.

Daisy's barking and yipping called to her as her friend danced around her feet after the shield withdrew. Healing the shield gave her an advantage over their discs.

The wind kicked up, flipping her hair around her face. She scrambled to pull it back and snapped a hair tie around it that she had on her wrist. Small vortices spun, pulling the ash into the air so fast she didn't have time to take cover before it was over. The pristine yard held no history of the Monarchs' presence.

"Father, I'll never get used to seeing You work."

She headed out to the coop.

Monarchs or no Monarchs, she still had lots of work to do.

She kept the chickens confined instead of letting them free range. Three ended up being something's snack last week, and one chicken's feathers were half-plucked from its back. Something got a hold of them. She and Daisy were spoiled by the fresh eggs every day and the juicy chicken dinners, and very much accustomed to them now. When she collected the eggs every morning, some snuck through her perusal and hatched, adding to her flock.

Her interior coop designing skills freely flowed to create nirvana for them. Walking the exterior of the outbuilding, she pictured where would be the best place to cut a hole in the side and attach the outside run to it and put in a small door to escape the elements.

Working in this capacity, building her visions with her own bare hands gave her a sense of accomplishment she'd never had, no matter how hard her day-to-day job got back home. But watching her creations take root in her mind and transform them into a reality turned out better than she fathomed.

She recycled what she had on hand since she couldn't go traipsing down to the local hardware store for supplies. She thought she did pretty good. She took off her jacket earlier and now swiped the back of her hand across her eyes.

Casey wanted her friends back. Would there ever be a time they were back for good? Her mind drifted to times before they lost Amanda. There was something about them. The four of them clicked. She felt empty without them.

Shaking herself out of her musings, she glanced up at the sky and hoped there would be a chance of rain so she wouldn't have to rely on the well water to give her plants a drink. With the cloudless blue overhead, her wish for the drops that would quench their thirst deflated.

Nodding, Casey stood back to admire her work. It looked good, even if she did say so herself. She chose the first stall across from the far side of the door as the base for the coop. She cut beams and angled them overhead to staple wire around them to keep predators out. With the cut-down bundles of grass she spread out, it looked pretty cozy. Now, she had to see if the chickens liked their new home.

She would also move the water and food inside. If it would keep her from taking a screwdriver and hammer to chip off the frozen layer of water every day, she called that a win.

Her mind drifted to how easy of a life she lived in her own house. Having Mason by her side had made her feel safe. Back then, she couldn't fathom any other life for herself. Now she wouldn't go back for anything. Even with all of the ups and downs. The death of her friends. The heartache. She would still pick this life over the other.

This struggle to survive only made her feel more alive.

"Come on, Daisy. I need your stealth herding capabilities." Casey let the chickens out to attach the outdoor area against the barn.

She would have Daisy work her magic and chase them back inside. The little ramp giving the chickens access to their indoor coop latched on the lip of the bottom of the opening with hooks.

Standing back, Daisy moved them back inside the enclosure after Casey butted it up against the slatted boards. She felt tickled when the first chicken ran right up the ramp and inside.

"Let's go check them out." Casey slogged her way around the side when she heard the chopper.

"Run!" Casey didn't need to tell Daisy. She already headed into the shaded opening of the barn while Casey still had half the distance to go.

She slid the door only partially behind her. She braced her hands against her knees, taking in gulps of air.

"Momma needs to work out more, baby girl." Daisy cocked her head to the side and stuck her tongue out panting.

She looked like she laughed at her.

This time, they never ventured closer than several acres away. What would the motivation be to search for so long? The fuel bill had to be astronomical. She would have to make sure she made herself scarce. If they stayed away from her, she would let them do what they needed to.

But if they didn't, all bets were off, and she would defend this new home she grew to love over the years and the back-breaking hard work she put in. With the calmer weather, this trip was one of the longest they stayed in the area, flying in almost perfect lines back and forth. Their determination to locate what they were looking for made her wistful for her friends. It must be worth a lot to them to persist for two years.

The relics roared to the front, no longer dormant. Her hair whipped around the back of her head as power coursed over every inch of her. The glyphs on her arms grew brighter as Daisy whined and darted behind a pallet.

As the helicopter steadily flew south, the relics calmed down and became a muted presence in her mind. She hadn't felt them so strong in ages. It gave her hope they would soon be at their full strength after this morning. Did that mean the Monarchs were headed back?

The chickens were in heaven scratching through the ground covering and munching on anything they found. She learned the year before that if she left on the porch light, there were tons of June bugs. Once they landed in glass jars she set outside, they were stuck because of the slick sides. The chickens almost got into skirmishes trying to gobble them up. The second time she came out with the jar of beetles, she laughed so hard she let go of the jar and let the chickens out to eat them. She'd never seen a chicken run.

She didn't have to use the jar on the porch to coax them up the ramp. Apparently, they were efficient in getting in and out of the shelter as they clucked at her when she headed to the house from their outdoor pen.

"Ladies, I'll be back." She snatched the jar off the railing and quickly let them enjoy their treats.

Casey was in a holding pattern. The parchment didn't help since nothing had been added in a long time. The first thing she used to do when she woke in the mornings was to check for new information. Now, she rarely checked at all. The relics humming under her skin told her there was about to be a change.

She let the static of both weapons play along her fingers, rolling it over and over and flipping it through her digits like twirling a pen, mesmerized by the action. Her eyes glowed blue in the reflection of the back window as she set the June bug jar back on the railing for the next night. The shield popped back out and she manipulated it, expanding or shrinking it to her wishes.

"Father?" Was the reactivation of the relics the telling of an approaching storm?

"Patience. I am with you always."

"I know." Casey secured the house and started for the stairs. Since Daisy arrived, she slept on a real bed instead of the couch downstairs. The smallest noise alerted the dog, and she would wake Casey.

Were Ben, Clint, and Amanda going to port again? Were they going to be the friends she loved or the barbarians she dealt with earlier? She wanted her friends back, and she would do almost anything to have them all living here with her. She wanted to scold herself for wishing they would come back, even the bulked-up trio, so she would have people to talk to. Yelling and reprimanding her counted, didn't it?

Twelve

"See, right there." Clint flung the reports across the table at Ben and Amanda, scattering the pages across the smooth black-coated surface. "Now do you believe me?"

Ben fumbled, trying to stop them from sliding off the slick table. He didn't want to, but the military reported Casey in the midst of the lawlessness that ravaged the surrounding states. The energy of the pulse knocked everything out, but for her to go with the Monarchs to massacre entire populations that had survived, was unreal. Quite a few residents hid, refusing to leave the only homes they knew. It was no different than if she tracked them down and pulled the trigger herself.

It had been a couple of days since their last trip out with the sphere. He felt different with every use.

"I don't know, Clint. You know the technology the Monarchs have. Look at what they did with the viruses. Do you have someone you know personally who witnessed this?" Amanda fingered the pages, not quite picking them up as she perused them. "These are words on paper and images of the aftermath."

"Guy stationed with me overseas; he saved my life more than once so you might say I believe him. The Monarchs tried to keep her out of sight like a secret they didn't want anyone knowing about, but he saw her." Clint scooped up the pages with Casey front and center and jammed them in the folder.

"That's not the Casey we brought here." It distressed Ben to see Casey capable of such heinous acts.

How had the sensitive, gentle woman he fell in love with turned into a monster? He would never be able to turn his back on his friends and switch to the other side, no matter what they did to him. He would rather die than turn on his God, family, and friends.

"Maybe they're forcing her. If we can go rescue her, maybe she will—"

"No! How many times do I have to tell you what I saw her do? If you don't trust my source, at least believe me," Clint muttered. "Neither one of you would do what she did no matter what the Monarchs put you through, would you?"

Ben and Amanda didn't answer.

"You would choose death over killing anyone much less one of us." Clint stormed out.

Ben interrupted Amanda when she started to argue her stance again. "Sis, I agree the woman God told me to bring here is not that Casey. They broke her. Changed her. Clint is right. We need to stop fighting among ourselves and work as a team again. Only then will we get answers."

Amanda slumped over the table and put her head in her hands. "I know. You're right."

"Of course I am. I'm the mighty big brother to you pipsqueak." Ben tugged her to his side as he pulled her to the cafeteria to grab food.

"Clint's not the same since he came back," Amanda muttered under her breath.

Ben agreed it would change anyone if they were held for months by their enemy. Clint alluded to the hours and weeks of torture he suffered at the Monarchs' hands. Clint endured another nosebleed this morning, which took forever to stop.

Clint drilled them about what happened when he saw the scars from their rescue attempts for the first time, his concern genuine. Ben had already glimpsed Clint's fractured mind. The light had gone out of his eyes. Some days he saw a hint of his friend while other days, he only saw the fractured shell of a man. They informed him they were in an accident and didn't elaborate. His friend was already stressed out enough. He didn't need to pile more on his plate when they were fine and had survived while Junior hadn't. It wasn't worth bringing it up.

Now there was only a coldness, the dark side of the soldier he fought to keep under wraps since his last deployment with the military. The internal battle ravaged him. Ben didn't see his happy trusting friend but rather a shadow of the man he used to be, one who never second-guessed Ben's loyalty or Amanda's.

They lost count of how many times they ported to gather information and resources. Clint had the bright idea that if they jumped back and forth, maybe they could collect more relics and each have their own weapons and shields.

With every jump, Ben found it harder and harder to care about Casey. He wanted it to be over. They were all exhausted and needed rest, but Clint's relentlessness kept them both up. The scheme to collect numerous relics failed. When they ported back, the weapon and shield disappeared before they finished the trip. Now, they were no better off than when they started all of this. This could have been handled and done and over with before now if the sphere didn't need recharging. It was never an issue before because they didn't try to jump continually. If one of them noticed the charge was complete, they'd notified the others so their ports were carried out as soon as possible so it could work on replenishing itself.

They didn't speak as they ate their breakfast. Both were engrossed in their thoughts. Ben didn't know how to try to fix this. The urge to kneel and call out to their Heavenly Father crashed into him like a cannonball to the gut. He couldn't remember a time he set aside for God lately.

Amanda wiped her eyes.

"I want to pray." Ben faced the room so he could see the doors.

"Me too," Amanda whispered.

"Father..." Ben had never been at a loss for words when he prayed before. He talked to God as if He were a dear friend. Now he fumbled with what to say after calling out to Him.

Amanda clasped his hand. "Father. We are floundering without you. Please help us find our way home to You. Amen."

Ben gulped and blinked away the moisture in his eyes.

"Short and to the point seemed the way to go." Amanda released his hand to finish eating.

"Not going to invite me to join you for a meal?" Clint forcefully set his tray down with a clatter. The fork jumped out of the molded section for silverware, landed on the table, and broke the silence.

Everyone sensed the change in Clint and kept their distance. If he walked into a room, they walked out. Ben knew Clint fought to not bring it up and point out people's hesitancy in trusting him. When they first arrived, everyone looked to Clint for guidance. He kept them alive. Now that dependence was gone.

Three people frantically loaded everything back on their trays and fumbled with picking them up before taking their half-full trays to their rooms, clearing out part of the group eating.

"I think we need to talk about our strategy when we finally jump to Casey." Clint shoveled potatoes into his mouth as he continued. "She will be jumpy, having been alone for so long. I think we should jump separately so one of us can ease her into our return before we hit her with the knowledge and the evidence of her becoming a traitor."

"How? We only have one sphere. You know it isn't available for another go immediately." Amanda pushed her tray to the middle of the table.

Ben struggled with the nagging pull that they were missing something.

"She will probably try to confuse us, pit us against each other. So, I was thinking...One of us needs to go through and scope things out. She might be alerted or warned when the sphere is activated. But say Amanda goes through first and holes up, staying out of sight. We deactivate it on this side. Casey won't be able to find Amanda or the portal, so she'll let her guard down. When several minutes pass, Ben and I jump." Clint didn't look up from his lunch.

"How do we join Amanda when the sphere won't be ready?" Ben balked.

"If we shut it down from here and no one jumps back, I'm hoping it will recharge faster."

"That makes no sense." Amanda shook her head.

"We have to try something to throw her off."

"Wait, she won't be able to explain away if she is alerted to a portal and just ignore it." Ben pursed his lips.

"Amanda is fast. She can hide before Casey knows one of us used the sphere. I say we can give you a sedative to knock her out, putting us on even playing fields." Clint smirked. "If you have to be one with nature for a few days if we can't come right away, you are fine with that?"

"Sleep outside? Unless someone has a gun to my head the answer is no." Amanda huffed.

"So, knock out Casey and then sleep in the house and wait for us." Clint shoveled another forkful of food into his mouth.

"What about when she wakes up? She is stronger than we are. Every relic is part of her DNA now. We only have one per person each." Amanda let her hair fall over her face.

Clint, with a gentleness Ben hadn't known him to have lately, placed a syringe with a dark solution on the table.

"What is that?" Chills ran down Ben's spine. He didn't like where this was going.

"It removes the relics. She has no protection if they aren't active, and I can end this once and for all." Clint tapped his finger on the glass cylinder.

"Is that what I think it is? The parchment said to use it with caution. And by, end this, you mean as in bring her back and help reverse what the Monarchs did, right?" Amanda darted a glance between the two of them before settling on Ben's face. She widened her eyes asking for him to back her up.

"There is only one way to end this. She needs to be taken out. Do I have to say the actual words?" Clint's nostrils flared.

"Come on, you're going a bit too far. Who did you get that from? Doc doesn't have access to anything even the slightest bit that lethal." Ben stood reaching for the elixir.

Clint's fast reflexes tucked it in the inside pocket of the jacket he wore. "Don't worry about where I got it. I have connections from my time in the military, you know that. We needed the upper hand and I got it for us. No, I don't believe it is going too far. We don't take prisoners. Are you in or out? I won't hesitate to do this myself if you don't have thick skin to cope with the harsh realities of life. This is war and she's the enemy. What if this were the Monarchs? Would you defend those around you who can't fight for themselves?"

"It's not the same. The Monarchs are psychos who get sick entertainment from what they do. Casey..."

"What Ben? Casey isn't one of them? What about the evidence you saw with your own eyes? Now you need to decide which side you are on. Are we fighting to break free of a genocide maniac, or do we put our hands up and wave a white flag? I won't be a quitter; I don't give up easily. How many times have we been knocked down, yet here we are, still standing? There shouldn't be a choice on what the best course of action is." Clint stomped toward the door. His knuckles turned white at Amanda's next question.

"What about God?" Amanda asked, trailing after him.

"What about Him? I don't think this is something He's concerned about. Once we have our relics and find the fourth, we will let Him guide us where we need to go and He'll give us the next steps to take down a terrorist group. The Monarchs are killing us. He doesn't have time to sort the small details. We have to take charge for once and do what needs to be done so He can handle the large decisions." Clint shrugged.

"Everything concerns God. But I agree. They are killing us and have been for years. Do you see a way to reverse what they did to Casey?" Ben's heart pulled him to his best friend. He still loved Casey, but the reports were hard to ignore.

"I wish there was. I want to keep my two closest friends safe. Amanda, I can't go through losing you again. The first time wrecked me. I believe God is giving us another chance to make it right, to undo what happened to you. Casey being a part of our group changed things. Maybe we were wrong to bring her to our time. Could that be the answer?" Clint retook the stool he vacated before they ate and squinted his eyes at the bright lights.

"What about the key?" Amanda put her chin on her hands, her elbows resting on the table.

"Maybe activating the relics and leaving should have been the extent of it. Go back to where she's from. Did bionic Casey seem to know us as if she never met us before? Maybe that is the timeline we are supposed to live in. Activate the relics to thwart the evils of the world. The three of us." Clint squeezed a hand on each of them, pleading for them to understand.

"You know that's possible." Ben agreed, but his heart craved for Casey to be in his life.

He refused to let his feelings put everyone else in jeopardy. Sending Casey home may turn the tide of the war. The more he thought about it, the more he agreed with Clint.

"So, is that our new plan? We jump at different times. Hide and when her defenses are down, we go in and render her use of the relics dormant. Transport her home so she can live out the life she's born to live." Amanda clambered on board with that idea.

"I can work with that. You know I want to take retribution for the lives taken." Clint's eyes glimmered for a second and Ben saw his old friend.

"If we send her back, they won't be lost. We come back here years before it happens. She can't activate the EM pulse that destroyed entire states and reverted them back to destitute pre-technology lives. We don't agree with ending her life." Amanda dug her fingernails into her palms.

Ben pried her fingers open before she dug her nails in. Clint frowned, concern flooding his features.

"You're right, we erase any evidence of her existence here in our time." Clint knocked his knuckles against the table and left.

The thought of never seeing Casey again once she went home didn't sit well with Ben, but he wouldn't admit it out loud. They found a way to save her and also all the thousands snuffed out by misuse of the relics.

"Will you be okay? I know you were developing feelings for her." Amanda was the only person he talked to about what Casey meant to him after they got Clint back from the Monarchs.

"Sure. I mean, we were together for only a couple of months. What a great suggestion. Every person restored." Ben hooked his arm around his sister's neck and rested his chin on top of her head. "Thanks, sis."

They talked over the details and the differences between their Clint, Junior, and the one ported back to their time. Technically he was still the same person, but what he experienced and saw changed him. Now with his escape from being tortured by the Monarchs, Ben hardly recognized his friend.

"Can I ask you something, and you won't tell your bestie?" Amanda tried to kid but Ben saw the seriousness in her.

"I'll keep it a secret as long as it doesn't interfere with what we are trying to accomplish." It was the best answer Ben could give his sister.

"I think the Monarchs did something to Clint." When Ben didn't interrupt her, she forged on. "He would never tolerate murder. When we used the sphere for resources and to steal more relics, I was angry and ready to act on his request. But..."

"Now that we are back, waiting for it to refresh, you don't have the conviction to follow through?" Ben wondered the same thing.

"Yes!"

"I don't know what to think. On one side, I agree. Look at what they put Casey through when they took her on the food run. If they had her any longer, I'm sure she wouldn't be the woman she is today." Ben realized deep down he still saw her as the woman he loved and the key to the prophecy.

"I don't want to think negatively about him. Just wanted to express my concerns."

"Sis, don't worry. You aren't the only one."

"I forgot to tell you, Mom and Dad called again." Amanda smirked.

"Ugh, what, don't tell me they want us to move out there with them? We already told them we need to stay and see this through." Ben nudged his sister to the door. They talked long enough he was shocked at the time; his hungry stomach announced lunchtime.

"Yep. And they want us to bring Clint. You know they worry about him too. They definitely picked the right time to move to the coast." Amanda dragged her heels against the floor as she followed him.

"Perfect timing." Ben hung a left.

"They also said they had a compulsion to pray. Specifically, for us. Said, God urged them to pray for us, so they were checking in. I updated them on a couple of things along with getting Clint back. That only spurred them on to all but demand we move there." Amanda balanced her tray with one hand.

"Why would they feel the urge to pray? There's nothing more going on than there has been since the invasion." Ben chose soup and two sandwiches.

"Because of deceit of the heart. Do you know what that means?" Amanda sat down at the last table on the left.

"Deceit?"

"Don't look at me like that. I'm as confused as you are." Amanda took a large unladylike bite of her burrito.

Mark stopped by their table. "Will we see you at Bible study tonight?" He lowered his voice. "It's been several weeks since you attended."

"Probably not. There are some developments we are still working out." Ben grimaced at the lame excuse.

"God shouldn't be put on the back burner because we're busy. You know that more than anyone. There's never a time when we tell God to wait while *we* figure things out. That's why He is there. So, we can go to Him, and He lifts us from the mire in our lives. We can't lift ourselves, hence the verse 'I can do all things through God.' God doesn't let us walk alone." Mark left before Ben or Amanda commented.

"Do you think he's right?" Amanda chugged her water.

"If we can finish getting a few things resolved, we'll be sitting in a better place." Ben put the crust over to the side of his tray to dunk in his soup.

Clint had an overloaded tray of food and stalked over, carrying two extra cups of juice with him. He didn't say anything as he pushed the cups in their direction.

"What is this?" Ben eyed the drink.

"They have extra juice and want to make sure it's drank before it goes bad." Clint shrugged and downed his before wiping the back of his sleeve across his mouth.

Ben and Amanda drank theirs as they finished their meal in silence.

Ben swayed on his feet as they walked to the lab. Amanda started to drop when Clint caught her.

"What did you do?" Ben's vision blurred.

"This way, you won't remember the conversation we had about sparing Casey." Clint heaved Amanda over his shoulder as he wrapped a hand around Ben's waist, helping him back to his room.

Clint disappeared with Amanda, taking her to her room on the other side where the women bunked. Ben tried to repeat they should rescue Casey over and over, hoping he would remember something about it before he drifted off.

Thirteen

An alert from Casey's glyphs on her arms announced a portal had opened. She ran to the front yard, her heart racing in anticipation but didn't see or hear anything. Rustling in the shrubs had her holding her hands up, ready to release shields. Would her versions appear today? The ones she grew to love or the hardened cruel excuses for her friends?

A raccoon hissed and spit at her when she walked closer. That didn't make sense. The relics warned of an opening portal, which had never happened before, and she knew the raccoon didn't travel through one.

No breeze stirred, and tweeting birds flew through the tops of the trees, checking on their nests. Casey checked her symbols again, but nothing glowed. Weird.

She went back inside and continued to dust the shelves in the den. A floorboard creaked. She held the duster motionless in her hand, only the end of the feathers quivered with the hint of movement.

She peeked around the doorframe; the house groaned as a wind stirred up outside.

Casey laughed at her paranoia and went on with her dusting.

Later, she made a quick lunch and ate outside on the front porch.

The tops of the bushes across the road shook as squirrels darted through them before scampering halfway up the large black locust, clinging to the bark with their sharp claws. Her glyphs lit up, showing the portal symbol. She held her hands up and walked down the steps to check the side of the house.

A whoosh behind her; she squatted and hurled shields around Ben and Clint, acting on instinct, her defenses on full alert.

She blocked the sound as they pounded on the sides. Clint's face flushed with varying shades of red as he clenched his hands into fists.

What did that mean that he couldn't walk out of the bubble on his own? She remembered when she put Ben and Clint in shields before, but to keep them safe. Now it kept her safe from them?

According to the prophecy, they couldn't use the relics against each other. They sensed the chosen DNA.

She shifted her hands to let a sound out when they calmed down. "Why are you guys doing this to me?"

"Nice try with the innocent act. We've been hunting you for a long time," Clint interrupted her before Ben said anything.

"Casey, maybe we should sit down and talk to each other." Ben put his hands out to his sides.

They looked different than the previous ones. Clint, aggressive as always but with a smaller build. She almost wondered if he shrunk. Ben didn't have the muscle mass he accumulated in the other version. They should know she was the key. She had a hard enough time believing in time travel when she was first taken, but were there different dimensions? Why were only Ben and Clint here? Were they the only two left?

"Casey, we can help you. There is a procedure to remove a chip in your body. It's making you do what the Monarchs want you to do." Amanda drew her attention away while Clint pulled a Glock and fired off several rounds.

Clint tilted his head to the side, closed one eye, and grimaced when none of them hit her.

Casey spun, ready to send a shield to cover Amanda, but Amanda shot her as she turned. The stinging in the shoulder didn't compare to the red-hot heat when she took a bullet. She reached back, only to find a cylinder sticking out of her shirt. She shook her head as her vision blurred. "You..."

The shields dissolved, freeing Ben and Clint.

"Do you have it?" Clint spoke to Ben.

"Yep, give me her arm and this will rid her of the power she has over the relics." He jabbed a needle in, not sparing her his harsh treatment of her.

Her skin was on fire from whatever the syringe injected into her veins as it traveled through her bloodstream. She opened her mouth, but only silent screams left her. Paralyzed with whatever Amanda injected her with, she couldn't fight the subsequent injection's torture of the worst kind.

Clint yanked her up by her arms and deposited her over his shoulder.

They stalked into the house and tossed her on the couch. These weren't her friends and the man she fell in love with.

"I'm starving. Let's see what she has to eat in here." Amanda, the first one to leave, stepped past her, coming close to knocking her off the sofa as she bumped into her legs.

Dishes clanked in the kitchen, and smells of something delicious wafted through the house, while Casey's nightmare engulfed her. Acid burned in her veins. She couldn't scream, couldn't make a noise. What happened for them to throw their friendship with her away? The men and woman she came to know were not who these people were.

Yellow flecks coated her fingers as they dripped out of her into a puddle on the floor. Clint smirked as the ring's power drained from her. With every drop, her heart slowed.

Next, the opal color swirled around her wrist, untwisting from her skin and crawling like a vine. It was trying to find purchase, but soon, there was nothing but a memory of its caressing touch. The red beam fired straight into the floor with all the pomp and circumstance of the finale of a fireworks display. She screamed as her skin split on her palm before healing back over when it left her.

Her labored breaths filled the air. Every grueling release of the relics tore another hole in her soul. She understood now how much they had sewn into her own being, metamorphosing into a permanent part of her. Like having a limb cut off, the loss of the relics left her hollow.

She cranked her head back as the blue healing aura surged from her into the den, bypassing Clint, who watched with fascination at her anguish.

They couldn't shove her to the side and cause inexplicable pain and toss her away as if she were trash while they ate a meal!

"She has canned apples!" Amanda's voice filtered through the fog.

Silverware scraped against the dishes as they stuffed themselves on all of her hard work over the past couple of years. She tried to figure a way out of this. Her mind went back to the day Ben kidnapped her and all she wanted to do was run away from him. Once again, they frightened her.

She doubted the three, who sat so close while she writhed in agony, would hesitate to execute her.

Clint perched in the recliner he used to sit in when the two of them made this their home while it sounded as if the other two emptied her food reserves. "Casey, are you still with us?"

"What's happening? What did you give me?" Casey groaned as she pushed to a seated position, twisting her hands together. How long did it take them to prepare dinner and take their own sweet time devouring it?

She'd been in torment the entire time.

"Do we need to restrain you, or are you going to behave?" Ben gestured to her hands as Amanda plopped down next to her on the couch.

"I want to know what's going on. I want to know what you did to my friends." Casey feared what they were going to tell her.

"Classic. Casey trying to be the caring friend we all know she isn't. We've been running from the Monarchs for years now. Until you came into the picture and took your place as the key." Clint scooted forward. His face scrunched and he pinched the bridge of his nose with his thumb and forefinger.

Casey pulled her brows in. “Yes, we all know this.”

“You also turned on us and got my other half killed.” Clint glared at her.

“I’m sorry. I don’t think I heard you right.” Casey started to stand but Ben and Amanda put their hands on her shoulders and tugged her back down.

Ben motioned for her to not try and get up again.

“You were taken four years ago. The night you escaped and ran, they swapped you out with a decoy. The one sitting in front of us. When I went back to bring Ben and Amanda to you, you turned off the sphere, trapping me in the past. All of this, a big hoax to manipulate the leaders of the resistance so the Monarchs could assassinate them.” Clint was supposed to be her protector.

“But if you were going to kill me, why go through the trouble of removing my powers?”

“I couldn’t take the chance you would take them to your grave. So, we proposed removing what is rightfully ours so you can go home. I wanted to give you a last opportunity to prove you aren’t the imposter I believe you to be. Maybe the Monarchs did something to make you turn on the chosen, your friends.” Clint huffed.

“No that’s not true. I’m still me just like you are still you even though there were two of you in the same time. You aren’t acting like the Clint I know; doesn’t that make you phony? The Monarchs never took me except the day in the old neighborhood where they tortured us three and when the grocery run ran into a bit of trouble, which you know about.” Casey couldn’t wrap her head around this, but she didn’t like it.

"This is going to be confusing so try to follow along. Casey, Clint watched a vidcast of what you did to Clint's other half while the Monarchs held them. We woke our Clint, dubbed Junior, after your Clint, Senior, walked through the sphere's phased-out field. Yeah, yeah, yeah, we know they are the same person but from different times. It was just confusing to try and keep them straight, hence the titles. You looked right at us and shut it down. We all watched you. There was no compassion in your eyes." Amanda squeezed harder holding her in place with her hand.

"Why would I stay here for three years fighting for my life? Struggling to keep this place so we can all live here?" Casey tried to use the shield to push them away, but nothing happened.

Ben chuckled. "The relics don't work for you. A serum in the parchment deactivates the key. Clint was lucky enough to know a scientist who could create it so we could take back what was rightfully ours. You aren't our fourth. The Monarchs have the real Casey, and we will get her back."

Casey looked down at her palms. No static, no red or yellow flecks of relics flowed in her body. She only felt a void as if they ripped her soul from her. An empty husk of the person she used to be. The friends who sat in front of her were not the ones she knew. What happened that made them hate her to the extent they refused to listen to her? Casey wanted to talk everything out. Dread gripped her worse than when Clint left her behind and abandoned her. More severe than the Monarchs' first attack happening here that she fought off.

This had to be a bad dream. She was going to wake up at any moment and find out she was still alone and had powers. She huffed at the thought she came to rely so much on them. Now, having them gone felt as if she were naked without any way to hide herself from their glares.

"Okay, I need you to listen to me. Like you guys did a long time ago. We would talk things through. For old times' sake, can we give it a go once more? Please listen to me?" Casey didn't know how to make them believe her.

Clint waved his hand at her, giving her permission to speak. How considerate of him.

"Clint, you and I came to your uncle's house years ago. You and I were the only two left. Amanda had been killed, Ben, taken out by a sniper's bullet while we buried friends taken out by the Monarchs. Please tell me you remember those events." Casey might stand a chance if his memories were still intact with what happened while they were together.

"I've already told them everything that happened before I ended up back in Amanda's room. Everything we survived." Clint rolled his eyes.

Casey cleared her throat. "Right so, the night you went through the sphere, it fell apart as soon as you ported, leaving me here by myself. I absorbed your relic like the others. The sphere surrounded the house and cocooned me into a safe bubble for a while. I think that was to allow me to get my feet under me and work through the shock of losing you also. You put the phone in your pocket so I couldn't call anyone to help, and no one came looking. Although it is interesting that you and—what did you call the other one—Junior, were taken by the Monarchs. You survive and are the only witness out of you three of my slide into being a traitor and killer. Yet no one is looking at the fact this all revolves around you."

Ben tilted his head, taking in her words. Something in his gaze told her he didn't buy it.

"I never left and teamed up with the Monarchs. I've been here, fighting for my life. The Monarchs kept sending wave after wave of those creatures and soldiers for the first couple of days. I was waiting for you to come through time and join me, since the sphere didn't work. I thought I would have to wait years until you returned, but now that you have a sphere, we can finish the prophecy." She stared down as she picked at her cuticles. She didn't want to think about how many people she harmed or worse to survive. Vibrating and bumping sounds came from the office.

"How did you defend yourself against so many? You're not military trained, and if I remember right, you could hardly shoot, much less take out an entire squadron of Monarchs. This is why we need to finish this; we need to get back to searching for the real Casey. You shifting the spotlight off of you and implicating that I've been converted isn't going to work." Clint stomped into the office his gun raised.

Drawers scraped against their rail system as they were yanked open and then slammed closed.

"Ben, Amanda, please listen. I could never hurt you much less work with the Monarchs or murder Clint. Tell me you believe me." Casey reached for Amanda, who leaped up and put space between them.

"Casey, we would like to, but with what Clint saw you capable of, I regret ever pulling you into the future with me. You have the coldest heart I've ever known. You have no remorse when you take a life. The real Casey we are fighting to bring back is the only one I care about. I don't know how the Monarchs were able to grab one of you, but it breaks my heart I ever trusted this copy of Casey." Ben stood as if he hadn't ripped her heart out.

A sob tore through her. "But did you actually see me do it? Or just Clint, when the Monarchs had them?"

"Be ready."

Casey sat up straighter.

"Ha, told you she was a liar." Clint marched back into the living room with the sphere in one piece.

Amanda quickly pulled a gun from behind her back while Ben pointed his barrel at her chest.

The sphere soared into the air and projected a glance at the house from a week ago. She remembered because a mother doe gave birth to a rare white fawn in the front yard.

Casey threw herself out of a seated position so fast they weren't prepared for it. She jumped in the air and stole the sphere as she propelled herself toward the shimmer. Shots pierced through the night and right into her as she tumbled headfirst into the past. The past for her but the future for the other three. By her calculations of the events, she and Clint survived, and they were still a year or two behind her in time, which is why they pursued her by porting to her future time. They initially brought her forward thirty-five years, yet now, ironically, they were trying to play catch up to her.

Casey landed on her back and stayed on the floor. She whimpered and tried to call on the healing relic to help her.

Nothing happened.

Whatever they injected her with had done its job. She couldn't sense or use any of the relics she absorbed. Her stomach was a sticky mess as blood seeped out of her. The hole by her shoulder started hindering her breathing. She probably punctured a lung.

Casey rolled over onto her stomach and saw the den through a hazy vision. She couldn't feel her legs. Was she paralyzed or in shock? The healing stone was her only option to make it. She set the sphere on the cushion of the chair and let it roll to the back so it wouldn't fall to the floor and shatter again.

She bent her elbows, using her forearms to pull herself forward, and cried out at the pulling in her shoulder. Casey rested her head on her arms as she struggled to breathe. A few more inches and she rested again. Her legs were dead weight she dragged behind her as she pulled herself along with her arms.

This continued for longer than she thought she should be alive for. Once in the den, she pulled herself up with her hands, using the legs of furniture, and forced the top back, but couldn't reach the crystal treasure chests they were kept in. Her fingers skimmed the leather desk mat she forgot covered the surface.

She curled her fingers, rolling the edge of the mat and giving it a tug. Everything crashed around her. She barely got her head covered with her hands when the healing relic tumbled out of the case. Her arms gave out as she shuddered through her next breath. She was spent and had no energy to continue.

She reached for the stone. Her fingertips brushed the cold dark surface with no hint of the healing ability in there. Did Ben, Clint, and Amanda seal her fate? Did she survive three years fighting the Monarchs only to be taken out by her friends?

Casey's body chilled from the loss of blood as a shiver flowed through her. "Father, I'm ready."

"Oh child, you still have much to learn about what I can do."

Daisy ran into the room and nudged her cheek with her wet cold nose. "Hi, baby girl."

Casey's fingers still sought purchase on the stone. Daisy sniffed the relic and prodded it until it flipped over, getting it within Casey's reach.

Warmth emanated from her fingertips. Her eyes flicked open, and she gaped at the blue in the stone as it crept and crawled up her arm. The hieroglyphs flickered to life as they journeyed their way up her skin, melding with her flesh. Casey whimpered as it mended, the wounds stitching her back together from the inside out.

It lifted her when it finished and surged into her once again. Blue glowing light blasted its way into the room. Her head flew back as her spine arched. The other lids to the rest of the relics flew open and they exploded into the air rotating around her.

One by one they amassed as one large bright swirling ray of light. All the colors intertwined. White from the shield, yellow from Ben's ring, red from Clint's weapon flickering as if a solid flame of eternal fire.

The shield burst forth, shoving its way past the walls of the house as it was unable to stay restrained in such a small space. The rest of the colors bled and flowed freely, melting into a kaleidoscope of tinted hues along with the healing stone.

Casey recovered from her injuries, and the healing stone surged into her again.

The symbols on her skin absorbed the three colors of the other relics. They weren't the hemp color but a brilliant ombre of yellows, reds, and blues.

For the first time in years, the full force of the relics and the main source of strength blessed from God coursed over her.

She checked her stomach. The scar and signs of her earlier injuries from the Monarchs that never healed completely, didn't mark her skin. Her body was now whole. The agitated relics calmed down as they welcomed her home. She would never doubt herself again when she received warnings of a portal opening.

They wouldn't know what hit them the next time they invaded her space. This was her home, and like with the Monarchs, she wouldn't go down without a fight. Until she found a way to fix what broke inside Clint, Amanda, and Ben, she refused to let them hurt her again.

"It seems as if you have chips, making you evil versions of yourselves. Wait. Is that why the shield works against them, Daisy girl?" Casey pondered.

Fourteen

Lightning zigzagged across the sky, backlighting the clouds into a macabre of flashes. The air crackled with static. Casey sat on the back porch with her knees pulled up so her heels sat on the edge of the seat. Her hands warmed by the hot tea-filled ceramic cup, she inhaled the aroma of cinnamon and chai spices before taking a sip. Ever since the storm that initiated her into farm life, she'd become an avid storm enthusiast. Under the roof of the covered porch, she'd sit for hours to clear her mind and just talk to God.

A hum filled the air. Casey used her enhanced hearing to try and pin down where it emanated from. Rain and thunder masked everything else. As she started to think she was hearing things, a small gray object swooped down in front of her. A red laser scanned the chair next to her and then settled its beam on her.

Casey threw herself to the floor, her cup shattered and shards bounced down the steps onto the rain-soaked grass. Three darts puckered the fabric of the chair she occupied seconds ago. Not wasting any more time, she hopped to her feet and threw her hand up. A yellow orb launched from her, disintegrating the drone.

She crept to the corner in a crouch to stay out of the window's dim hue of light that filtered through the old plastic blinds. Shadows slunk from tree to tree across the road. No engines alerted her that they were the Monarchs. More than three people were working their way to her so they weren't her friends.

She deployed the shield to conform to her.

"I'm shocked at how well you seem to be doing." The android voice that haunted her nightmares spoke from her left.

She never heard it approach. "And here I thought I disintegrated your circuits...more than once."

"Yes, you seem to enjoy doing that." He strolled past the balustrade and kicked at one of the shards of stoneware at the bottom of the steps.

"I don't enjoy dealing with a group of bullies who probably picked on kids in school." Several shapes shifted out of the shadows to stand behind their boss.

He held up a finger, telling her to give him a minute.

She laughed and crossed her arms to hide her shaking.

"He has her attention. We should strike now," a wheezy voice said from around the side of the house.

"No, he said we wait for his signal."

"Can you imagine our reward if we capture her and do his job for him?" A cough had the other waiting to answer.

"Or he will kill us."

An arcing band of light struck behind the group and split a tree in half. The Monarchs dropped to their stomachs. In the same instance, the leader struck out with a disc. The shield collapsed and his hand wrapped around her throat.

Casey cried out and then silenced as the pressure closed her windpipe. Red static blocked her vision. She held her palm out, and static slunk up his arm and around his neck as the ring defended her from his attack. He screeched as his hand separated from his arm and fell from his body.

Casey yelped and sidestepped as it crawled toward her. The two men she heard before jumped out, and each grabbed an arm.

"We got her for you!" His wheezing got worse the louder he spoke.

"Let her go. You both are dead since you didn't wait for my signal." Android man's eyes spun to black.

Their grips tightened, giving her the leverage to swing her legs up and kick out, knocking their boss over the railing.

She zapped them with Clint's weapon, and they slumped over each other as she swung over the rail landing on the rain-soaked lawn with a squish. Drops coursed all over, her clothes clung to her frame.

The leader rose slowly and flexed the fingers of the hand that had reattached itself. When he removed a syringe from his inside jacket pocket, her blood froze in her veins. It was the same dark solution that Ben and Clint used to remove her powers.

"I don't think so." Casey refused to believe they received it from the Monarchs.

Could she trust anyone?

"Trust me."

Casey smiled. "Always, Father."

Three men approached and swung their fists. She dodged one and used the stun weapon on another but wasn't fast enough to keep the third from hitting the side of the head. Her vision swam. Casey's left knee hit the ground, water soaking into the worn denim.

The boss studied her as he grabbed her arm and rested the needle into the crook of her elbow. "This will hurt."

"I don't think so. Been there done that." Casey roared, shoving up with her right arm, and knocked the syringe away.

She stepped on it and the glass cylinder cracked, the small tinkling sound almost drowned out by the downpour if not for her modified hearing.

A bullet hit her side, skimming along her skin and gouging a deep groove. Warm blood ran down her side and leg. Casey lifted her head. The leader smirked, blowing at an imaginary wisp of smoke at the end of the barrel.

She filled her lungs and then pulled every ounce of power she could feel to her palms. God's strength coursed through every relic. The healing relic wanted to do its job, but she shoved it to the side. Yellow and red static played across her as the shield conformed to her body, recharged and ready to go.

Two Monarchs in the back turned to run when the leader shot them, killing them.

"Hmm, interesting how a machine gets its feelings hurt when his men turn on him. Kind of pathetic if you ask me." Casey sent out the combined charge and took out six men on her right. "If any of you survive tonight, tell your leaders, this is what will happen every time you come for me. This *thing* will not win."

The leader jumped for her but then fragmented into a pile of liquid metal from the power of God's relics.

The rest ran. She remained still until she no longer heard their footfalls. Interesting that they didn't use vehicles. What electronics were sacrificed from the EM pulse? Was that why they hadn't returned since then?

Their visit put her on edge. Now she would have to deal with the Monarchs and her friends. Ben and Clint using the same serum on her that the Monarchs had tonight only confirmed she couldn't trust them until God told her they were back on His side.

"Once they can navigate the shield, they are once again part of the Chosen."

Fifteen

Casey hauled the basket of wild raspberries over her arm, switching it up as it weighed more than she thought it could. She did a happy dance when she spotted the berries a few years ago, but the wildlife had picked them clean. She left them that year but placed markers so she would know where to find them.

She wanted to make jams and freeze a bunch so she would have a delicious healthy snack whenever she wanted without feeling guilty about splurging to satisfy her sweet tooth.

A branch cracked to her right. The shield popped up in that direction. The sun set about fifteen minutes before, the dark sky rising in the east as stars winked on in the heavenly expanse. She got good at reading the sky and knowing when she would be out of her element in the darkened woods around her. She didn't mean to wait so late in the day to scavenge her favorite fruit, but plucking the chickens took longer than she planned. Two of the hens developed bumblefoot. She decided that instead of trying to find a way to cure it, butchering them just opened up more spots for younger laying hens.

Shuffled movement through the dry undergrowth caught her attention. She didn't want to deal with Clint, Ben, and Amanda so she prayed a wild animal tromped through the underbrush so she could ignore it and head inside.

She flinched when someone spoke up behind her. “Hello, Casey.”

Clint wore a pair of night vision goggles. Not fair. She hesitated long enough for them to get closer before she abandoned the berries and flipped her flashlight beam into his eyes and hurdled over a log. He screamed as she darted around another tree. She couldn’t see the other two to engulf them in shields and toss them back in time.

Almost silent, Clint pursued her after letting his eyes adjust to the brightness she blinded him with. She didn’t know how far he was when she stumbled and fell forward, her hands taking the brunt of the impact, embedding pine needles into the delicate skin.

“Come on, Casey. Give it up. There are three of us and one of you. We want the powers you keep reabsorbing. We will be on our way and find the other Casey, who didn’t turn into a mass murderer.” Clint’s words cut her worse than she wanted to admit.

“Have you ever thought you were in the wrong? When in all your infinite wisdom did you think to ask God for guidance over the last year? My true friends would have asked me what happened, but say I did what you said I did. They still would turn me over to the authorities to be punished for those crimes. They aren’t vigilantes.” Casey brushed off her hands as she stood.

“What authorities? There are none left! I happen to have gotten a rude wake-up call. I found out you were chummy with the Monarchs.” Clint aimed at her.

She wanted to laugh but if she let it out right now, she didn't think it would be laughter that bubbled out of her. She refused to break down in front of him and let him see her weakness.

"Answer me one question." Casey faced off with Clint. Ben and Amanda came in from the left as if taking a nice stroll down a beach while on vacation.

Amanda sneered at her. "Oh, this is going to be good."

Clint bowed his head at her to ask. A noble gesture to a poor peasant like herself. She scoffed under her breath.

"Which Clint are you? Because the one who lived in this house didn't condone murder. He loved Amanda and wanted to see where things could go with her. He respected her brother as if he were his own flesh and blood kin. His anguish reflected my own pain, and he told me he would do anything to make sure the Monarchs didn't come back for us. He would die for me. So that tells me something went wrong when you went through the sphere. Maybe the two of you can't occupy the same space. If we can figure out what happened, maybe we can fix this once and for all. I don't know about you three, but I'm tired of this. I'm tired of a solitary life. I miss my friends and my boyfriend." Casey's voice dipped at the end.

Ben lunged forward and Casey threw a shield around each of them, encasing them in their own bubble.

"This isn't the way to convince us you mean us no harm." Ben pounded on the inside.

"This isn't harming you, drama queen. If I wanted to harm you, don't you think I would have, in the two times I transported you back? I want to say something and tell me, once you let it rattle around in those thick skulls you all seem to have, if you don't agree." Casey waited until they were all listening.

"Per the parchment, we can't use the powers against each other, correct? They are not meant to harm any of the chosen but to fight side by side, harnessing the powers to use in conjunction with each other's assigned relics." They all nodded.

"If you are the chosen ones, you are destined to be part of my team. Why can I suspend you if you are on God's side? You should be able to walk through the shield. We have popped in and out of the shields, except for the two times when I had to move you out of my way or heal you. Both of those actions were in direct correlation to helping my team. Despite the fact you hunt me like wild game, I only defended myself without hurting you. So, go on. Come join me and show me you mean me no harm because your heart is in the right place to do God's will."

No one spoke.

"Who are you people? How did you turn from God and become these shells of the friends who were once devout believers? Don't you remember how we helped each other through Ben's death? It devastated me! Did you pray about what to do and what steps to take, or did you let your anger brew into hate and take over, turning you into murderers?" Casey planted her legs wide and glared.

No one said anything. Amanda refused to meet her eye. Clint pressed two fingers into his left temple. This wasn't the first time she noticed him uncomfortable, possibly in pain.

"Clint, you're previous military. Tell me this. If I'm someone who, without any remorse or second thoughts, massacres so many people, why haven't I done the same to you?"

"You're right. All of those are great points. I may have jumped the gun." Clint put his Glock away.

"Don't trust them yet."

Casey studied each of their faces. Ben, with his brilliant blue eyes that seemed a shade darker. Evil lurked in his gaze. This man was not the one who held her close during the loss of her family. He forgot the sound of their Father's voice when He spoke in the small whispers encouraging them not to lose hope.

Her hair kicked up behind her as she spun to take in Amanda. Her best friend was no longer in there. She hid it better than the other two, but there remained no connection to the friend she loved like a sister. Was this the outcome of not being a united front as the chosen ones?

"Take their powers from them before they go. They have not listened to the warnings of misusing the relics. It is time they see for themselves what it would be like to live without them."

Casey held up her hand as the relics slipped from each of them and floated toward her.

They started yelling at her, asking how she stole the relics, and they told her it proved their point that she couldn't be trusted.

Tears dripped down her cheeks. She would trust in God and follow Him.

"Father, please select the place you want them to go." Casey turned to the portal.

The flashback of Casey when she chipped away at the paint on the window surfaced. A vision of them sneaking up on her to keep her safe and from harm. Ben's arms anchored around her to keep her from hurting herself. The injector was in Clint's hand as he depressed the trigger when he forced it to her neck.

Clint and Ben had gone quiet. The flashes through their eyes told her they remembered how her fear propelled her into running. The Clint and Ben from her time were in the vision, caring for her after they sedated her.

"These are the men I want back. The ones that wouldn't listen to Satan's prideful lies. The ones whose hearts are so big, that no one doubted their love for Jesus Christ. You are nothing like these two." Casey motioned to the scene playing out in front of them.

With a flick of her wrist, they flew into the past.

Casey finally let the tears fall. She was tired of fighting them. Of being the only one fighting for herself. Would her words penetrate and give them something to think about? She marched back to where her basket was and scooped it up. Maybe tomorrow would be a better day.

A thought came to her. What if her Clint being in the same place as the original Clint started the downfall? Did it have something to do with the two of them not being able to occupy the same space? She would research it tomorrow. Sending them into the past put them right back in line with the relics.

"Father, please help me through this. Open their eyes and let them see. Let their hearts feel." A peace washed over Casey she hadn't felt in a long time.

That told her He hadn't left her, and He never would.

She hated her need for reassurance because she saw it in the gifts around her. He bestowed them on her, which she didn't deserve.

There were chores she had to tend to. She thanked God for the mindless tasks to keep her mind from wandering to the dark, lonely, depressed woman she refused to be as she dumped the raspberries in the sink to soak.

Once done, she picked up the relics she tossed in a bowl on the back porch to place them in their own storage cases. The relics she absorbed from her time were missing, she saw when she opened each lid. She nestled each one in the soft fabric to cushion them.

So, no two of the same relics can occupy the same space? More research needed to be done to make heads or tails of what all of this meant. She ran her fingers over the sphere. Was it the root of the evil as the chosen misused it?

All of this back and forth only drained her emotionally. She needed a vacation. She couldn't bring herself to laugh at her own poorly thought-out joke.

Daisy whined from the doorway.

"Come in, pretty lady." Casey kneeled on the hard floor.

Daisy's lower body wriggled in time with her tail as she inched forward and placed her head on Casey's neck as if hugging her.

"Thanks, baby girl. I needed that." Casey ran her fingers through her fur.

She stood in a daze at the sink while soaking the ripe red berries. She plucked one out of the water and tossed it in her mouth. Sweet juices burst to life making her hum in satisfaction. Taking a deep breath, she tried to understand how they misused the sphere, turning them into who they were now. Did she get through to them? Would they consider all she said and come up with the same conclusion? That she could be trusted?

Casey wanted her friends back. They were at the point where she chose to make a life with Ben and accepted the fact she couldn't go back to her time. Now she wondered, if she left all this behind, would she be happier? She would rather be in her time with her family and friends. The sphere worked sporadically so she would test it out, starting tomorrow. If she could go back and live her life in the past of this world, she'd take it. Ready to walk away from fighting the Monarchs.

And Ben.

Sixteen

"Ben, come on. We're going to lose our chance to take her out if you don't hurry!" Clint hollered from the next room over.

"What if she's right?" Ben sat hard on the chair in the corner.

"She's not right. Why would the three of us feel the same and see the same things if she were right? What does it matter which one of me she executed? Let's leave that out of the equation. Look at the number of innocents she snuffed out all with a tantrum, trying to take out the Monarchs. She is reckless and careless with her powers. They have gone to her head. We don't put civilians on the line to take out the snake in the grass. Why is it so hard for you to trust me? I can't take her on by myself with how strong her powers have gotten. I need my best friend." Clint slammed the bathroom door.

Ben put his head in his hands. "But what if?"

"Ben, the Monarchs didn't take Clint until after his other self came through the sphere, telling you and me to follow him into the future to *help* Casey. When we got him back after his time in the custody of the Monarchs, he refused to talk about what he saw. Only now we have to kill Casey because she killed him. He's changed since the

Monarchs." Amanda bumped into his shoulder when she squeezed in next to him.

"I think so too. It's like her words opened up a huge chasm in my chest. My heart hurts at the thought of how lonely she's been for three years and how she watched both of us die. Could either of us make it that long without talking to another person? Well, you would have to be put in a padded room after a day so no." Ben chuckled as he put his arm around Amanda and tugged her to him, kissing the top of her head.

Amanda sighed. "Do you think..."

"Think what?"

"Did Clint love me in her time? You know what, never mind." Amanda tried to stand but Ben stopped her.

"Yeah, I think it's possible. We need to go back." Ben kept an eye on the door Clint was behind.

Amanda started for her shoes. "I think we owe it to ourselves and Casey to see what we can figure out."

"First, we have to ditch Clint. He won't let us try what we're attempting." Ben slung the bag with the relics sphere over his shoulder.

"You going somewhere?" Clint held a gun in his hand.

Ben hadn't heard him open the door.

"Clint, what do you think you're doing? Are you going to shoot us?" Amanda put her hands up. "Ugh, you are such a Neanderthal!"

Ben placed himself in front of Amanda. "This is what Casey talked about. You have never threatened us. Something changed in you and with every use of the sphere, it started to change things in us also."

"I can't believe you want to listen to that woman. I don't want to shoot you, but I have to do what is right. I don't know how else to make myself clear. What happened that you decided to listen to someone besides your best friend?" Clint grasped for the strap on the bag.

Ben dodged out of his way and covered Amanda with his body when the gun discharged.

"Ben?" Clint's voice wavered, sounding like his old self.

This was the first time since they started hunting Casey that he faltered in anything.

"I'm okay, I think." He slid the bag off his shoulder. A glow oozed from around the flap.

Clint removed the sphere. The glow bubbled out of it. It crawled up Clint's arm, small black strings twining over his skin. He tried to wipe it off, but it only transferred to his other hand, spreading faster the harder he tried.

Liquid transferred to the towel Ben tried to wipe the ooze away with. Soon it covered his elbows.

"Ben!" Amanda held out her hand.

"Run." Ben didn't know what would happen to him and Clint, but he didn't want it to happen to Amanda also.

"I'm not leaving you." She hooked the bag over her shoulder until it settled in place.

Her eyes glistened as she shook her head no. "Amanda, for once in your life listen to me and run!"

AMANDA DARTED THROUGH the door but stopped; she couldn't leave her brother and best friend.

"The chosen are intended to be four. Open your eyes and see what you are doing to the key. These tendrils of venom laced throughout the sphere are your doing."

Ben cried out when power surged into his heart.

"Ben." Clint collapsed on the floor.

Amanda didn't have a choice. She ran. The further she got, the faster the glow overtook her.

Blinding light enveloped her, knocking her unconscious.

Amanda ached when she rolled over. God spoke to them. She smiled. It had been so long that she almost thought she dreamed it until she found herself on the floor outside Ben and Clint's room.

"Oh, my gosh." Doc clumped over to her with his cane.

"I'm okay. Do me a favor?" Amanda used her enhanced hearing, and steady heartbeats let her know her brother and friend were okay but not awake to hear her request.

"Sure."

"I need to talk to Chloe. Is there a way you can secretly tell her to meet me in the lab whenever she gets a chance?"

Doc patted her on her hand. "Of course, deary."

"Don't tell anyone." Amanda didn't miss the look on his face that showed that he had questions he wanted to ask.

Doc's clomp of his cane let her follow his progress down the hall.

On unsteady legs, she stumbled to the room and found Ben and Clint unconscious. The sphere lay on the ground near Clint's hand. It didn't look any different.

Amanda's hands shook as she kept her brother and Clint in sight, their breathing steady streams in and out, and yanked out drawers to shuffle through the contents. Was there something to help her figure out why Clint changed so much? Clint twitched and she yelped, frozen with the next drawer pulled halfway out. When he didn't move again, she rummaged through the next one.

There was nothing here. No secret communication devices, no papers with traitor instructions. Something changed in him, and she was going to find out what so she could get the man she loved back.

Ben groaned. "What happened?"

She squeaked and shuffled over to Ben and grasped his hand to pull him into a seated position. "Do you need Doc?"

They didn't have the key to heal them, and with Casey having confiscated the relics, they also didn't have powers. The sphere and parchment remained the only two left.

"What are you two yammering about?" Clint shook his head as his nose started bleeding.

Ben tossed him a towel and motioned to his face.

CLINT FELT FREE FOR once. Casey confiscated their relics, and it was a relief that she kept them from using them against the chosen and other innocent lives. Now, if only he could stay in control and get a message to Ben and Amanda to not trust him.

Darkness pulled at him. No, he had to talk to his friends. He couldn't lose control yet. He screamed, pounding his hands against his cage as he was relegated to the depths of his subconscious mind to be a spectator with no voice in his life.

Clint pinched his nose and held the towel below it to keep from making a mess. "What happened to the sphere? We have to go back."

"That's the first thing you think of? Going back and hurting Casey? I almost hope the sphere is broken. Did you not hear God scolding us about the key? The tendrils of venom?" Amanda stomped out of the room.

He should care more but he couldn't summon the right feelings to follow through. They were muted, like someone flipped a switch, turning them off. Not for the first time, he wondered what the Monarchs did to him. He wasn't sure what she was talking about God speaking to them.

The only thing he cared about was finding Casey and killing her for killing him. If he didn't keep her as his main focus, it became excruciating. The thoughts of her dying kept it at bay.

It was wrong, but he couldn't stop the urge to wipe her off the face of the planet. The old Clint would argue with him about it, and there were moments when he wanted to go back to his old self. The protector and leader. The one everyone turned to, to guard them.

"How many of those have you had now? Did they do something to you?" Ben motioned to the towel, now stained red.

"Don't worry about it. I'm fine." He gritted his teeth, waiting for Ben to push.

Shocked when he didn't, he left without saying another word. He tossed the ruined fabric in the trash. A memory assailed him. The vidcast of Casey pulling the trigger as Junior begged for his life.

No, that can't be right.

Something seemed wrong now.

A blinding pain pierced him right behind his eyes, and he let himself float away. It was the only way to manage the throbbing.

Seventeen

Quiet ascended on the farmhouse as Casey lugged her heavy legs back up the steps. She took another look around, taking in the serene fields she grew to love over the last three years. Now it felt tainted. Hardly any leaves were left on the branches of the trees. The cool touch of air told her she would need to be ready for the harsh season that didn't concern itself with its brutality.

She was tempted to leave so they couldn't find her until she figured out how to bring her friends back, but looking at her surroundings and everything she accomplished changed her mind.

She missed them but could she ever trust them with how they turned their backs on everything they believed in?

Casey pulled the parchment out, and the hieroglyphs lit up and seemed to dance on the paper. She unrolled the bottom where the sections were blank before, now full of writing. A pen poised over a piece of paper; she started translating as the script updated, adding several new texts. If the prophecy kept it up, she would have an entire book on her hands.

The translation went easier than she thought.

"The sphere will spell doom for those who misuse it. Designed to bring the four chosen together. Using it other than those specific designations will taint the users, hardening their hearts. Creating tendrils of venom. Once one starts down that road, it's harder to bring them back from it." Casey shivered with the pronouncement.

As she read the words, the glyphs on her arms lit up. The entire prophecy covered her arms. Starting at her left wrist, she matched everything between the parchment and herself. How had she not put two and two together? She was the walking talking copy of the foretelling of the relics and how it affected them. On instinct, her excitement to share the news with Amanda withered, knowing she couldn't.

Casey choked back a sob. Her friends didn't exist. Deep down, their black hearts ruled their bodies. They must have been using the sphere to jump more often than she thought. How did they get the sphere to work in their time? This one stitched itself back together as if God wanted her and Clint to bring the two back into the fold and finally face the Monarchs head-on.

After a bit, Casey kept reading as she documented the new additions, but her mind kept wandering to a certain line. God mentioned in the parchment the hard road to travel to bring them back from evil. Did it mean the damage could be reversed?

Her arms flashed as the symbols glowed in alternating patterns. She couldn't keep up with the ever-changing fluid motion.

The word for *chosen* flared to life as she hissed at the searing skin as if it were branding her. She almost tripped over her own feet, extricating herself from the chair as she stumbled to the kitchen. She plunged her arm under the faucet and blasted it with cold water.

The cool liquid didn't do anything to abate the stinging sensation when it abruptly halted, and she finally took a breath.

In times like these, she missed her friends and needed someone to talk to. She hung her head but refused to let herself cry.

Determined not to let it break her, she shook out her hand as blue flowed to the mark and cooled it down. This better be a one-time event, and she hoped all these marks wouldn't singe her skin. Her next course of action included finding a cure for the sphere's dark side.

Eighteen

Clint slammed his fist into the door, knocking the lock loose in the process. "How dare she send us back again. She didn't let us say anything!"

Amanda never saw him this mad. This man was not the friend she grew up with. Nothing she said would calm him down, only anger him more, so she kept her mouth shut and pulled out the case for the sphere to stow it away. It would take several hours before it was ready for another trip. They attempted to transport themselves to the farmhouse, but Casey delivered them back without talking to them. She was always one step ahead.

"Come on, you can't say you were shocked she tossed us right back here. She seems to know when we're going to appear. Amanda, does it say anything about the sphere portal alerting the other side it is opening?" Ben propped his feet on the table after settling on a stool.

"Nope." Amanda knew the prophecy inside and out, backward and forward.

"Nope?" Clint towered over her. "That's all you have to say: just nope? Our lives are on the line, and a stupid four-letter answer is all we are worth?"

"Back off, Clint. I'm not lying. You towering over me to intimidate me is only gonna get you a boot in your butt." She stalked into the storage room for the parchment.

Ben's mouth fell slack as she kicked the door behind her and turned around.

Amanda looked at the two of them before Clint burst out in laughter.

Ben seemed to release the tension in his body, sure Clint would blow a gasket. They had seen too many times how the smallest irritation set him off.

Clint yanked her into a hug and kissed her cheek. Now, this hinted at the man she loved. Nope, she wasn't going there. It would only end in her broken all over again. These small glimpses of her friend were becoming fewer and fewer. She wondered when he was going to disappear altogether. A more thorough search of his room didn't net her any information as to what she was dealing with so she'd have some idea of how to bring her friend back from the brink.

"You're right. I don't know why I'm so mad. I get tunnel vision and can't see anything else." He rubbed his eyes with the palms of his hands.

"What did the Monarchs do to you? You weren't like this before." Ben asked the question she wanted to ask for the last several months.

"Ben, I love you, man, but we are not discussing anything to do with that."

"Clint, you holding it in isn't making it any better. You have to admit you are over the top, which never happens. You are the king of cool and collected. You reason through every situation like a computer tabulating every possible outcome. Now, you are all bent out of shape over the smallest setback. Seriously. You need distance to get some perspective. You're too close to the situation so you're missing what we all see." Ben kept his voice calm.

"Too close to the situation. Of course I am. I *am* the situation! You don't get any closer, since I'm the person it's about." Clint turned to leave.

"Wait." Amanda rushed forward.

He didn't move but also didn't turn around to face them.

Amanda put her hand on his back. His muscles tensed, becoming harder than concrete under her fingers. He'd worked out relentlessly since being taken and only bulked up more, adding to his already intimidating size. "You know we love you, don't you?"

"Come on, I don't need some girl crushing on me and trying to guilt me into changing who I am. If you don't like it, you can leave." Clint slammed the door open and left Amanda standing there with her chin quivering.

"Sis." Ben hugged her as tight as possible without cutting off her air supply.

"I didn't mean it that way. Why is he so mean now? He never would have said something like that. I miss Junior." She tried to keep her voice from shaking but failed.

Ben slipped the lock back in place so Clint couldn't barge back in. "I know. We can't keep going like this. If we can maybe go through to Casey without him knowing, do you think she would talk to us?"

"It's worth a try. She may have information our future selves don't know about yet since she is two years ahead of us." Amanda pulled out the sphere again but there were no signs of life in the orb.

"Ben." Amanda pointed to the drop of blood on the floor.

He only shook his head. No matter how many times they tried to convince Clint to see Doc about his nosebleeds, he only muttered and walked away from them.

"I'm going to grab something to eat. Did you want anything?" Ben peered down the hall around the door as he opened it.

"Not hungry." Amanda unrolled the parchment.

She read the symbols for the millionth time, but the text remained exactly as what she and Chloe had deciphered.

"Knock knock." Speaking of Chloe, she stuck her head in the room.

Amanda rushed to the door and closed it behind Chloe.

"I heard you were looking for me?" Chloe propped her feet up on the highest bars on the stool.

"I need you to call your uncle. Have him investigate when the Monarchs had both Clints."

"I need a reason, so my uncle knows what to search for." Chloe grabbed her UniSat.

Amanda pressed her ear to the door and held up her finger. Chloe patiently waited. "I think they did something to Clint. He isn't the same since they held him."

"That's it? My uncle won't have much to go on."

"Just trust me he isn't my Clint. Our Clint." Amanda shrugged.

Chloe started for the door. "I agree. He hasn't talked to me once since he returned. Normally he checks in on me. But not since they held him."

Her soft lyric voice was greeting her uncle as she left.

Amanda peered at the parchment.

Wait.

The key.

Comes from the future?

She grabbed her notebook with scribblings of nonsense when she initially tried to read the writings after finding the hidden rooms and tunnels under them. She found the page where she doodled different styles of old skeleton keys along the edges. The key will come from a different time and place. She assumed it meant the past since the sphere initially dialed in to Casey in their past. But now it read from an approaching time and place.

"Oh my gosh!" Amanda hopped off her stool.

No one was in the lab with her. Where had they gone? She remembered Clint storming out and Ben mentioning food, but why hadn't he come back? They were going to discuss meeting Casey on her terms. She wasn't the killer Clint proclaimed her to be.

Looking at her watch, she saw that several hours had passed. Her pulse skyrocketed. Did something happen? She chucked everything back into the satchel and scampered to put it away. She locked the storage room door when she heard footsteps behind her.

She was thrown down over a table, an arm pressing against her shoulder blades. Were the Monarchs here? Was that why Ben and Clint hadn't been back? Were they captured? Dead?

"You keep siding with Casey, and this is going to end very badly for you," Clint whispered in her ear; his hot breath sent goosebumps parading down her back.

She pulled in air to scream when pressure on the side of her head told her he held the barrel of a gun to her.

"Clint."

"We've known each other since grade school. Do you think it doesn't gut me that you would throw me to the side like trash? I never should have friended you. I tried to tell myself the pesky baby sister of my best friend would eventually grow out of her annoying puppy dog, I-have-to-follow-you-everywhere phase. But you didn't. You only grew more aggravating the older you got. Some snot-nosed brat who wanted something between us. What a joke. I am so far out of your league, you couldn't fathom how far outside the line you were." Clint's words tore through her.

"You're a jerk; you know that. Maybe it would've been better if you hadn't gotten away from the Monarchs instead of becoming the man you are. *My* Clint would never say such hateful vile things to another human being, much less one of his friends. He wouldn't think them either, which tells me right there you are not my Clint. They did something to you, and you refusing to have Doc look you over doesn't help us fix it." Amanda breathed hard by the time she finished since he increased the pressure with every word out of her mouth.

"Let me get this right. You would rather they tortured me more instead of escaping because you don't like who my true self is. How barbaric, even for you. This all could have been handled differently if you'd only followed my lead. Casey won't hesitate to prove you wrong, and where will we be then? You'll be dead. Don't think I don't know someone has been going through my stuff. Has that been you?

Looking for something to use against me?" Clint shoved off her back, thumping her head into the desk.

"You are such a disappointment. You make a horrible Clint clone, because that is what you are. Casey is right. We have walked away from God, and He should be front and center. I found a change in the prophecy. You were right. It is changing." Amanda's adrenaline spiked and she jerked back when Clint surged forward. She had been meticulous when she searched his room. How did he figure it out?

"What changed?"

Amanda slapped at his chest. "You will never know. Where's Ben?"

"What do you mean?" Clint leaned away from her.

Amanda squinted at him; he was responsible and the reason for Ben's absence.

Ben stumbled into the room, holding his head as it bled.

Amanda rushed to him. "What did he do to you?"

"Clocked me when I confronted him about what his intentions were if he got his way and exacted revenge on Casey." Ben winced as he pressed harder on his scalp.

"What do you mean?" Amanda turned to Clint.

What else could go wrong? What if he took the sphere to the Monarchs? The only comfort she had was that he hadn't yet, with all of his trips from the warehouse, so maybe he wouldn't.

"I think it's time to let the people wage war for themselves. I'm tired of always defending people who take it for granted. Once Casey is taken care of, I'm packing up and heading north toward the mountains. You can stay here and watch over these sniveling idiots all you want, but it's not worth my effort." Clint shrugged his left shoulder.

"See, right there. I am done trying to make peace with such a jerk. You have to walk on eggshells around him because you never know when he is going to blow up at you. I don't regret saying it would have been better if you never escaped the Monarchs. My Clint wouldn't turn his back on people. You are a pitiful excuse of a soldier too." Amanda bared her teeth, knowing she had gone too far.

His fingers grazed her temple gently above her left ear. A storm brewed in Clint. She almost saw the internal conflict. There was a sadness in his eyes he didn't normally have since coming back.

"Sometimes I wish it failed. If only my system failed like Junior's did. All of this could have been avoided." He moved so fast pricking her with a syringe, her knees gave out before she registered the sting.

CLINT DIDN'T LET AMANDA fall. At least the last few hours would be erased when they woke. Now, how to carry them back to their rooms with no one seeing them? He would wait for lockdown tonight and sneak back here. With how much he was using, the cocktail would run out before he completed his mission.

Something about the way Amanda railed against him bothered him, but he didn't know why. They didn't understand. They would be saving so many people if they snuffed one inconsequential human from the world. The needs of the many, right?

Heat seared through him. He stumbled to the wall, catching himself. He couldn't take in any air. What happened? His heart—not his head, like all the other instances—raced with a weight sitting on his chest. Hoping it wasn't a heart attack, he lurched to his room and chewed a handful of antacid tablets.

His breaths drew up short, and he couldn't draw in air. An anxiety attack. He witnessed several of his fellow soldiers have them when they fell into despair after their military tours. He didn't have anything like that going on.

This wasn't that.

No way.

Except he couldn't erase the image of the angry look on Amanda's face. Why couldn't he file it away like he did his concern for Casey? No, not concern. She didn't mean anything to him.

Clint tried to stand straight but failed and fell to the mattress.

Free from the prison the chip kept him in, Clint pulled in a lung full of air. Before he lost his hold on his body, he grabbed a notepad and pen.

Ben and Amanda,

There is something wrong with me. I think the Monarchs took over my mind. I'm still in here. Don't give up on me. I'm trying to keep my darker self from completing his mission to kill Casey. I am trying to reserve my strength for those times he is close to her so I can control my limbs and make his aim inaccurate. Don't let me have access to the sphere while alone. I don't trust him to not use it and fulfill his assigned task. Pray for me and stop using the sphere without God's guidance.

Clint.

Clint fell to his knees and crawled over to Ben's Bible slipping the note into gold-leafed pages of Psalms 119, one of Ben's favorite chapters to read. He felt the other side trying to take over. He shoved him back until he replaced the book and lurched to his side of the room before the prison bars surrounded him again.

Nineteen

Casey hadn't slept for more than an hour or two in the past week. She was beyond tired. Her nerves were frayed, and she wanted to curl up and cry. The Monarchs and Amanda, Ben, and Clint had visited on multiple occasions for the past six days. At all hours of the day and night.

Sometimes only minutes passed between either group showing up, and other times, hours gave her a small reprieve. She was always on guard, not knowing when they were going to show. Her fight or flight system shifted into high gear, never shutting down. The smallest movement or sound ramped up her anxiety.

The parchment now twisted to a new reason for the use of the sphere. It foretold of friends being led astray and using the sphere for harm more than good and with more use the farther they drifted from their former selves. Casey had instantly used the shield against them, sensing the danger Clint, Ben, and Amanda posed when they came through the portals, following God's instruction that when they can walk through the shield, they are back as the chosen.

Casey sat in front of the unrolled parchment and curiously watched as numerous symbols appeared and several more paragraphs were written.

They were able to use the sphere to change the past and target people they wanted to. The initial goal to take out the Monarch leader, before he put together the means to bring his wrath down on the US, took a back seat to Clint's revenge. The sphere's design, to unite the four chosen to take on the enemy, carried out its task when Ben brought Casey to them.

According to the prophecy, they weren't supposed to use the sphere out of anger or vengeance. The user's soul would darken by those negative feelings. Every time someone used it with undesirable wishes, it would destroy a little bit more of their good side until in the end only darkness persevered.

A black void could never be filled with love or positive energy. Porting to the instance they initially took her, may be a way to stop them from using it for personal gain. Her true friends would have never done something so self-serving.

She wanted to know what event led them to think this was the only way out.

The house vibrated and she wanted to cry. Only a couple of hours passed since they tried to take her again. The shield kept them isolated, but the drain it put on her to keep them suspended until she tossed them back through a time loop exhausted her. Ever since the shield overinflated and cleared out the surrounding states, she didn't overheat anymore while using it.

Not wanting to become the shadow of herself, she refused to activate her sphere. She had to find the portal they came through. They learned quickly after the first couple of times she tossed them through it. Now they tried to hide it from her, so she had to locate it before she ported them out until the next time.

A shift in the floor told her they were closer than they'd been before. She peered through the front windows but didn't see anything. She gasped when she heard boots thudding against the hardwood floors.

Clint used a pulse that wrapped around her wrists. Red static coursed up and down her arms, immobilizing them. Clint found himself a new toy. Since she removed the relics, and they sat nestled safely in their containers, this didn't belong to the chosen.

Casey flicked out the shield for it only to be thrown back at her.

Amanda smirked and tilted her head to the side. "Not so fun being on that side of the weapons, is it?" In her palm lay a circular apparatus similar to how what the Monarchs had used to defeat the shield's barrier.

Clint yanked her forward with the red strands. His hand snapped around her throat, cutting off oxygen when she stumbled. The toe of her shoes barely scuffed against the floor. Casey clawed at his hands only for him to manipulate her restraints and move them so she couldn't reach him.

Black dots danced in front of her eyes.

Ben yanked Clint away from her. She fell to her feet as Ben and Clint faced off. "You promised this time we would talk to her."

Clint smirked. "How else can I lure you here to help destroy her once and for all if I didn't tell a little white lie? Now move out of my way!"

"We don't lie to each other. It is one oath we took as friends. If we start lying, how are we going to survive? As soon as we lose our trust in each other, it will only be a matter of time before they win."

"Clint, how can you do something like that?" Amanda stormed up to him and craned her neck back, glaring at him.

"If you won't listen to reason what else was I supposed to do? You denied me access to the sphere to come through and handle this myself," Clint growled.

Casey threw out shields as they bickered with each other. For the first time, they were at odds among themselves. "I have an idea. How about we try something different."

Clint's face and neck flushed while a vein throbbed in his temple.

Amanda motioned for her to go ahead.

"You stay here for the foreseeable future in those bubbles until I can rest, and you guys listen to me." Casey flopped into the recliner Clint claimed as his.

His anger flared. "You can't keep us here indefinitely."

"You enjoyed a nice dinner last night so that gives me, oh, nine hours until you are really hungry. I'll send you back after I take a good long nap." Casey leaned back, extending her feet, and shimmied back and forth as if burrowing into the soft fluffy chair.

"We ate at breakfast, so ha!" Amanda yelled.

Ben reached toward his sister. "Now she won't feel guilty about holding us longer!"

"Oh." Amanda dropped her chin.

Clint lowered his head. "How about both of you shut up for a minute and let me think."

"You thinking is what got us into this mess!" Oh, how Casey missed Amanda's spitfire attitude.

Casey held back the giggle she felt bubbling up. It was a release to the tension that overflowed from the past week of constant barrages from her friends and the Monarchs. "I could always put you in the same bubble and let you have a go at each other."

"You wouldn't dare." Clint shifted from one foot to the other.

They all began yelling as she started to drift off. She twirled her fingers around and silenced their floating cells.

Hours later, she stretched her arms over her head and pointed her toes. The sun had set. She popped the foot release and jammed the bottom, clicking it in place. "Great nap. I feel so much better."

Casey left them where they were and pulled together dinner. She braced her feet on the coffee table and made obscenely loud chewing noises while she enjoyed her meal. She didn't bother addressing them as she overemphasized how delicious the flavors melted in her mouth.

She continued her evening ritual. Except she permitted Daisy to stay out. The dog avoided being around when they ported in. Was that a good or bad sign? It kept her from being underfoot, trying to defend her and getting herself shot or worse.

This Clint wouldn't hesitate to squeeze the trigger on a poor defenseless animal. The fact Daisy made herself scarce worked in Casey's favor. Otherwise, she would be distracted and make a mistake that could cost her everything.

"Are you guys thirsty? No? Okay, make yourselves comfortable. We have a few things to discuss." Casey shimmied back into the cushions of the recliner and waited for the others to quiet down to begin.

When they didn't appear to be in a hurry, she opened the Bible and started reading aloud. Passages of God's never-ending love. The sacrifice of His son Jesus dying on the cross for them. Amazing with how quiet it got when she got to what Jesus went through to save them from eternal death.

"Do I have your attention now? Would the Casey who did the things you say she did, Clint, read with such devotion our Father's words?" She couldn't stop the tears.

She needed them to understand what they were doing, to be on the same page, or the Monarchs were going to win. They would obliterate the entire country if they were given free reign.

Ben looked properly chastised. "Can we have a civilized conversation?"

"I've been trying for months. Yet Clint over there, Mister Neanderthal, comes tearing in, muscles flexed and ready to go head-to-head with a tyrannosaurus. I know I have short arms, or at least they feel short, but I'm not the monster here. You brought me to this world. I'm not supposed to be here. I wanted to go home, but you convinced me I'm this magical key that answered your prayers. Sent from Heaven to turn the tides of this war.

"Did you forget I didn't ask for this! You brought me here, you made me believe, you gave me hope I meant something to you. You made me want more than my boring dull life I led back home. I felt special, unique. I was the key. Clint, you were my protector. You held me when I broke down when we buried Ben. You were stoic but never let me feel less than you, a soldier, because I devolved into a weepy mess. I couldn't breathe without you, Ben. I fell in love with the man who followed God's voice and managed to do the impossible. You loved me back. I've never felt that kind of joy in my entire life. Do you know how huge that was for me?

"Amanda, you made me grieve for not having a sister like you growing up. You light up a room by walking in it. This silly yet sensitive soul who I couldn't help but click with. We were twins separated by several decades. When I met you, you knew me better than I knew myself. My brother didn't even know me that well. The one wanting adventure, excitement. And boy, did you guys deliver. Running for my life to pick up groceries. Fighting terrorists. Having secret powers. Every buried dream inside me I never recognized I wanted. The three of you drew me out of my comfort zone, and I proudly stood beside you. To hear God telling me which way to head.

"Now all you want to do is destroy everything good about us. No one could separate us, yet all of a sudden you did. From the inside, you dismantled our family and shattered my trust. I didn't think that was possible. I'll say it again. Do you still hear God? Because I do. The still, calm voice keeps me going when my walls are crumbling. He holds me up. He provided the produce you see growing, the chickens that feed me, the ability to solely thwart the Monarchs' continued attacks. You three used to anchor me, but not anymore. I ache at the future you willingly destroyed."

Amanda's tears streamed down her face. Ben covered his eyes with his hands and bowed his head. Clint didn't say a word, working through his own demons, but not broken up about what she word-vomited before they interrupted her. Sadness dwarfed his features. He cleared them and put his mask of defiance back in place.

"I'll keep praying for you. You can count on it. It is a promise I'll never break. The parchment says if someone uses the sphere for personal gain or vengeance, it will harden their heart. Shocking, I know, but I can say with utmost certainty it has happened."

Casey leaped to her feet. The blades of the dreaded helicopter were muffled by the house, but she definitely heard them.

"Is that a..." Ben bounced against the shield, trying to see.

"Don't go out there!" Amanda's concern shocked Casey.

"It's not a military bird so it's probably the Monarchs. They finally came for you," Clint boasted.

"They already did but I'm still standing. This stupid determined pilot who keeps coming back is searching for something or someone." Casey peeked through the blinds.

"You mean they never set down and only fly around?" Clint rubbed his chin.

"Yep."

The chuffing sound got louder than it had in a long time. "Did you lead them here?"

Clint smirked. "Wouldn't you like to know?"

"Enough." With a wave of her hand, she slung the shields through the portal.

If they leaked her location, so be it. She could only handle one enemy at a time. She didn't need the distraction of her friends, who she hoped listened to her words today, breaking free and helping to take her into custody.

Scratching noises at the back door froze her in place.

Finally, she was able to move when Daisy's whine followed. She opened the door a crack for her to wiggle her lithe body through and then slammed it shut.

Judging from the growing noise, they were hovering over the house or they were going to land. She ran from window to window trying to figure out what side of the house they were on. She couldn't see them so they must have been off to the side. She took the steps two at a time and hit the landing hard when she ran to the second floor.

Those window's curtains were open. She crawled across the floor to peek over the sash while still staying out of sight.

The downwash, as they hovered above the fields, damaged her plants. She wanted to go out there and ask how they could destroy all of her hard work but held herself back. She had more self-control than that. After what felt like a lifetime, they lifted the bird and flew toward the north.

Casey leaned her head back against the wall under the window. She would wait to make sure they left before she checked the vegetation.

"Father, use my words to open their minds. Let them know the truths I spoke. There is something wrong with Clint, and it is more than the mishandling of the sphere. He's angry, but also scared. I've never known him to show so much of himself. He's not normally vulnerable. Let them find You. Speak to them the way You still do with me. I know they may have turned their backs on You, but Your voice is a balm to my soul. In Jesus' name, Amen."

Daisy's snores tickled Casey. For such a sweet pup, she sure sawed some logs. They were so loud the first time she heard them, they woke her from a dead sleep. She'd assumed someone broke in, looking for a place to crash. People would have to try hard to make the kind of racket she did.

"Come on, pretty lady. Let's go check our plants. Should I throw rotten eggs at them the next time they try a stunt like that?" Casey wandered toward her crops.

Three cornstalks were bent, but hammering in stakes next to them might salvage them. The rest were low enough they probably would have had to set down right on top of them to damage them enough they would have to be pulled. She panned the flashlight over the crops.

Clint made a good point. It wasn't a military chopper. She counted three people when they were low enough to see heads backlit by the lights on the instrument panel, but she couldn't make out their features. They were determined. To continue flying in all these years later and still not land to investigate was curious. With each flyby, she got less and less tense. Who knows, maybe one day she would have the courage to go out and wave at them.

She chuckled. Not happening.

"Come on, girl. What do you want to have for dinner? Rufus is trying to dominate the new roosters; we need to separate them." They weren't quite old enough to butcher yet, so she built a separate pen she moved them to.

She outdid herself by expanding the paddock. Adding a second cordoned-off area for the young intended for meat instead of egg-laying helped to keep injuries to a minimum.

Daisy put on so much weight Casey found herself watching how much she dished out for the loyal friend. The freezer was stocked to the brink of overflowing every year before the cold months took over. The feasts she enjoyed seemed to taste twice as delicious. There was nothing like fresh produce and chicken. She always fancied eggs but was now addicted to the hot-off-the-nest ones she collected every morning. Chanterelle and morel mushrooms added flavors so mouthwatering, she would continue to increase her stores of foraged delectables.

Last month, she separated Rufus the rooster from the hens. They were sitting on too many eggs. The hatched chicks overran the outdoor paddock she expanded once already. She quickly put a stop to it while it was still manageable.

She easily had enough plucked frozen birds to feed her and Daisy through two winters. Next year, she would concentrate on her egg recipes and how to preserve them. She wasn't brave enough to try pickling them yet. If only bribing her friends with a roast chicken would work.

"Come on, girl. We're done for the day. Let's go." Halfway up the steps to the house, the chickens let out distressed calls from their yard.

She ran but Daisy beat her to the fence. Her growls spurred Casey on to pick up the pace. Another growl, definitely not Daisy, answered her dog's warning.

She skidded along the dirt when she came to a stop. A fox partially dug up the corner of the wire. Casey yelled and waved her arms around, charging after the animal.

"Go find your own food. Those ladies are mine!" She was tempted to feed it one of the butchered birds inside, but it would only encourage it to return whenever it was hungry. Better chase it off now and deter it from returning. There were an uncountable number of jingle bells in a box in the attic. Attaching them on the perimeter would sound a warning when something startled her hens.

She spoke to them for several minutes to soothe their fears before she went in for the night. Tomorrow's new day hopefully wouldn't include any visits from the three other chosen ones.

She never would have guessed she would pray for them to not be in her life for a short while. Nothing she could do about the circumstances now, so why worry about it.

Casey's knees popped as she kneeled next to her bed. "Father, never in this new world would I conceive of asking You to give me a rest from the men and woman who came to mean so much to me. I need a break, if only for a little while. With every encounter, it breaks a piece of me. I want my friends back. The chosen, who You put in my life in a most fantastically engineered way. Please help me have the resilience to withstand the trials headed my way. In Jesus Christ's name, Amen."

Twenty

Casey cried out when a large bee stung her on the back of her hand. "Oh, come on. I gave you these wonderful plants to grow you flowers to pollinate, and you go and sting me."

She gently lifted the stinger out of her hand with her fingernails. The swollen irritated area burned. The sun beat down on her neck, and she readjusted the sun hat.

She still struggled with the quiet. The birds singing and the nightly crickets were a symphony for her, but she missed having a conversation with a real human besides the constant bickering when the other three chosen ones decided to visit. The Monarchs had been quiet. Some would find comfort in the calm, but it only fueled her suspicions that they were gearing up for something big.

Casey would keep an eye out for the mid-summer plants to be ready to harvest in the coming months. Practically salivating at tasting the large, mouthwatering tomatoes the dainty, bright, sunny yellow blooms grew into. She was in awe of how such large red plump fruit came from such a small flower the first year she planted them from her harvest the ravens delivered at her feet and the sporadic germinated seed from the packets from the cellar. They weren't kidding when they said the percentage went down every year after expiration dates.

She abandoned trying to keep track of the time of day, especially when she toiled away with her plants. The sun on the horizon dipped lower each second while the pile of weeds grew. The chickens would love their treats. Daisy loped alongside her as she delivered the wilted leafy greens to the clucking brood.

The hieroglyphs glowed on her arms, alerting her they were on the way as Daisy disappeared into the underbrush. She raced back to the house, dropping her hat on the kitchen table after she made it inside, and slammed the door, locking it.

It wouldn't keep them out for long, but she wanted to make sure to set the trap so they couldn't get to her like last time. She turned on the electric blanket she'd wrapped around the dummy she found in the attic that was used to sew clothes. Around, that she put an emergency blanket, with a sleeping bag over that.

Casey laughed, thinking back to the day she found several in a box under the weather radio. She opened the sealed plastic bag, shook out the aluminum foil blanket, and thought what the heck did someone cook that involved an oversized piece of aluminum foil to cover it. Once she read the description on the small slip of paper included did she understand.

Casey backed away, trying to go slow so as to not draw attention to movement in the house. They might cheat and use technology she didn't have, but it didn't mean she couldn't set up some of her own tricks to try and survive.

She'd been tempted to try and use the sphere to go back and rejoin them when Ben first took her. The forewarning from the parchment to not use it for personal gain stopped her. Maybe they would come to trust her again. Or never stop trusting her. She only confused herself when she tried to think of time travel and how it pertained to the past, to now, to the future. She shook herself out of her musings when the glare from the symbols on her arms beamed at her.

She slipped into the closet and pulled the door, so the latch didn't quite click but still let her see what took place. The constant attacks physically and mentally drained her. They wouldn't know what hit them today once she set her plan in motion. She needed a break, but Clint kept coming at her, trying to wear her down.

Being military, he saw some of the worst life had to offer, from the battlefield to the Monarchs and the empire they were trying to build in the US. Clint's body was acclimated to not getting sleep and being on an adrenaline high for days at a time. She needed serious shuteye. She was just a woman from a bookstore ripped from her life and taken to the future.

A knock at the back door laser-focused her eyes on the hallway. A shadow passed in front of the door she hid behind, and she sucked in a breath as her body jerked in shock. They were already in the house. A weird green glow reflected from around Clint's face before he stepped in front of her. She couldn't see around his back and broad shoulders.

Casey remembered when that broad-shouldered back protected her. Her friend, who she thought of as a brother. She would die for him, but now? Yes, she would still die for him. If only to allow him to straighten his life out and turn back to being a soldier in God's army. Her eyes stung behind her closed eyelids as she silently prayed this would go off without a hitch. She may not be military, but she was nothing if not ingenious.

The relics seemed to only strengthen themselves with every use. She hardly concentrated on utilizing their powers. They became part of her.

Ben stalked around the corner from the kitchen and stood in front of the couch with the dummy Casey. He too wore weird goggles that emitted a faint glow. “She’s asleep.”

“Good, we can take her out before she wakes and shoves us into those stupid shield bubbles.” Clint’s shoulder bumped Ben out of the way as he raised a Glock and aimed at her. Hesitation gave Casey hope. His arms shook as he took aim.

Ben shoved Clint. “We aren’t killing someone who is asleep. This isn’t who we are. We came to take Casey back with us so we can figure out what happened before our future explodes, like we saw in the sphere.”

“Quiet, you guys are being loud,” Amanda called from near the front door.

Casey didn’t have eyes on Amanda since the door opened toward the entryway.

“Clint, we don’t murder people in their sleep. Since when is it okay to behave no better than the Monarchs? Maybe we need to take a step back. What if Casey is right?” Amanda whispered.

Casey’s heart swelled at the thought she might break through to them. Could kidnapping one of them and keeping them here sway them back around to the friends she treasured and who loved God with all of their hearts' work? She hadn't thought of that before.

But who would she keep? A smile pulled at the corners of her mouth. How poetic to keep Ben. He kidnapped her to bring her to the future. God put this in her hands?

"Don't let him go."

Casey bowed her head, letting God's love wash over her, renewing her spirit. He was always in charge, and everything would work according to His will.

"I'm doing this. It's the only way to protect ourselves from her poisonous actions. I've personally seen what she is capable of. Her finger squeezed the trigger like I'm about to do. With no hesitation or remorse when she did it. She smiled." Clint gritted his teeth.

He believed her responsible for what happened to him. She straightened her shoulders, her hands palms up. Three small shields popped into existence. Now or never. If the real Clint pulled the trigger, he would never forgive himself for being in the frame of mind to end an innocent person's life. Would she be able to bring him back from the brink? She stepped out from behind the door, the bottom of the wood swishing against the hardwood floors.

Amanda gasped and started to yell at Clint about a trap when she wrapped her in a shield. Casey quickly did the same to Ben and Clint, who were turning to face her. With no warning, they didn't have a chance to react.

Clint yelled and banged on the inside of his shield. Casey muted him.

"Clint." Casey waited for him to notice she addressed him.

"Casey, let us go." Amanda's eyes were wide. She didn't look away from Casey's hands.

Casey looked down as red and yellow static danced and shimmered over her skin. She nodded. The powers were a part of her like her blood, bones, and tissue. They would never fail her. She believed in them and herself. Most importantly, she believed everything happened for a reason with God right beside her the entire time.

"Clint." Casey ignored Amanda.

Finally, he acknowledged her with a glare. "This proves what I've been saying all along. You are not to be trusted. You attack us and expect us to fall in line? We know what the Monarchs are capable of. They have been in our world a lot more than you have."

"Says the person who wasn't going to hesitate to pull the trigger on a sleeping person who couldn't defend themselves. This is not me attacking you. This is me trying to stay alive and salvage the chosen ones before it's too late. Clint, look up." Casey kept her words calm.

He glanced at the ceiling. "What am I looking at?"

"Do you believe God is still up there?"

"Of course I do. How dare you question my loyalty to God?" Anger seared his words.

"So, He told you to kill me?" Quiet oozed through the room.

Amanda and Ben exchanged a look, telling Casey all she needed to know. She had to get through to them one at a time and open their minds to what they were doing.

Amanda tried to step forward but didn't take into account the bubble situation. "Clint, maybe..."

"No! Don't let your guard down. She's trying to lure you in before she strikes!" Clint shook with anger directed at her. He sniffed as blood dripped over his lip onto his chin, and he grabbed his head and then used the bottom of his shirt to wipe away the blood as if nothing happened.

The sphere flew into the room from the den and hovered above Casey's hand. It nestled into her palm. She let God decide where to open the timeline. Once it displayed the mess hall, she determined it was time to say goodbye to her friends.

"Amanda, you once told me you considered me the sister you never had when growing up. I believe you feel in your heart, like I do in mine, how real that statement still is today. I love all of you as if you were my blood family, and I'll never stop loving you. Clint, reach inside you. I know the protector of the key is still in there. You saved my life more times than I can count. Don't let hate darken your soul. Dig into those snippets of what happened to you. Clear your mind. What does your heart tell you I'm capable of?" Casey didn't wait for them to answer.

The portal sucked in their shields before it turned off again.

"Amanda!" Ben beat on the inside of his capsule.

"Ben, I merely sent them away."

Casey put the sphere back into its crystal treasure chest as it turned dark once again, dormant until the next time God decided she needed it.

"Are you hungry?" She walked to the kitchen.

Ben followed but not of his own free will. She deposited him above a chair, dropping the shield to include the seat.

"Oh, I'm allowed to sit?" Ben scoffed.

"I'm not completely heartless." Casey pulled out fresh chicken thighs in the marinade Ben taught her how to make, while she heated the oil to fry the succulent meat.

As she worked, she hummed some of her favorite hymns as a child. She added several chunks of veggies to skewers and drizzled oil over them along with dried herbs she cultivated the previous year.

"How long are you going to keep me?" Ben fidgeted.

"At least until they come for me again. I don't want to fight my friends. I'm tired. Mentally, I'm beyond my limit. I can only keep going because God is on my side. The day I walk away from Him is the day I know I will fall. He is the only thing holding me up because I'm not strong enough to do this on my own." Casey sat hard on the chair next to Ben.

Concern clouded his features. "How long have you been out here?"

Casey furrowed her brow as she thought back to when Clint first disappeared through the sphere, leaving her by herself. "At least three years, I think. No, it's been four. This will be the fifth winter season since..."

"You have been alone." Ben finished for her.

Casey nodded as she got up and flipped their sizzling meat in the oil. She put plates on the table along with silverware. Over four years. That was a long time, she had to admit when she let herself stop to think about it. She tried to never do that since it tended to overwhelm her.

"You haven't talked to another person since?" Ben seemed to finally understand she posed no threat to them.

"Well, if you don't count the Monarch attacks and your lovely visits, no. Of course I talk to God. Sometimes He's quiet but I know He hasn't left me." Casey pushed a plate over through the outer shell so Ben could eat.

"Why didn't you call Chloe, or someone else?" Ben hummed in appreciation when he took his first bite only after seeing Casey take one of her own.

"Clint had the phone on him when he left." Casey cut off another chunk and enjoyed the flavors.

"Casey." Ben tried to reach for her.

She didn't return the gesture. Only having him here for a short time kept her from being ready to trust him so soon with her life much less her heart.

Ben seemed to sense her heightened emotions of realizing she'd had no one for so long and pulled his hand back, and they finished their meal in silence.

"Did you need to shower or anything?"

"And how do you propose I do that?" Ben raised an eyebrow.

"Like this." Casey walked in front of him and tossed a change of Clint's clothes into the bathroom before stepping to the side and letting the shield expand to the walls.

She secured the door, making sure the shield didn't extend past it. He would have use of all necessities except the door to escape through.

"Come on. Casey!" Ben pounded on the wall.

She cleared out everything in the downstairs bathroom except non-deadly items such as soap, towels, and other blunt objects.

"The hot water heater has been acting up. I'd make it a quick shower if I were you. Yell when you're done; I'll let you out." Casey smirked as he continued to rant.

She was unsure how to turn his trust back around, but maybe it started with a hot meal and a shower.

With the dishes put away and no leftovers, she counted dinner as a success. She sat in the chair in the den listening for Ben and pulled out the parchment. Her arms glowed as she read. She stopped when she came to a quote not there before.

When the four are reunited, will they be whole, in heart and mind? God's armies will charge into battle with His chosen leading the conflict. Those who do not believe will fall to the side. Beware, for the day of judgment is coming.

Casey couldn't believe it. There it mentioned again the four of them being back together. "Father, thank you for the hope You continue to bestow when I so greatly need it. Open Ben's heart to You. Let him see what he needs to see to bring his heart back to me. I miss my friends and the man I fell in love with."

"Be ready and speak the truth. They will join you soon. The stone can heal the heart."

She scrubbed her hands across her cheeks when Ben called out from the other room.

Casey jogged to open the door and let him out while she kept him suspended off the floor.

"Have you been crying?" Again, Ben reached for her.

Casey wiped her eyes again. "I want to show you something."

Ben nodded and she lowered him enough to walk of his own free will, but if anything happened, she wouldn't hesitate to scoop him back into his jail cell.

Ben peered over her shoulder as she showed him the new script telling of their union as the chosen ones again. "Is this still rewriting itself?"

"Yeah. Look here, after the Monarchs took Clint. I found this a few months ago. It talks about the misuse of the sphere. It will harden the hearts of those who use it for their own purpose. Ben this is what's happening to Clint, you, and your sister. I don't know what he saw that makes him think I could take his life, but I think you know deep down he has a darkness in him, twisting the way he thinks." Casey waited for him to acknowledge her. Of course, it couldn't be that easy.

"You know I can't read hieroglyphs. It's probably all made up. Trying to separate us and pit us against each other. Nice try. I refuse to be used against Clint and Amanda. You playing mind games isn't going to endear me to you." Ben crossed his arms over his chest the shirt pulling at his biceps.

She couldn't believe how much bigger he and Clint had gotten. As if they exercised nonstop for the last four years. Amanda was lithe and fast. She moved with an ease Casey could only dream of.

"I think that's all you can handle for the day. I'll put you in Clint's old room. We can continue this in the morning. I don't think I'll get through by talking you to death." Casey stopped. "Okay, wrong choice of words to use here."

Ben chuckled, sweeping his arm for her to show him the way. She knew his familiarity with the old farmhouse since, as small children, he and Amanda visited Clint in the summers.

Her steps were light as they traversed the stairs. She stood to the right of the doorway before expanding his cell. She allowed access to the bed, but not the windows or door.

"I want you to know I do miss the Casey I first met. If I could go back and find her again I would in a heartbeat," Ben confessed.

Casey folded her hands together. "Therein lies the problem. I'm still the frightened woman God told you to not let go. You know what He told me downstairs?"

Ben swallowed, his Adam's apple bobbing in his throat. "No."

"He told me to not let you go. Sound familiar?"

Ben sat hard on the edge of the mattress. "He did?"

"Yes. It's no coincidence He chose the same words He said to you?" Casey wanted to go to him.

"Do you think we can talk tomorrow? Put everything on the table?" Ben walked to the shield and held his hand up, letting it rest on the barrier.

"I'd like that." Casey placed her hand on the outside, mirroring Ben's.

Casey clutched at her chest as a blue arc flew through the shield into Ben. He screamed at the same time she did.

"Stop this. I can't believe I thought I could trust you." Ben fought as the beam started to withdraw.

Filament strands pulled from Ben's chest right over his heart. Hundreds of thin strands turned a dark shade of gray as they retracted. Gray turned black and slowed from being pulled from his chest. The strands leaped and pulled against the healing stones' strength. Barbs like fishhooks sprang from the sides of the threads.

Ben's eyes rolled into the back of his head.

Once the healing relic's power siphoned the final black from his heart, his eyes popped open. She saw the old Ben in there. The one who couldn't stand not being in the same room with her. Her Ben, who held her hand every chance he got. A light lit in his eyes again, his rebirth. Darkness didn't haunt his features.

"I feel free, from the chains that dragged me down." Ben stared at his shirt and took a deep breath for the first time in a long time. "You were right. There was something in me."

"Goodnight, Ben. You may not believe me but your death, it broke something in me. I wasn't the same after you were gone. Neither was Clint. Watching you...With how you...I missed you. I still love you and I always will." Casey wanted to say more but didn't want to overwhelm him with the flood of sensations she kept at bay.

"The misery and despair inside you, now it's your turn to let it go. Open your heart to the chosen ones again and let God heal the damage. It's like you had a heart transplant. God is your anti-rejection meds. If you take them every day by reading his words and praying, you can keep your heart. Your real one, the one that loved me." Casey shifted back and closed the door.

Casey clasped her hands in prayer. "Father, thank you for showing me how to heal their tainted soul."

"It can only happen to the ones who know deep inside themselves the truth. Their eyes need to be opened to the possibility of change before it can be used."

Exhaustion pulled her under, and she dropped off to sleep in seconds.

Twenty-One

Ben lay there, unable to fall asleep. Casey's words tore at him. She still loved him. She sounded so much like the Casey he held as he kidnapped her. The woman he couldn't live without. He shook his head. The abundant opportunities to hurt them were there, but she never acted on them, only sent them away. Heck, she even fed him and let him clean up. Was he ready to open himself up to her? Take the gamble to put himself out there again?

He ran his palm up and down his sternum. The anger pulled from him dissipated, yet he wasn't sure where this left him.

Clint had been his best friend since they were kids. Stronger than friends, more like brothers. If Clint said they couldn't trust her, he wouldn't. Except what she said about the prophecy sounded familiar. He felt lighter than he had in months. Full of hope. What had she removed from him? They looked like the tendrils that escaped from the sphere when Clint accidentally shot it.

Ben flipped to his side and reached out, pressing against the shield. Glittering static pulsed around his hand as he ran it up and down. Just enough to know if he tried to push it, it would give him a jolt he would feel for days.

He huffed out the air in his lungs and turned to his back again. A chuckle rippled out of him when he paid attention to what stuck to the ceiling. Glow-in-the-dark stars shone from absorbing the light in the room before he turned it off. He remembered the year they put them up. They didn't ask for Clint's aunt and uncle's permission and balanced a chair on the bed to reach. Ben tried to hold it steady, but Clint moved around so much as he was overreaching to put up the last of the stars. The chair tilted, taking them both down to the ground in a loud thump along with the bookshelf.

His aunt ran up the stairs and gawked at the mess they caused by the tipped-over large bookcase jammed with books and tubs of toys he got too old to play with.

She quickly left and came back with a ladder and put her finger to her lips as she silently slipped back out of the room, not reprimanding them for breaking the shelves or the chair.

Memories like those were the Clint he remembered. Fear unlike anything he experienced coursed over him as Clint held the gun to Casey on the couch downstairs, ready to end her life. Nothing in his response when he stated so matter of fact that she had to die showed his concern with taking a life. Yet he faltered in his conviction and didn't pull the trigger in time.

Ben flipped over again and punched the too-soft pillow. He shouldn't be this comfortable while his sister and friend were worried about him. He didn't tell Casey they hooked up the sphere to a power source and manipulated the timeline. Was the parchment right?

No, he refused to believe. Because it meant his best friend was wrong, which also made him wrong. He blindly followed Clint instead of listening to the voice in his head telling him it went against the sphere's intended purpose.

Not to hunt down the person who gunned him down. Casey did seem like herself, and she never used the sphere to come after them. If she were this Monarch-controlled puppet, the sphere would be at her beck and call, and not stored in its container.

Each time they used the sphere, they aimed for five minutes before the last time. It never helped. They only grew angrier with each failure, seeking revenge for their own mistakes, taking them out on Casey.

He thought of his chosen relic. The ring of truth. Casey called it right; he hadn't let God guide his life since they got the second Clint back from the Monarchs. He was a darker version than the friend he grew up with. All the tours he survived through the military hadn't changed him like this. A grimness brewed in his friend.

Ben gave up on getting any rest and opened the Bible on the nightstand. It had been too long since he read from the holy book.

For the first time, Ben wondered if God left him.

"I've never left you."

Ben choked on the quick inhale, filling him with more than a breath of life. "Father."

All his feelings for Casey when he stood in her house and their Father said for him to take her, flooded through every part of him. The death of his sister. How had he forgotten? Casey's lifeless body as Clint carried her into their underground housing while Ben stayed with his sister. Everything he'd been through, the ups and downs of falling in love with Casey, the grief that tried to drown him when Amanda died. This wasn't his history; but the other Ben's.

The one that left the warehouses and found a way to live without his sister as he fell more in love with Casey and fought the Monarchs with Clint.

The sphere. It took from him what made him who he was. It darkened his soul. Another stain to scrub clean every time they used it beyond its design. He knew in his heart what God expected him to do. He had to convince Amanda and Clint. Stealth without a doubt was the way to go. He couldn't go in guns blazing and start spouting off everything after he spent one night with Casey. They would think she got to him and warped his way of thinking.

Clint would be the hardest one to win over so he would make Amanda his primary target. The next time they came for Casey, he would coordinate with her to separate Amanda and keep her behind. They would both work on showing her they chose the wrong path.

The malevolent side of the sphere, which took root in a person's soul, was no match for the healing relic to flush out.

God's love invaded Ben in a crushing blow as if His arms wrapped him up, welcoming him home again. The prodigal son finally saw his ways were distorted, and he needed to turn his life around. To fight for their Savior. For the innocents who couldn't stand up for themselves.

Ben's finger twitched as yellow filtered into the room. The ring glowed, filling the void between him and the sheer walls of his prison. It floated through the shield and landed in his hand. He placed it on his finger and felt complete for the first time in ages. Always destined to be his.

"You've always known the truth in your soul. Now show the others. It's not too late to free them before they are too far gone."

Ben kneeled beside the bed; his anguish at being misled and hurting the ones he swore to help protect overwhelmed him. His sobs hiccuped through him. "I'm so sorry, Father."

By the time Ben crawled into bed, the sun started to show through the tan, geometric print curtains. His body hadn't experienced such a sense of revitalization since he'd been a kid and would drop off at a moment's notice and sleep all night.

Fatigue was the norm nowadays; his renewed soul took him to levels he hadn't known for a long time. He heard Casey moving around in her room. He wondered how she kept the shield around him while she slept.

He rammed his feet in his shoes and waited for her to come. Energy course through him. He was on board with this.

"Ben, are you awake?" Casey lightly tapped on his door.

"Yeah."

Her head poked in. Ben's heart stuttered. He'd been looking at her through the dingy glasses of his murky soul. The most beautiful woman he had ever seen he now saw in such vibrant colors.

"You look different." If Casey saw the change in him, it gave him hope for their future.

"I am. Casey, I'm so sorry for what we put you through. Clint's wrong to come after you for revenge. He said he saw you pull the trigger, ending his life. Or not his but Junior. Okay, see, now I've already done too much thinking for it being so early in the morning." Ben smiled when Casey chuckled.

"Junior?"

"Amanda and I couldn't keep track of which Clint we were talking about, so she came up with Senior, your Clint, and Junior, ours." Ben relaxed the more he talked.

"That's right! Hilarious. Come on, you can help me in the garden before it gets too hot for the day." Casey didn't wait around. "Freshen up and I'll grab breakfast."

Casey left him alone while he closed the bathroom door behind him. This time she extended his shield to include the door but he still couldn't move farther than the shield if he tried. The journey to gain her trust when they first met would be twice as hard to do a second time, and he had no one to blame but himself. As he opened the door, he tried to lighten the mood.

"You're letting me out of my prison?" he joked.

"Oh, if you think I am naive enough to believe so quickly, you are sadly mistaken, mister. You are staying in there," she waved her hand up and down in front of him, "until God tells me I can trust you."

"God, not you?"

"To be honest, I don't trust myself. My heart is ready, but my mind can't wrap around the fact just yesterday you sided with Clint to kill me. You let yourself be led astray. I'm not ready to put my life in someone's hands, who is all too eager to believe I did those things Clint said. I thought you knew me enough to make a better decision than to follow blindly as someone hunted me down, no matter what your best friend believed. Someone who the parchment said would protect me with their dying breath and who did so many times." Casey grabbed a horrendously large hat and settled it on her head as she clomped down the stairs into the yard after they stood at the counter and splurged on fresh toast and jam.

"What on earth?" Ben couldn't stop his laughter.

"Oh, come on. This is one flashy fashion statement." Casey did a small pose, pulling down the sides of the large hat, so they touched her cheeks as she pursed her lips.

Ben followed as she turned and giggled. He stopped as his feet touched the edges of a very large garden. Plants of all shapes and sizes sprung up from the soil. Tomato plants chest-high to him and over Casey's head. The large cucumber plant blooms overwhelmed the corner, overrunning the grass taking over.

He turned to see corn stalks already in the silk phase of their growing. They still had two months before the harvest. What a massive undertaking for one person. Respect for her grew, knowing all she accomplished without any help.

"Where did you come up with all these seeds to grow this much produce?" Ben turned, taking in yet another row of corn.

"Funny story, actually. In a low place, with nothing to eat the first year after Clint went through the sphere, I decided to forage for my meals. The woods gave me access to a lot of nature's storehouses. There is a walnut tree growing about a mile in that direction." Casey motioned.

"Walnuts?" What did a tree have to do with her garden?

Casey smirked. "If you would let me finish. About an acre over there are raspberry bushes. They are full in the late summer and early fall. They freeze well so I can have fruit all year round. I found those because ravens delivered overripe veggies at my feet one day while I was out trying to figure a way to survive. I figured they came from somewhere, so I went hunting. I never did find where the ravens got their bounty, but God guided me to a place where there were other resources for me. Including chanterelle mushrooms. God looked out for me." Ben respected how she never wavered from her love of God. Even when at a low place.

"Isn't there a passage in the Bible about God feeding Elijah with the help of ravens?"

"Yes, I thought the same thing." Casey grinned wide and her eyes gleamed.

"Wait, you mean to tell me you got all of this from them?" Ben didn't believe it.

"Yes. Well, no. I dried out the seeds and hoped they sprouted the next year. I rationed the food Clint and I gathered before...well, you know. I made it through a pretty skimpy first winter. I tried to teach myself how to hunt deer and such a horrible failure it turned into," Casey joked.

"Did you snag one?" Ben tried to picture petite Casey dressing a deer.

"No, I lost my four whole arrows the first week. I rationed myself down to one meal a day. When I found the raspberry bushes, I heard animals on the other side of the trees. When I cleared the brush, a large buck lay dying. The rest of the herd ran off into the wild. I butchered it how the books explained. With more than enough to live off, I upped my rations to two meals a day. The next spring after the last frost, I planted the seeds. I was so ecstatic when the first sprouts came up. I tilled and weeded the soil every day, babying the plants so they would produce something edible. Such a proud moment for me when I bit into my first homegrown tomato. I did something by myself when I'd never grown anything in my entire life. I can't even keep a succulent alive."

"Casey, I'm so proud and impressed. What about rabbits or squirrels?" Ben wanted to hug her, but his personal dome of distance held him back. Frustration coursed through him that she had had to limit herself to one meal a day.

"Thanks. I barely got through the deer butchering; I didn't want to learn anything else. I was in the mindset that I was okay at the moment, so I put off trying to obtain other meats. So, over the next couple of years, I learned what to plant where and what did the best. I also learned how to pluck a chicken like you ate last night. The freezer is full and the last of the canned produce will last until the next fresh crops are ready." Casey turned to him.

"I'm not sure I would have been able to do what you did. No way to reach out to anyone. In the middle of a ranch, unsure if the Monarchs would find you. Us coming after you time and time again. I'm sorry, Casey. I should have been here with you, not coming after you. How have the Monarchs not found this place?" Ben put his hands on his hips and surveyed the fields surrounded by trees.

"They did." Casey turned and didn't expand further as she started working the soil, tearing out weeds so they couldn't choke out the roots of the plants she wanted to survive.

Ben didn't say anything. He dropped down in the row next to hers and went to work. If she could do it, he would help her in any way he could. He didn't wish to go back. He wanted Amanda and Clint here to reunite the four chosen ones the prophecy foretold. Back to who they were when he first took her.

"Casey." Ben waited for when she took a break.

"Yeah?" She twisted around to him.

"We need to convince Amanda first, that we lost our way. I think she's almost there on her own. She's been talking lately about our faith. Once Amanda's on our side, we can approach Clint as a united front. But we have to be careful. He's angry. I've never seen him like this. He swears he was shown a vidcast of you ending Junior's life. It already started worrying me before you kidnapped me, for my own good, though. I'm scared we won't get the old Clint back." He was honest for the first time in a long time about his buddy, and Ben felt good to get it off his chest.

"I was never there." Casey gripped the edges of her hat and repositioned it.

"I know that now. He saw something. I'm just not sure what the Monarchs did to get him to believe something so ludicrous about you. Amanda's convinced they are controlling him, but she hasn't been able to find anything."

"You're being honest, aren't you?" Casey pushed off the ground.

Ben slouched as his chin trembled because of the way things ended up. "Yes. There's no way I'll be able to fix what I broke between us, but I'll prove it to you through my actions."

The popping of the shield startled him. He ran his fingers over the surface. His eyes met Casey's. They widened as he stepped through. Finally, he stood face to face with no barrier to stand between them. She couldn't use the relics against him.

He couldn't stop himself if he wanted to. He swept her up in the best hug he ever had. Her choked sob tore through him.

"Sweetheart, I'm so sorry for what you've gone through." Ben tightened his hold when she gripped him harder.

"Let's devise how to nab Amanda during the next portal opening. Do you think she'll be on our side?" Casey shifted away and he missed her already.

Ben clutched her hand to keep the connection between them. "I saw her Bible out for the first time in months the other day. It's hard to explain how using the sphere for personal gain rips a piece of you away each time. It forms a callus around your heart. Every time the layers build up thicker and thicker until all you know is anger and hate. I was still in there, because here I am, but it scared me. I knew it was happening, but I didn't care enough to stop it. Like a drug you're addicted to. You know it's wrong, but you still want the rush that high, and you put that ahead of anything else in your life because that's all you care about."

Casey shook her head.

"It's not an excuse because I still walked through the shimmer every time, but it became harder and harder to care. It tore my soul from my body piece by piece. I guess I'm messing up how it happened. I haven't always been so eloquent with words." And Ben's fell short, describing how it took over their lives.

Casey closed the distance and tilted her head back. "I understand what you're trying to say. It's scary it causes such a rift in you; you aren't concerned with what the consequences are."

"You have no idea." Ben cupped the sides of her face. Finally home, he found the place he belonged.

"Come on, let's work out a plan to kidnap Amanda. We can leave Clint for last. I think he's going to argue till his dying breath on this."

"Hey, I've been meaning to ask you. How were you able to use the shield against us?" Ben thought initially it was because she turned against the prophecy but now, he realized it was because he had.

"I don't know." Casey's brow furrowed.

Ben suspected she had an idea, so he forged ahead. "I say it was a way to protect you from us. At first with Clint's accusations, I assumed you stepped away from God's will and the prophecy so it enabled you to use them against us. Now, though. We walked away, we used the sphere for our own personal gains, not how it was intended. The shields were your way to keep you safe from us but also so nothing happened to us so we could find our way back to God."

"Maybe it's why the shield popped like it did. It felt you were on my side again, and it reverted back to you being part of the chosen. God told me when you guys could walk through the barrier, I could trust you." Casey had a good point.

"Perhaps it's why God gave this back to me." He wiggled his finger where the ring sat.

"How did you..." Casey backed away.

Ben grasped her hands, stopping her retreat. "It floated through the shield as I prayed last night."

Casey rubbed her fingers back and forth across the ring.

Ben held the door for her as they started planning the next stage in rescuing the other two chosen ones from the draw of the corrupt side of the sphere.

It was kind of like two sides of a coin. The relics have their two sides also. It originally said the relics couldn't be used for malicious means, but the sphere had. Dread pervaded his thoughts of a dark tunnel that still dug its claws into Amanda and Clint.

Twenty-Two

Amanda paced back and forth while waiting for Clint to come up with a way to rescue her brother. Casey had to be stopped before she did something to permanently ruin them. Did she hurt Ben? Casey set a trap. What a conniving, horrible woman. She never should have thought of her as a sister.

The hate in her heart wanted to spill over. Listening to her excuses of missing her and how she thought of her as the sister she never had planted this small seed of doubt in her mind that they had been wrong this whole time. When she was thrown back and Ben left in her clutches, the anger jumped into the forefront of her thoughts. Amanda chucked a bottle of water across the room as Clint walked in. Luckily, he batted it away. He raised his left eyebrow and waited for her to say something.

"Sorry. I'm worried about what she may be doing to my brother. Is she turning him over to the Monarchs? Will we get to him in time? Clint, I can't lose him. I can't." Amanda barely held it together.

"Breathe, sweetheart." Clint pulled her into a stiff hug and awkwardly patted her on the back as she tried to bring her rage to a low simmer.

"There has to be a way to stop her." Amanda chose to let Clint handle Casey the way he always wanted to since being tortured by the Monarchs.

"I'm thinking. She surprised me on our last trip. I didn't expect her to be so cunning. I'll be better prepared for her next time. We have to hope she hasn't turned Ben with her lies and he won't side with her."

Amanda gasped. "Do you think she can? Ben would never go against us, would he?"

"I don't know. She's good with her deception and gaining sympathy by playing the victim. Isn't that why you've been second-guessing me lately?" Clint crossed his arms.

Why did it feel like being torn in two? It had been a while since she spoke with God and heard His voice in response. That is why she started reading her Bible again. She felt closer to Him when she read His word. Shouldn't Clint be happy she wanted to put God first in their lives again? Amanda tugged at her hair. Honestly, she missed Clint junior.

"Amanda. The truth is all I've ever wanted. Do you have your doubts about me and what I witnessed her do?" Clint tilted her head up with his hands on the sides of her jaw.

"No, I'm with you. I never thought her capable of doing anything so vengeful." Amanda noticed Clint becoming more focused on only one thing: ending Casey's life. It scared her.

Clint held on for a few more seconds before releasing her. "Good, because I won't fail in my mission."

Amanda nodded and headed to the cafeteria. She hadn't eaten that morning. Too nervous about her brother, she didn't think she could keep anything down. Now her stomach grumbled some sort of cadence, marching right through her. She took her lunch back to her room.

She sat cross-legged on her bed and enjoyed her sandwich and chai tea, adding more honey and cream than she probably should have.

Amanda couldn't help herself and pulled her Bible from the drawer. It always gave her comfort to be engrossed in the scriptures.

A knock brought her out of her thoughts. She quickly moved the tray with her lunch to the dresser and opened the door.

"I think if we head back as soon as the sphere is ready, we can sneak up on her and rescue your brother." The forced smile on Clint's face didn't fool her.

"Have you ever wondered why the sphere seems to need to recharge after using it?" Amanda started to question everything, at least in her mind.

"Probably when Casey broke it, a cataclysmic failure occurred in the power grid. She did it on purpose. How else do you explain it? We brought her into our fold, and she tried to tear us down from the inside." Amanda suddenly realized that Clint was so immersed in his hate of her, he couldn't think with reason.

"Clint, do you hear yourself? We scared Casey to death when we brought her here. Her fear was so intense she crawled through the ceiling trying to get away. You were her champion. The one assigned to protect her by the prophecy. Now look at you. All you want to do is believe she is this evil incarnate and there's nothing good about her. We took her whole family from her. We carried her to a time she didn't belong to. She didn't know about the relics until Ben kidnapped her. The healing stone absorbed into her. Directly from God. Her being the key turned on all the other relics. She helped us take down Polson..."

"No, you are not going to turn on me too. What did she do to you? Did she inject you with something? Scramble your brains a little?" Clint pushed Amanda up against the wall hard.

"Clint, you're hurting me." Amanda kicked at his shins. "I'm confused. I want to believe she can be saved, but I don't want to lose you or my brother in the process."

Clint ran his hand through his hair and walked to the door. "Stop going against me. We can't be at odds, or she'll win. I'm the only one left on your side. I'm trying to save the two people I care most about in the world."

"I care about you too. You are one of my best friends." Amanda put her hand on his cheek.

Clint's eyes lit up and he leaned into her hand before they darkened again, and he stormed from her room.

Amanda settled on the chair. "Father, help him. He's so angry."

Clint fought his own war waging in himself. She got flashes of the man she fell in love with before the blackness would tug him under.

She pulled a picture out of the back of her Bible of the three of them as youths walking through his uncle's fields as his aunt called them in for supper. They spent all day down by the river that ran through the neighbor's property. He let them play there anytime they were in town. Catching frogs and lizards. All three were smiling as if they didn't have a care in the world. Back then they didn't; they were young kids playing and enjoying life. Clint's dimple was prominent in the photo.

Amanda hadn't seen it since he came back from the Monarchs. Who could she talk to about mind manipulation or brainwashing?

A knock made her cringe. She was not in the mood to deal with more of Clint's negative conspiracy theory.

She opened it to Chloe on the phone. She motioned her in and peered down the hallway to make sure no one was around before closing the door.

"Thanks, Uncle." Chloe hung up.

"Okay, you don't look happy." Amanda patted the bed for Chloe to hop up.

"James is still alive. They only made it look like they killed him. After the Monarchs imprisoned both Clints, James met with an undercover agent in the Monarchs. The agent blocked his signal as he tailed him after the meeting. They took him into custody, so we're safe for now," Chloe said in one breath.

"Doesn't necessarily sound like a bad thing. Why the scowl?" Amanda frowned.

"James said he isn't the only mole in here."

Amanda clambered to her feet. "We have to tell Clint!"

Chloe bolted to the door, stumbled over her feet, and slammed into the cold hard metal with a thud. She put her back against it, blocking Amanda from leaving. "Clint's the mole."

All the air rushed out of Amanda, and her legs weren't able to hold her up. "No."

Chloe kneeled next to her and took her hands. "They messed him up. He hasn't given up our location. But he's feeding them information on who is here and how many weapons we have. He mentioned the relics."

"He wouldn't." Amanda refused to believe the man she once had a crush on worked for the very people who wanted them all dead.

"My uncle said he thinks they implanted something in his brain. It's controlling the empathy side. Friends of my uncle are sending a scanner if you think someone can get close enough to use it. Technically, a chip would have to be inserted for them to hijack his system. They have a new technique. A small incision scar in front of the left ear will confirm an implanted chip. The concern they left some sort of foreign electrical component to regulate him is higher if there is a mark there. Amanda, they can mess with his recall of events and insert false ones." Chloe started to cry.

Amanda squeezed her shoulders with her right arm. "Tell your uncle to be concerned."

"What? Why?" Chloe stuttered.

"I've seen the scar." Amanda didn't wait for a response before she left. She would need to hide the sphere from Clint. If she denied him access, maybe it would liberate him from the Monarchs' hold. She hesitated, hearing a swish of boots against the floor. Was she being followed?

She took a few more steps when she heard it again. When she stopped, so did they. Did someone listen to her and Chloe? She speed-walked to the lab. Her heart told her Casey wasn't the poison he claimed her to be.

He was.

She made it without running into anyone. After quickly locking the door behind her, she lifted her leather satchel and unlocked the back storage door. She relaxed for a fraction when she saw the sphere in its case. In seconds, it was stowed away in her bag, and she hurried on her way.

Amanda glanced both ways and listened for foot traffic. Someone in thick rubber-soled boots headed her way. Those steps were Clint's. She lived with hearing them long enough she could pick him out of a line of men walking toward her with her eyes shut. His steady steps had an air of authority and purpose.

She took off at a fast clip around the corner and into an alcove. A key rattled in the door. She waited until she heard the click of the door closing before she hoofed it to the next hallway and sprinted to the end, keeping her footsteps as light as possible.

Amanda stopped Chloe from closing the door to her room. "I got the sphere and parchment. We need to hide them before Clint comes looking for them."

Chloe clung to her hand and hauled her in the direction of her room but bypassed it. Amanda followed, not sure where she was headed, but they kept a steady pace. She hadn't been on this side since they secured it from the homeless, trying to use it as a home.

Ben and Clint hadn't been over here since Casey tried to leave through the overpainted window, the day she ported in with Ben from her closet in her house. At least Ben and Clint caught her, forcing her back for her own protection. Clint was scared she would get out before being vaccinated.

Amanda was determined to get him back. The boy she grew up with. The young man she crushed on. The man she loved more than anything. If he never saw her in the same way, she would still rescue him from what the Monarchs did. If he never reciprocated how deep her love ran for him, she'd be okay as long as he survived.

Chloe opened a filing cabinet door taller than her. "No one knows about this. It's an escape route my uncle has been working on in case the Monarchs surround the building."

"You never told anyone about this?" Amanda couldn't believe she kept this from her.

"My uncle swore me to secrecy. It is a last resort when there is no way else out. The other side isn't finished yet. It's about a mile and the lights aren't connected, so once someone goes in, they are shrouded in total darkness. We have flashlights but they are solar-powered, and if they haven't been docked into the panel on the roof, they won't last until the end."

"Whoa, it's that long a tunnel?" Amanda didn't think she could handle feeling her way around and having to put her hands on who knew what kind of bugs and insects.

Chloe laughed. "He said it's far enough down that phones don't work in it."

"I don't think I can do that. What if the Monarchs find it?" Amanda took a couple of steps back. "Won't the ceiling cave in, burying me alive?"

"They don't have scanners to reach that depth, and no, the tunnels have been shored up to keep them from collapsing. If my uncle can't find it with all of his technology, the Monarchs surely can't." Chloe beamed with pride.

Amanda shook her head. "I can do this. What's a simple little tunnel? We've been through worse, right?"

"Yep, but you need to go now before Clint notices you gone." Chloe handed her a large lantern-style light.

"You didn't say you had one of these!" Amanda chuckled when she took the handle.

"Why do you need a light?" Both Amanda and Chloe shrieked at Clint's voice behind them.

Clint glared at Amanda and the pack she wore. Legs planted wide as his nostrils flared. She'd never seen such cold hate in his eyes. She locked her knees to hide the trembling. Sweat dampened her palms, making her hold to the lantern slick.

"Well, after the surge the other week, Chloe's uncle gave her one since they stay lit longer." Amanda tried to move and cover the tunnel opening.

Clint stormed over to her and grabbed for the bag. Chloe vaulted off a table onto his back and twisted her right arm around his neck, applying pressure. Clint struck her arms, trying to dislodge her.

She hung on for dear life as Clint collapsed.

Chloe screamed at her. "Go!"

Amanda sprinted several feet away into the dark with the light being swallowed up by the sheer volume of shadows. Her heart rate exploded into a staccato rhythm.

"He's out, keep running. There will be a door at the end where light filters through. It comes out in a field. My uncle will have someone waiting for you. Don't stop, whatever you do, keep moving." Chloe's voice faded away as Amanda's feet pounded against the ground as she increased the distance between them.

A scream ripped through the air straight to Amanda. Goosebumps told her Clint did something to Chloe, but she couldn't turn back. What if Clint took the sphere to the Monarchs? She couldn't allow it to fall into enemy hands. Chloe said he hadn't informed them about their powers; they, unfortunately, vanished when Casey took the relics, but she couldn't take the risk they got through the last few walls he kept their secret hidden behind.

Boots sounded behind her, getting closer with each step. He was going to catch her. Pushing herself harder, she tried to widen the distance between them, but his faster and lengthier gait caught up to hers in no time.

A shriek bubbled up her throat and wanted to escape, but she held back when he hit her hard from behind. Clint's massive body tackled her like a linebacker. The air whooshed out of her lungs when she smacked the ground, knocking a yelp out of her. Clint yanked her arms behind her back so hard they screamed in protest.

Soon, he relieved her of the satchel she worked so hard to keep from him. She struggled to move her hands around to the front to push off the ground but found they were restrained at the small of her back. His long fingers wrapped around her bicep and pulled her up.

"Shouldn't have run from me, Amanda. Your actions show me I can't trust you now." His hot breath was against her ear as he whispered.

"Did you hurt Chloe?" Amanda tried to stop the flow of tears as fear coursed through her.

"She got what was coming to her for attacking me. All I'm trying to do is keep everyone safe. Is that so hard to understand?" Clint, none too nicely, helped her over the threshold.

Chloe slumped on the floor, her eyes glazed and her mouth gaping.

Amanda sucked back a wail for her friend.

"Oh, settle down. I taught her she should never touch me."

Amanda saw blood on the floor under Chloe's head. She surged forward only for Clint to spin her around and throw her over his shoulder.

"Come on, we need to have a talk. I'll send someone to take her to Doc and get her checked out. I'm not completely heartless." Clint's voice belied that with how chipper he sounded.

"We're meant to be under your protection. How can you be so glib about it? This isn't the Clint I grew up with." Amanda shook her head to combat the dizziness from hanging upside down.

Clint didn't say anything to her as they continued to his room. He dumped her on Ben's bed, and she bounced a couple of times before settling. He slipped a panel in the wall to the side and set the bag in. She didn't know they had a secret compartment. She didn't like everyone keeping secrets from her. First Chloe about the tunnel and now Clint.

Amanda raised an eyebrow. "Secret panel? Next you will tell me you're an undercover agent spying on us, turned double agent and still working on the side of good."

"Try switching it around." Clint removed his shoes at the end of the bed and relaxed back with his hands folded over his stomach.

"What are you going to do with me?" If she was honest with herself, she didn't want to have that question answered.

"I haven't decided. They transported Chloe to a hospital for her uncle to pick up. It would look a little suspicious if she woke up later on that side of the building, so I hinted in passing to Mark that I hadn't seen Chloe lately. His curiosity took care of the rest," he explained.

Amanda was glad Chloe would get medical help for her injury. "Aren't you forgetting something?"

Clint quirked his mouth up. "Nope, gave her a sedative, wipes everything out for two hours before the injection. She'll wake up in the hospital and not remember having a conversation about the tunnel."

"How could you?" She didn't know which way was up.

"Speaking of." Clint pulled open a kit and pulled out another dose.

"No!" Amanda lurched to her feet and made it two steps before Clint pulled her back against him, jamming the needle in her neck.

"Sleep, Amanda. It's either this or I have to kill you. I'm sure you prefer this way as opposed to the other. You know too much and will spoil the plot to take Casey out once and for all. I don't have a choice. My head hurts all the time."

Amanda couldn't feel when Clint picked her up and placed her on the bed or when he untied her hands. She floated on a cloud of bliss as her eyelids drooped.

The last thing she heard was him whispering, "I wish things were different, but they aren't. The Clint in charge is not the man you love, and I can't go back to not existing."

The sphere's green glow from the shimmer wavered out of reach. Clint looked back at her once before he stalked through.

Twenty-Three

Clint brushed the hair off Amanda's forehead; she was still comatose. His little side trip didn't take as long as he figured, and he made it back before she awoke. He came close to killing her. He didn't want to have to answer to her brother what he'd been forced to do because of his sister's stubborn streak. He gripped the sides of his head.

Clint was finally in charge for a little bit. Amanda lay on Ben's bed. He cupped her cheeks and kissed her forehead. Always stepping into it ever since he had known her. He couldn't count the times he bailed her out of a jam growing up. Ben would call and they would team up to get her out of whatever party she snuck into or hiking trip someone reported her missing from. One thing or another got his adrenaline pumping until they got her to safety.

Ben told Clint, while deployed overseas, about her troubles he dealt with on his own. At least his harsher side stopped her before she reached the end of the tunnel. A niggling thought in the back of his mind told him the Monarchs staked out the entrance and found it after he escaped. He would hate her walking into the trap at the end that the Monarchs had set up for anyone who traveled through the underground. Chloe and her uncle thought it was camouflaged; they were wrong.

He wanted to pull her into his arms and hold her until everything was back the way it was. They all trusted each other without second-guessing their ulterior motives. He didn't have much time. He already felt the other one stirring, shoving him to the back. Seconds later he only saw the haze around him, locked in his cell.

Clint senior hated losing snippets of time because the other one was front and center.

Chloe and Amanda didn't know he listened to their little clandestine meeting in Amanda's room. Chloe told her about a chip in his head. He would remember if they performed such an invasive procedure. He commanded his own mind. No one hijacked it, and no one would convince him differently. So what if he had a scar he didn't remember on the side of his head. His finger traced the bumpy ridge over his left ear. This didn't mean they could control his mind.

He pulled the sphere out and placed it in the case. Clint shook Amanda. She didn't acknowledge him. He placed the relics in their corresponding chests and loosened a panel in the wall to the side. With replacement relics stashed in the secret compartment, he replaced the false wall. If Ben and Amanda earned his trust again, he would fill them in on his little side trip to replace what Casey stole.

His mind wandered to Casey when a sharp pain doubled him over. He pulled his knees up to his chest as he curled into the fetal position. He concentrated on blanking his mind so the hurting went away. The extreme bolts of agony only increased his anger toward Casey. A vision flashed through his mind, transporting him through his memoirs.

They dumped James in the trunk and were on the road in a matter of seconds. Air raid sirens cut through the silence when they were only a few blocks from the underground parking. They turned down an alley behind more businesses, the car's engine pushed to its limit as they cut corners faster than the car was designed to do. A shockwave rolled through the city, blowing out windows and raining glass everywhere.

They made it to the ball fields with no further incidents. They were ready to question him about Casey when he thought he heard her voice.

"What was that?" Already on the move and halfway back to the car, Junior ducked when shots rang out. Was she within range for their earpieces to pick up a signal? They ducked behind the front of the car when several Monarchs lurched through the shadows.

The Monarchs rained blows down on both of them until Clint passed out.

The next time he woke, he sat strapped to a chair. If he wasn't mistaken Casey sat bound in this the very same chair when the Monarchs took her when she went on a grocery excursion. He knew where they were. Now to survive long enough to get them both out of here and back to his friends.

The door opened and a plump man walked in. Blood dotted his shirt and he wiped his knuckles on a torn towel. "Never got to operate on twins before. This should be fun. Your brother didn't last long before he caved into a whimpering mess."

Clint growled. "You are the worst liar."

"Whose blood do you think is all over my hands?"

"Doesn't mean you broke him. You forget we're twins so I know what he's capable of enduring." Not bothering to explain he and Junior weren't twins, he played along with their mistake.

The first punch came faster than he thought possible. His head snapped to the side. What blood he wasn't able to spit out dribbled down his chin. He was already sore from the beating he took when they were overrun in the lot.

"When I'm done with you, you'll not only tell me everything I want to know, but also be my good little doggy. Your mind won't be yours. You can watch the festivities but won't be able to do anything. With a flip of a switch, you will murder who I tell you to and when I tell you to." His fist connected with the other side of Clint's jaw.

The realization he would turn on his friends sent fear coursing through his veins. Did the Monarchs have such technology?

"I see you understand there is no hope for you. Your mind belongs to us. If you are lucky enough to withstand the constant frying of your synapses while you are near Casey, the rebellion's secret weapon, a flick of a switch and your whole brain will be fried. Slowly and painfully, your body will shut down, organ by organ."

A man pushed a cart into the room, covered in white linen. He stopped to the left of Clint. With a dramatic flair, he flipped the sheet off the medical instruments that reflected the bright overhead lights off their smooth polished surface.

Clint pitched himself back and forth in the restraints until a needle pricked the skin on his upper arm. The lights danced as his vision blurred. Vertigo sent his stomach churning.

"Knock him out before he pukes everywhere. I'm not cleaning up vomit," the man who punched him ordered the other man.

"He has to be partially conscious, or the insertion deteriorates within seconds. Do you want to tell the leader why his prize-classified experiment is dead?"

"Fine, fine, get on with it. I can't wait to test this baby out." He cackled as he left the room. "Imagine shutting off sympathy on the subconscious level so you are left with nothing more than a robot going through the motions implanted in their mind, unable to think for themselves. It's genius!"

Clint felt pressure on the side of his head but no longer controlled his limbs. His body, paralyzed with the sedative, kept him aware of what they did to him.

"Easy does it. There it is." The man spoke to himself incessantly.

Liquid dripped from the side of his head down his arm. Clint was unable to scream as a sharp twinge made his eyes water and sent him into tunnel vision. He saw a small pinprick of light at the end of his line of sight. A scream burst from the other room. It was disturbing to hear your own voice. They were probably doing the same to Junior.

"Just a little bit more. You are taking the implant better than I thought you would. Imagine if we can implant these into any of the leaders of this country. There will be no limits to what we can achieve." Clint hoped the surgery failed so he wouldn't be the cause of his friends' deaths.

To be locked away in your mind, knowing everything happening around you but not able to stop it, was more than he could handle.

Another scream echoed into their room but cut out. Running feet stopped outside his room. The door didn't have time to creak in the hinges before it slammed into the wall behind it. "He's dead."

"What happened?" the man beside him growled.

"At the first image we displayed of Casey, he fought the process so hard it damaged the neurotransmitters. He stroked out before we could do anything to stop it. How's it going with this one?"

Junior didn't make it. He prayed the same would happen to him. Then they couldn't use him.

"We'll see once I'm done here. Go clean up. You look like a B-rate horror movie character."

"Yes, sir." Footsteps took the other man out of the room.

"I was afraid of that. Sometimes the urge to protect those you hold dear is too much for someone to handle when they're tasked with their demise. Let's see if you are as faithful to them as your twin." He chuckled as the pulling of his skin told Clint he closed the incision.

Squeaky wheels in desperate need of oil traveled toward them. The man who came in before, telling their scientist Clint died, maneuvered a large screen in front of him.

"All done. Load the vidcast while I fine-tune the settings."

Casey's smiling face appeared on the screen. Sharp stabbing coursed through his skull. Clint screamed.

"Every time you see her face the consequences of not putting a bullet in her will be misery unlike anything else," the man stated quietly in his ear.

The other man came over carrying a Ruger and put it in his right hand. Before he lifted the barrel to aim at his captors, the weight of it told him there were no bullets in it for him to take out the people in the room. Casey's face lit up the screen, sending another jolt through him.

"Pull the trigger. The suffering will go away if you do," the man taunted him.

Clint released the gun.

"Oh, come on. Stop being a hero. Look at what she did to your twin, your brother, your own blood." A very dead Clint, who suffered through hours of torture, appeared on the monitor before Casey's face replaced his.

"Murderer." The man pressed the button.

Clint screamed, his voice hoarse from the strain.

"Pull the trigger." They put the automatic pistol back in his grip and flashed her face in front of him again.

Clint dropped the gun before dropping his head forward, sucking in deep breaths to combat the torment.

The man sighed. "This is going to be a long day."

"Mapping his receptors takes time or he'll end up like his twin next door. The leader wants this done correctly, or it's our heads that will roll. I personally like mine where it is, attached to my body." The man to his left grunted.

Soon the days turned into weeks, the weeks turned into months. Clint couldn't remember half of the days as he drifted in and out of his mind. He would be coherent one minute when the other, who he now called his weaker side, would slip in and take over. He pulled the trigger more times than not. The weaker Clint tried to stay aware, but it was more than he could bear. Stories about children who have a stronger version of themselves that takes over so they can live with the trauma became his very real, vivid life.

Now, thinking about Casey without pulling back the lever sending a bullet into her delivered excruciating convulsions through his body as his synapses revolted at not getting the result in the death of Casey.

This week they would let him shower. As long as he stayed in control, he may have a chance to break away. If the other side, the Clint clone, took over, it would be useless to try.

He blanked his expression as they shuffled him down to the old school team locker rooms. They sat a stack of laundered clothing on the bench by the stall and told him to hurry.

Murmured voices spoke of the Monarchs working on a disc that could render the shield useless and that if they could reproduce it, they would send one with Clint if he passed his training.

What disc? It wasn't something he could worry about now.

The hot spray splashed his skin for mere seconds before he dried off to tug on his new duds. They took his shoes before he ever regained consciousness when they first took him. He left the water running and scaled the side of the wall to the small, slatted windows.

Clint looked back, making sure the coast was clear or he wouldn't make it far. He thanked God the night held no moon so it would hide his movements better than if the sun shone. Inch by inch to stop the unused hinges from alerting the Monarchs of his breakout, it took forever before the pane tilted up out of his way.

If he hadn't lost so much weight from his time here, he wouldn't have been able to squeeze through the opening. Since the window sat at ground level, he rolled across the grass and out of the way to lower the sash into place. He gave himself only about six minutes before they would realize he got out.

Murmured voices around the corner stopped him in his tracks. Two Monarchs pulled long drags on their cigarettes before letting the smoke out through their noses and mouths to curl around their faces. They turned and started back toward the front of the building, letting him take the gamble to sprint toward the row of trees.

Clint skidded on his bare feet. He hopped on his left foot to extract a twig embedded in the arch of his right before taking off again.

An alarm sounded and search lights lit the mortar-and-brick school. Clint sprinted off before they panned the light his way. Several miles from his group, he kept his friends from his thoughts so the pain wouldn't incapacitate him.

Large vehicles scoured the area. He would make it a block unseen only to have to hide for the next several minutes before he moved again. At one point, he passed out from the jolt he got when he thought about where he left Casey behind to use the sphere.

He woke later as the sun hovered on the horizon. Not moving a muscle, he listened for several minutes before lifting his head and taking a look around. This neighborhood he knew well. It was where they built in the lower levels of the houses for them to move to. He made it farther than he thought he had.

Picking his way from building to building, he got back before the sun started its descent into the west. Ben and Amanda got through on his communicator. He traversed the stairwells and tunnels and pushed in the brick to open the hatch above his head at the top of the ladder.

The cool air chilled his skin as Ben helped him step onto the linoleum floor.

Amanda yelled his name and barreled into him slinging her arms around his neck, holding on for dear life.

"I'm okay. I'm back. It's going to be fine." Clint wasn't sure who he tried to convince more.

Ben clapped him on the shoulder. "Good to have you home. Where's our Clint?"

Clint fell away from reality, a sharp inhale the only sign of being relegated to the back of his mind. Words not spoken by him uttered. "Casey killed him."

As soon as he said her name he blacked out.

When Amanda woke up in a few hours he would have to come up with a believable lie she wouldn't question. Chloe missing would take a more elaborate story for her to believe. The poor kid thought she could take him down. He liked her. She was strong-willed, and he admired that about her. Although with her out of the equation and no memory of him being there, he breathed easier. He was back on track to port to Casey to rescue Ben and end Casey's existence.

Maybe they would stay. Casey grew a nice little salad on the far east of the house. The urge to protect her overwhelmed him, when a jolt seared through his brain again, knocking him for a loop. He cracked his neck to the left and the right, the uncomfortable burn still coming from the left side of his head.

He blanked his thoughts and took himself back to his childhood playing at his uncle's and how his aunt hid the fact that he and Ben broke his bookshelf as he scaled the room from every angle. They propped the chair against every usable surface and glued stars to his ceiling.

His childhood summers flooded his mind. Cancer took his aunt later the same year.

Someone shook him. He must have crashed after dealing with Amanda. He cracked open his eyes to see her standing over him, her hands on her hips.

"Is there a reason you are shaking me like the San Andreas Fault?" He stretched his hands over his head.

"Why am I in your room, and why haven't we gotten my brother back yet?" she huffed.

Clint couldn't stop the grin. He did love the miracles of drug companies helping him cover up his actions. "Well, you fell asleep, so you missed the hoopla. Someone attacked Chloe and we transported her to a hospital. Her uncle took over her care, and she won't be coming back. I wanted you to be able to say goodbye, but you were out cold. I first thought something happened to you too, but when you started snoring, I knew you'd be fine."

Amanda smacked him on the arm. "I do not snore!"

"Says the person who sounded like a chainsaw." Clint dodged the next time she tried to slug him.

"Do we know who hurt her? And how bad is it?" Amanda bit the inside of her cheek, never able to hide her feelings very well.

"No, Doc stabilized her, but she took a knock to the back of the head. We transported her as soon as possible and notified her uncle which hospital we were sending her to." Clint put his hand on her shoulder.

Amanda sniffled but held on, refusing to cry.

"I want you in here with me until we know what happened. Once Ben's back we'll reassess the sleeping arrangements. For the time being, you get to have a sleepover with your best friend. But seriously, if you continue to snore, I'm going to hang you upside down." Clint pulled her up and into a hug. "Let's go eat. I'm starved."

"That's nothing new. You and Ben both can put away food like nobody's business." Amanda rubbed her wrists where he restrained her the day before.

Clint discretely took a peek, relieved there were no marks to confuse her about what happened. "Ben is probably pulling his hair out being kept back there."

"I think it's kinda funny." Amanda elbowed him in the side.

"How is your brother being held against his will funny?" Clint pulled them out of the hallway and to the side as he towered over her intentionally.

"You know." Amanda didn't appear to be taking him seriously.

"No, I don't know. How about you tell me."

"He kidnapped her, now she kidnapped him. She is a tiny thing and she outsmarted him. Come on, it's a little funny, isn't it?" She shrugged and kept walking.

Clint chuckled. "You have a point."

"Of course I do. I'm brilliant." Amanda wriggled her toes in her fuzzy slippers.

"Not sure you adorning your feet with those means you're brilliant. Goofy maybe."

Amanda ignored him and rammed the doors to the cafeteria so they both opened, announcing her arrival with a flair.

The people who knew her antics cackled as they entered the room. He only shook his head and joined her in line. After they ate, he would convince her whoever attacked Chloe must have gotten the relics' location out of her and stole the cases. Except, of course, the sphere had conveniently been left behind so what needed to be done could be done: put Casey down, once and for all.

They sat with several others at their usual table, and Amanda chatted with them as if he hadn't knocked Chloe out and tied her up, also robbing her of her thoughts. He grunted along at the proper places, but his distracted mind prepared to rescue Ben. Once they had him back, could he welcome him back into the fold without argument?

He wouldn't be made a fool of again.

Finally, they excused themselves and made their way to the lab. Amanda made a beeline to the storage room they locked the relics in. Her screech had him rubbing his ears. "Do you always have to be so dramatic?"

"The relic cases are gone, except for the sphere." She gingerly held the box in her hands.

Clint gritted his teeth and placed his hands on his hips.

"Do you think the same person who attacked Chloe took them? Did they hurt her to force a location out of her? Do you think they're still here?" Amanda turned around in circles, expecting the boogeyman to jump out and grab her.

"I didn't want to be the one to tell you, but it was Casey. She left the sphere maybe because she had her own? We saw her on the cameras." Clint bowed his head, hoping the lie held. "Maybe she lost her cases for the relics and needed ours to put the stolen ones in?"

Amanda gripped the edges of the sphere's case. "No! How could she?"

When Amanda stormed out, Clint couldn't hide his enjoyment of her being right where he wanted her to be. On his side of the war not batting an eye when he took Casey out. He would deal with the aftermath of convincing Ben it was for the greater good. Ben would come around, They'd been best friends forever. So, he told a small lie about her on the security system. It didn't change the facts of what she did to him, and if he had to exaggerate the truth in other matters, so be it.

Clint already had an idea for getting back to the farmhouse and sneaking in to break Ben out of her clutches before Casey warped his mind. He wanted to develop a trip without Amanda. If she didn't go, she wouldn't have to live with the trauma of witnessing someone she once trusted dying.

He struggled with a strange sensation in his mind. Almost like another person. He concentrated on pushing them into the background. Casey preaching at them the other day bothered him, but he refused to let the other two see it.

So much of what she said made sense, but on the other hand, anytime he thought of not pulling the trigger a jolt coursed through him. What if what she said was right? Was there something wrong with them?

Clint's fond reminiscence of times past with his aunt and uncle filled his mind, but in the blink of an eye, it slipped through his fingers and dissipated into nothing. A building to sustain them, nothing more nothing less. He had no desire to stay there and *make a life*, as some people would say.

The small voice sounded like his, but he wasn't like that anymore. He converted into a shell of his former self. He couldn't bring himself to care for something he may have lost.

Protect the key.

Clint shook his head and hit the side of it with his hands. That right there proved something was wrong with him. How could he protect someone he had the urge to kill?

The only way to stop craving to be the person she wanted him to be, would be to end her suffering. He would convince Amanda to join his side, and they would arrange their jaunt out to the country without Ben. He'd seen Ben's eyes when Casey told him he was no longer the man she fell in love with.

Clint pulled a phone out and dialed his contact. "I need to know of any flight patterns over the last couple of years around the area at certain points of latitude and longitude."

He disconnected after giving his contact the location. If his friend couldn't find the information, no one could. Clint slid the slot on the wall to the left and hid the phone again. He never told Ben and Amanda. He kept the little gem from them and updated his military friend with delayed reports of the Monarchs' activities.

He could claim he learned of the intelligence but was unsure of the accuracy of it, while still keeping his source working for him.

Clint pressed his hand against his chest. A sharp pang roared to life at deceiving his friend. He shook it off and headed toward the cafeteria. Looking to eat in peace, he didn't tell anyone where he headed. His tray balancing on the palm of his right hand, he unlocked the entry to the docks, and then he set his tray on the floor. He scooted until his back hit the wall. His roiling stomach caused him to slide the dish away. He gulped the water to comfort his dry throat.

The void in him threatened to dominate his thoughts. His convictions for what Casey did sounded hollow, even to him.

Twenty-Four

"Do you think this will work?" Casey wasn't sure of Ben's plan.

"Of course it will. I learned from the best military planner and executioner of those plans. Clint taught me to think outside the box. Helping to know the enemy is key to outsmarting them. No one knows Clint better than I do. I promise this will work. If we can convince Amanda to commit herself to God again, we might flip Clint to our side." Ben grimaced when their ears picked up the sound of the portal opening.

"Ready?" Ben winked at her.

She had a shield around him as Amanda and Clint walked through the front door.

"Let me out! You can't keep someone in one of these forever!" Ben slammed his fist against the shield.

Amanda lurched for her brother when Casey sent shields to her and Clint.

Casey shook her head. "When are you going to learn? Clint, I will never hurt any of you."

"I've seen differently. You are a cold and unfeeling, cruel human being. I can't believe we ever trusted you." Clint aimed at the shield and emitted a pulse.

Like in the basement. Though the shield wasn't around her, a numb, tingly sensation traveled through her arms and to her chest. She flexed her fingers while Clint added the setting for when they knocked someone out. Her eyes drifted closed for a second before she stumbled on unsteady legs to the front door. How did he get a relic?

Activating a portal, she flung Clint through it as he hollered he would be back.

She put her back to the door and slid to the floor.

Ben walked through his bubble, making it disintegrate. "Sweetheart."

"What is this?" Amanda shrieked.

"Can you turn her volume down until we check you out?" Ben bobbed his eyebrows at her.

Casey reached out as if she were turning a dial, and soon, quiet settled around them.

"I thought you said we can't use the relics against each other." Ben pulled her to her feet and held onto her hands until she stopped swaying.

Casey stamped her feet and shook out her hands. "Remember in the basement houses, I described it like my hand and arm were asleep?"

"No, I don't think I remember that." He rubbed her hands, helping to dispel the sensation.

"Oh, right, you're the Ben before we lost Amanda and moved. Well anyway, it's the same as when you sit on your foot, and it falls asleep, sending those prickly tingling pains up and down your skin except more so. I think it's because he's a shadow of his former self because of the mishandling of the sphere. Somehow, he tracked down another weapon. He must still be using the sphere to time-hop, trying to find an advantage against me."

"Yeah, but he still used it against you."

"Technically, it was against the shield. But they are all tied to me in one form or another since I absorbed them. When you severed the connection when you injected me, I still felt them on some level." Casey pointed to her arms. "These never went away; they are a part of me, and it's the prophecy on the parchment."

"He'll only come up with another strategy with that knowledge under his belt. I guarantee he is learning and calculating his next move with every encounter. Soon, he will beat you. We have to turn him." Ben crossed his arms.

Casey flicked the volume to normal levels as Ben turned to address his sister.

"Amanda." Ben didn't finish her name before she screamed at him.

He patiently waited her out as she word-vomited her opinions about her current situation.

Ben rolled his eyes at Casey, who almost snorted. She missed this, the banter, the camaraderie.

When Amanda took her next breath, he cut her off by holding his hand up. "You done?"

"Let me think." She tapped her index finger on her chin and pursed her lips. "Yes, I'm done, but I request the option to revisit the topic later on grounds I may think of some great rebuttals."

Ben motioned around the room. "What do you see?"

"Um, a room? What do you see, oh dear brother of mine, who I'm thinking of disowning?"

Casey kept a snort quiet but covered it with a cough and lowered her head, so she looked at the floor instead of Ben's frustrated facial expressions accompanied by a heavy sigh.

"Listen here, brat. I'm trying to be serious. Really. What do you see?" Ben pleaded for an answer.

"Okay, I guess I'll play your game. There's a couch," Amanda gestured to the seat by her. "An ancient stereo in the corner, probably doesn't play music pods. The fireplace is nice..."

"No, the most obvious thing in the room." Ben walked in circles around her.

"Wait, why didn't you put him in confinement and only me?" Amanda jolted when she tried to step forward but bounced off the inside of her shield.

"Casey, bubble me up, babe." Ben winked at her.

Laughing, she did as he asked. He promptly walked right back out, then back and forth through the outer layer.

"You were right?" Amanda would have fallen if Casey hadn't moved her to sit on the edge of the couch, the first item she listed in the room.

Ben walked into her bubble and put his hand on her shoulder as he crouched in front of her. "Jesus is still here with us. He is waiting for us to find Him again. We are not meant to use the relics for our own purposes. There's a malevolent vengeful side usually overshadowed by the good in the ones who use them. We crossed the line when we sided with Clint *against* Casey."

"But she..." Amanda vigorously shook her head.

"She what? Come on, say it out loud. Trust me it sounds as obscene as you think it does." Ben smiled broadly.

"She assassinated Clint." Amanda's voice lessened in confidence as she said it.

"Dumb huh?"

Amanda rapidly blinked.

"We were wrong, sis. The relics, like everything in life, can be influenced for good or evil. It's our job as the chosen to do God's will, not our own." Ben grasped her hands and held on tight.

"But the prophecy said they can't be exploited for evil."

No matter how fast she fluttered her eyelids, she couldn't stop the waterworks.

"Amanda, there is something I have to do but it won't feel good." Casey pulled the coffee table closer and sat facing her.

"What do you mean?" Amanda shook her head, no.

"Come on, Case. We are all being honest here. It sucks." Ben bumped her shoulder with his.

"Ben." Casey scolded.

She didn't want to alarm Amanda and have her refuse help.

"Remember her mentioning the parchment came with warnings. The use of the sphere for any personal gain, whether for payback or to promote oneself, darkens the soul. Casey extracted my dark threads of sin, the venom, once I let go and gave it all back to God. I admitted my wrongs, and we need to follow Him." Ben's voice was unsteady as he recalled the emotional moment.

"What do you mean by dark threads? Like to use in a sewing machine?" Amanda nervously bounced her foot.

"Only the key can bring back the chosen from the sinister side of the relics. The catch is, you have to be genuine in your repentance. Only God can let the key heal you if He finds you truest of heart. Once you start down the tunnel, it is hard to turn back to the light. But that is what's so amazing about God's love. We don't have to do everything ourselves to pick us up out of the mire. God will meet us there and lift us out. All we have to do is reach for His outstretched hand and follow Him in all His ways." Ben nodded to Casey. He turned back to Amanda and placed his hands on her knee stopping the nervous action. "Let it go."

She nodded as tears spilled over her long dark lashes. "Father. I'm sorry. How bad did I mess up?"

"Nothing that can't be undone. Give yourself to me once again fully, and you will be free of the chains of bondage sin holds over every soul. I am the only one who has the key to release you, but first, you have to release yourself to me. It's that simple."

"Simple." Amanda choked out a laugh. "Father, I am yours, now and for all of eternity."

Casey felt the need to bring the black fibers out of her heart. She raised her hands as the blue aura weaved the finest translucent thread. Amanda started to move back, but Ben halted her movement.

"I'm right here with you. Deep breaths will make it easier." Ben rubbed his hand up and down her back.

"You went through this, right?" Amanda flinched as the end touched her.

Amanda gasped. She held her breath as the first tug started to remove the darkness disguised as an innocuous filament.

"Don't hold your breath." Ben coached her through it.

Another thread joined the first, pulling and tugging at the blue as it was trying to keep its grip on her.

"You have to release all of the lies and anger." Ben never stopped encouraging his sister.

"It hurts." Amanda tried to yank her hands from his.

"Nope, I'm not letting you go. You're stronger than this." Ben crouched half in half out of the shield the entire time, not letting Amanda go through it alone.

Several minutes later, Amanda melted into a puddle of worn-out muscles as the last of the tension left her body.

Ben stepped away from her and motioned for her to join him. She cautiously stood and strode toward the shield. It gave way under her pressure to walk through it.

"Thank you!" Amanda flung herself into Casey's arms.

Both women wept as they rocked from side to side.

"My internal light dimmed, but it's back. The misuse of the sphere made us capable of sliding into oblivion." Amanda's stomach growled when she sat again.

"I've got this." Ben stood and headed into the kitchen.

Casey regaled Amanda on what she had been through since Clint went back. "You have got to see the parchment. I swear it is larger and probably twice the prophecy than before."

Amanda followed Casey to the den.

"This is crazy!" Amanda ran her hands over the page and started talking to herself in whispers, translating the new sections she hadn't seen.

Casey sat back and let her work through everything. She was enjoying the time with her friends. She'd missed this. The friendship between the four of them. Now that left Clint and they would all four be back. Watching Amanda work on the translations always held her in awe of how fast her mind worked reading such an ancient language. Casey knew Amanda went to archeology school and Chloe was a quick learner with the discovery of the parchment.

"Do you think there are different dimensions?" Amanda blurted out.

"Well considering I never expected time travel to be real before I met you, I'd say it is a possibility. I encountered different versions of you. You guys were all buff, and I swear Ben and Clint almost looked twice the size they are now. A wicked scar cut across your cheek." Casey shared her fears of them not having any recollection of her and how lonely she felt.

"So, are you saying I was some crazy wild female warrior?" Amanda smirked.

"Who is crazy?" Ben's eyes twinkled as he set a tray on the corner of the desk. It was loaded with food.

"Did you tell Ben about our other selves in different dimensions?" Amanda plucked a raspberry and popped it in her mouth.

"Dimensions? Oh, please don't tell me we have to not only deal with the Monarchs but also with other variations of ourselves." He slumped into the only chair left unoccupied.

"I guess we haven't been the only visitors." Amanda talked around a mouth full of food.

Ben looked at Casey for her to enlighten them.

"The three of you in the group and their relics controlled the elements. They didn't need a key to activate them and seemed to be only fighting for themselves. They said the Monarchs won and they were ordered here to live out the rest of their measly existence. It was very disconcerting to see them beaten down like they had no choice but to comply with the ruling passed down to them." Casey shivered as she remembered that day. "I think something happened to them because when I first tried to send them through the portal, Clint activated the sphere in his shield and ported out. They reappeared seconds later but their bodies were broken or something."

"Have you seen them since?"

Casey shook her head. Did she kill them?

"Until they reemerge, I say we put that on a back burner. We will address it if they show up. What are we going to do about Clint? His nose bled before we came back here. They're becoming more frequent." Amanda frowned.

"We need Casey to use the healing relic on him," Ben suggested.

"I can't force the healing to draw the threads from someone. It is going to be like the two of you. He has to be ready to back away from the craving to use the sphere and get his life back on track." Casey wanted more than anything to take away Clint's grief of watching himself die. It would mess with anyone to have to witness their own demise.

"Not that. I think the Monarchs did something to him." Ben's voice cracked.

"They did. He has a scar and...and...it's like there is something on the tip of my tongue having to do with it, but I can't make myself remember. The scar is above his left ear. He didn't have it before they took him." Amanda rubbed her eyes.

"I think I can heal whatever it is, but he will have to take the first steps for me to extract the sphere's threads. This could work. Is this why he's so bent on taking my life?" Casey hoped to redeem Clint, or she would crumble.

Without Clint as the fourth chosen one, they would all fail.

Twenty-Five

Clint silently edged around the corner. He ported in with one task, to rescue Amanda and Ben. If he had to take Casey out of the equation, so be it. Doing both on this trip, all the better. He stood outside her room, gun in his hand. A quick shot and it would be over. They would search for another key.

He eased the door open. Casey's blankets tucked up and under her chin left only her head uncovered. The barrel was searching for the best shot.

His heart stalled at the thought of hurting Casey or worse. He backed out of the room and continued to Ben's as he rubbed the palm of his hand against his chest. Fear unlike anything before overwhelmed him and took him down to one knee. A jolt triggered his defenses, telling him to take the shot.

He took a couple of deep breaths to slow his racing heart. Static charges coursed through his brain as he thought of letting Casey go, yet his whole body shook when he thought of harming one hair on her head.

The skin on his hands tingled as they trembled. He willed his body to calm down, clenching and unclenching his fists. After a few short minutes, he seemed to be back in control. When he pictured Casey, he wanted to exact his own judgment for what she did to him, though his heart told him to protect her.

He remembered the blinding misery coursing through his head if he accessed any memory of their time together after Ben died and he and Casey were running for their lives.

Wait, he protected her. He bit into his fist as he tried to keep the cry of agony from waking anyone. Once the worst of it passed, he pressed both hands against his head. The pressure engrossed his every thought.

Kill Casey.

His body moved of its own free will to the room she slept in.

Clint locked his legs to stop his forward movement.

How had he known which room was hers? It was a memory, right? No, he was never here with her so how would he know where she lay her head? The ghosts of him and Casey living here fluttered through. Praising God when they survived a tornado. The sun lit cross on the side of the house.

He mentally berated himself for letting his heart make any decisions his brain didn't agree with.

Snoring from his left told him which room Ben dozed in. No one snored like his best friend. He had to spare Ben from the same destiny of his other self's fate at Casey's hand.

He tried to call up the vision of when she essentially electrocuted him with the relics. The Monarchs grabbed him when they took James out of the car. He squinted to clear up the blurry image. He made out her silhouette in a foggy dreamlike state. He couldn't distinguish between fact and fiction.

The pain he felt when his other half died. Static coursed over his body, sure his skin shredded to ribbons.

Casey yelled at him, "You can't use relics against chosen ones."

An image of him, Ben, and Casey in a small cove of houses hidden by trees, made him smile. A pulse passed through her in the tunnel with the creatures that attacked Ed, Brandon's friend. Wait, it passed through her and didn't injure her, so he didn't use it against her. Frustrated that he couldn't keep his mind straight on previous events, he shook his head. The shield passed over him and dismantled the creatures trying to end his life. Clint refused to release the scream as his thoughts jumbled over his belief that there was nothing good left in her. The Casey he trusted murdered him in cold blood without a moment's hesitation. If she could do that to him, then his friend's lives were at risk. And he would never allow her to do the same to them.

She tore apart the surrounding states. The aftermath of the EM pulse ruined so much for everyone.

He straightened and opened Ben's door. With a hand on his shoulder, he tried to wake him as quietly as possible.

"What?" Ben turned toward the wall.

"Ben." Clint tried again.

"Clint?" Ben sat up.

Clint held a finger up to his lips to silence him. They didn't need Casey to interrupt his rescue plan. It surprised him she didn't know the shimmer had opened and let him in.

"Come on, let's grab Amanda and go before she finds out I'm here and I have to do something you won't be able to forgive me for. At least not yet." Clint motioned for him to follow.

Ben dropped his feet to the floor and scooped up his boots as he tiptoed out after him.

Amanda dozed under a blanket with a pillow on her head, her hands and feet peeking out. Clint never understood how she slept outlandishly sprawled out like that. It felt like being smothered with all the pressure on his head, making it too hot for him.

Ben sat at the foot of the bed and put his boots on while Clint approached Amanda.

"Amanda, wakey wakey. Time to go home." Clint clamped his hand over her mouth when she sat up and started to yell.

Her arms came up and she got a few good slaps in before he convinced her she was safe with him and Ben.

"Shh." Ben motioned for Amanda to follow them.

She nodded and slipped out from under the sheets. "What about Casey?"

Clint shushed her again and guided them to where the shimmer from the sphere hovered.

"Clint, stop. We can't leave Casey. Do you know what she's been through? Can you imagine not having anyone to talk to or seeing another human being for months at a time?" Had Amanda been swayed to Casey's side?

"You want to stay here with her when she did what she did to me? Whose side are you on?" Clint got in her face.

As teens, if he took his commanding stance with her, she backed down, but dang if she didn't stand toe to toe with him and look up in his eyes with her hands planted on her hips. "I'm on God's side! Can't you feel it? The darkness by misusing the sphere? You said she killed you, but how's that possible when she's been here? Maybe you need to hear her out."

"You're my best friends, little sister, and I've known you our whole lives, and you want to take her side?"

"No, I'm saying the only side I'm on is God's, and she happens to be there also. We walked away from something amazing. We can still fix this!" Amanda walked over to Ben.

"Ben, do you agree with her?" Clint never thought he would see the day when his friends balked at following him. He slipped a weapon from his back and turned toward Casey's door.

"Let's go back and we can talk about it. I want to hear the evidence you have on Casey again." Ben swung his hand toward the shimmer for Amanda to go first and nudged her forward.

Amanda nodded and shifted through time.

Clint held Ben by the arm. "Is my word not good enough? It used to be. One pull of the trigger would free us of her."

"Don't put words in my mouth."

"What are you saying? Because if you don't trust me, why are we fighting this together?" Clint stomped through to the portal after Ben and felt the pull as he shifted through to the past.

Amanda raised her eyebrow at Ben. "What? Did you need to have a conversation without me since poor little Amanda doesn't get to be in on the big decisions because I'm a woman and not a tough strong man like you two?"

"If you want to know, I asked Ben if he didn't trust me and if I need to set out on my own to take down the Monarchs." Clint started to push past Amanda when her arm snaked around his waist, and she pulled him into a hug.

"We have always been a group. Best friends and siblings. We followed God and His teachings. We put Him first in our life. When was the last time we did? Have you heard Him in the last couple of years since we started using the sphere to go after Casey? Maybe we need to ask ourselves why." Amanda kissed his cheek and left to head to her room.

"Clint, she has a point. I know you don't want to hear this, but Casey asked us the same question. When was the last time we prayed for His help? Asked Him for His guidance? I miss Him. I'm completely incensed at what you said Casey did to your other side, but this is so much more beyond that. I haven't seen her attack any of us. It's not who she is. If she was so bent on taking us out, why has she never ported here?" Ben bumped him in the shoulder before he allowed him to his thoughts.

Clint shook his head. Had he been wrong this whole time?

No, Casey was a cold-blooded murderer, and she had to be stopped whether Ben and Amanda consented or not.

Something lurked in the back of his mind about a day spent in the Monarchs' clutches. He passed out and when he woke, he lay on the floor not restrained. Clint made it to the room next door. They got rid of the body, but the coppery scent of blood in the air made him gag. Especially since he knew who it belonged to. A disembodied voice announced Junior stroked out. No that wasn't right. The vision of the vidcast of Casey had him stumbling to a wall. If he fell, he wouldn't have the strength to get up.

Footsteps forced him back to his room. He wasn't strong enough to take them on yet, but he would be soon.

They held him for a few months. Or at least that's how much time he was able to keep track of. Would the others still be in the last location? He wouldn't blame them if they moved on; he would have. He ordered Ben to set out for the next safe house if he didn't make it back. Knowing they would be tortured for the location of the resistance group would have them move everyone to a safe location.

Clint fumbled his way out into the cool air, and he seemed to get his second wind. He would never forgive Casey for what she did. The flashbacks faded and blurred in his mind. The reminder of the pain inflicted was enough to flare his anger toward the one he swore to protect in the prophecy as stated in the parchment.

Clint jerked, his back hitting the wall next to him. Her protector. Everyone expected him to make her safe. She was the key. Fear of the Monarchs finding her raced through his veins before the image of the vidcast flooded his system again. He couldn't sort out his memories; some contradicted each other. Casey needed protecting one moment, and then the pain would hit.

No, she wasn't the same person. She had to die, and he would make sure he was the one to end her life. He shook his head from side to side. Accessing the roof, he let the cool night air flow over his skin. He didn't remember where Ben and Amanda went after Ben bumped his shoulder. He had to gain his faculties, or he would be no help to his friends.

Blood dripped down his shirt as his nose bled.

Twenty-Six

Breakfast was about ready, and Casey wondered when Ben and Amanda would be down. Eager to wake them, she flitted around the kitchen. They weren't quite on solid ground yet, but she thought they were making headway in restoring their friendship.

She glanced out the window in time to see several wild turkeys waddling across the yard. Something startled them and they took flight. A smile crept up on her when Daisy tried to box in the massive birds. She couldn't wait to show her to Ben and Amanda. They would love her. She was a pro at hiding when strangers were around, but since she was here, maybe that meant she was ready for an introduction.

She let her footfalls sound louder than normal, so neither of them would accuse her of spying. She tapped a few times on Amanda's door. When she didn't get an answer, she knocked harder. The hinges were silent as she eased the door fully open. The bed was empty, the covers tossed to the side sliding off the mattress.

"Amanda?"

Next, she went to Ben's room and found the same thing there, or lack of.

They were gone.

No wonder Daisy reappeared.

She wanted to sit down and cry. She thought they made so much progress. To finally put everything behind them was an answer to her prayers. Reinfection from using the sphere was a harsh reality. Now what? She couldn't take on the Monarchs single-handedly. She didn't know where they were or what they were plotting for the next attack, that could come at any moment.

Casey sat hard in a chair and popped a piece of fruit in her mouth as she looked off in a daze. What if God only had this for her, being alone?

No, she refused to think that. She saw for herself in the prophecy her designation as the key. They were the chosen ones. Four of them to take on God's enemies, who were on the same side as Satan. The prophecy never altered the number of the chosen. At least that section never varied, unlike the powers of the relics. It would only be a matter of time before the three of them came for her again. The short period she spent with Ben and Amanda fanned the flames of hope. Patience was never one of her strengths. She would have to pray God would lead her in the right direction in His time.

So much needed to be done with the coming season ending, and the harvest would soon be ready. If winter was as bad as the last two, she would need enough reserves for her, Daisy, and the chickens to make it through. The first year, afraid of running out of canned goods, she rationed herself to one meal a day until she went out and gathered her own food. The first time she found edible plants, she gorged herself on mushrooms and made herself sick even though she told herself not to. By the second winter, she did well in pacing her wild plant intake.

The next season blessed her with chickens and now fresh eggs she cooked for herself and the dog and chickens. She ground up the eggshells when she made a batch for the clucking brood, and they devoured it in a matter of minutes. The calcium helped the laying hens produce hard shells over the eggs. The roosters she would grind up, with a hand grinder she found in the cellar, for Daisy. The dog ate better than Mason did, her Rottweiler from before.

This season would be the largest with corn, due to being a huge part of her feed for the chickens through the wintery months. In the summer, she let them forage for their own food, and they kept the insects at bay in the yard around the house. Daisy would chase them back to the roost at night, and Casey locked them in. Running loose in the summers led to three missing so far. Casey was now the proud owner of at least twenty chickens, and anytime the eggs hatched out a rooster, she let it grow to full size before butchering it to keep Daisy stocked up in vittles. The slow-producing hens went into the stock pot, and she cooked bone broth for soups and stews, which froze perfectly. Large batches gave her hot quick meals when chilled from working in subfreezing temperatures to keep the coop clean.

Confident with Ben and Amanda on her side, she looked forward to their help with the chores. Why did she feel more isolated now since they were gone again?

Casey bowed her head. "Father, keep their hearts and minds faithful to You. Don't let them be lost to You again. I never knew what the true meaning of being alone meant.

This has definitely taken it to a whole new level. I'm not sure I'm strong enough to keep living this life, never knowing if the friends I grew to love will come after me. In Jesus' name, Amen."

"Patience."

One word was enough to know she wasn't left to fend for herself. God never left her, but there were some dark nights that felt as if she were the only person left in the world. The stars dotted the sky and were so much brighter than anything she'd seen as a kid in the suburbs with all the light pollution. It didn't hold a candle to the beauty of a country sky.

She ate her fill of the food she prepared and put the rest in storage tubs since she prepared enough for three people. She smiled as she put on her gardening apron and set out to check her crops. It soothed something in her. Watching the work she put in to bloom, grow, and produce some of the best foods she ever tasted was so satisfying. Grocery stores had nothing on providing fresh goods.

Casey weeded the fertile soil for several hours, and when she glanced back over her work, she couldn't help the corners of her mouth lifting slightly at what she accomplished with God's help.

Loud squawks from the chicken pen had her running with Daisy at her side. Her feet squished in the grass as she rounded the side of the barn. Casey flipped the latch on the door and strode into a mass of startled flying chickens. Excess feathers floated around while they were trying to make their way out of the pen.

Another chicken screeched from inside. Casey jogged around the enclosure to access the inside coop. A large black snake with its jaw unhinged and wrapped around an egg sat in the middle of the nest one of the brooding hens had occupied. She clucked incessantly, cornered by the reptile.

They weren't aggressive by nature, but a nice, fat, six-foot black snake didn't rank as her idea of a good time. She flipped over the rake by the door and gently prodded the tines under the serpent's cold, scaley body. It hissed and coiled into a ball. Quite a few attempts later, it finally draped over the rake, and she walked, keeping it as far from her as possible.

She let it go in the field on the other side of the backyard. It slithered faster than she was ready for into the tall grasses. She yelped and backed away. Snakes were always a possibility when having a coop so she read a couple of books on the subject. She knew peppermint oil would keep them away. She would mix up a spray from the essential oils Clint's aunt got into when she battled cancer. Casey found her labels and empty bottle stash along with instructions for each one she sold.

She didn't have enough to treat the whole area around the pen, but she would make more since extra ingredients lined the shelves in the cellar.

The drama had calmed down by the time she made it back, and Daisy lazed in the sun with one eye open, keeping watch over her charges.

"Have they settled down, pretty girl?" Daisy lifted her head and gave an enthusiastic tail wag.

"Might as well muck out the run while I'm here and the rake is in my hands, huh?" Casey had a system that worked well for her.

She sifted the sand in the outside enclosure first then she continued inside, so the heat of the day didn't beat down on her back. The non-air-conditioned building shaded the chickens, who camped out inside on the hottest days of summer.

Half a dozen old plastic kiddy pools had balanced in between rafters in the loft. She'd filled one with water, perfect to cool them down, and she packed another with sand for a dusting area. A huge success the first time she put it out.

She trained the rooster to stop charging her when she entered his territory. Oh, he tolerated her because she fed them, but if he wanted to, he wouldn't hesitate to try and chase her out.

Well, he counted as the second rooster since Daisy brought the flock to her. The first one attacked the poor dog so badly. Casey patched her up and made sure she didn't wander far for several weeks. The rooster's spurs had done a bit of damage, and some of the dog's fur hadn't grown back over the scarred skin.

The rooster had been her first butcher, and she still shivered at the thought of how she had wrung its neck and plucked the thing. Her stomach quivered as she thought back to the process of making dog food for Daisy

This little guy seemed halfway accepting of her presence in his space. She giggled as she called him Chuck because, of course, she had chicks, so it seemed appropriate to name him Chuck.

Casey cleaned the pen, and she sweated up a storm. A pitcher of sun tea beckoned her. After a shower, she braided her long hair. She was tempted to cut it, but she never saw it as a necessity, and now it flowed halfway down her back. Condensation rolled down in rivulets on the tea glass. She spent most of her days outside even when her tasks were done. After thinking of the dress mannequin she used to trick them, she rifled through the fabrics in the attic making herself a hammock out of old jean scraps. She let the wind rock her as she enjoyed having an afternoon off.

The sun started to drift down on the horizon. After dusting off her clothes, she started dinner. Casey again let her mind wander to Ben and Amanda. Clint must have come after them. Why he didn't try to take her out stumped her. She never heard him arrive or the three of them leave. The sphere's ability to turn the user's heart worried her. Would they revert to before she pulled the dark threads from them?

She didn't want to start over convincing them she wasn't the bad guy.

Twenty-Seven

Ben rapped his knuckles against Amanda's door. He hadn't seen Clint yet this morning, and he wasn't sure how he would react to them believing Casey.

"Come in," the muffled response instructed.

"Hey sis, you got a minute?" Ben peeked his head in.

"For you? Always." Her weak smile didn't fool him.

"What are we going to do about Clint? Casey is right. We have to give this all to God. Our anger at the assault we thought she carried out darkened our hearts. I was wary of using the sphere but didn't think it would cause us to stray from the path God chose for us. I wanted to be there for Clint after what he went through at the Monarchs' hands. I should have spoken up and voiced my opinion. When he tugged his Glock from the holster, I thought I was going to have to fight him to keep Casey alive."

Amanda held out her hands for him to join her on the bed. He sat at the footboard while she sat farther up by the pillows. She clasped his hands in hers and bowed her head. "Father. I know it's been a while since we have sought Your guidance. We are defeated; I don't know where to go next. The prophecy says we are the chosen ones. I remember Casey unlocking the other relics and her being the key, but our hardheadedness blurred time for me. Please clear our thoughts and help us see the truth and Your will. Help us hear You again. I've missed you."

Hiccuped sobs shook her shoulders.

Ben scooted up to hold his sister, who he loved more than life itself. He could never handle her upset and definitely not when she cried. Like any normal big brother, he wanted to fix everything for her.

"Welcome back, my children."

"Father." Ben couldn't say anything else.

They sat and absorbed their father's love as the room stilled to an eerie silence that almost seemed to block out the whole world still living outside their room.

Ben gasped as a rush of consciousness flooded his mind. He remembered the day he died though they never left the warehouse in this timeline. He helped to bury one of their group and her small daughter. One minute he reached up for Clint's hand, then nothing.

"Ben, what is it?" Amanda lifted her tear-stained face.

"I remember."

"Remember what?" Amanda encouraged him to go on.

"Dying." Ben locked eyes on her.

She shook her head. "No, you didn't. I did. Or you told me I did."

"It's coming back to me. Oh, my gosh. We were so wrong about Casey. She's been by herself all this time. She was there when I died. What she must have gone through. Clint—how his heart must have ached after losing you and me. We have to go back to her. We have to end this now. The Monarchs have held onto their evil for long enough. How do we tell Clint about this?" Ben paced back and forth.

"Can Casey withdraw the darkness from him like she did for us?" Amanda swallowed hard.

He understood what she went through. The thoughts of the other experiences he had lived rushing through him almost swamped him, tearing the sanity from his mind.

"Only if we can convince him we're right. If he can let go of the anger." Ben didn't know if Clint would be able to. There were hints that something more was going on.

"That's not possible. Look at how he reacts every time we bring up anything with Casey where she isn't the bad guy."

Amanda's sob cut off as she pulled her knees up, wrapping her arms around her bent legs.

"What is it?" Ben gave her a minute to regain her balance.

"I remember."

"Remember what?" Ben hoped she didn't have flashes of the day she died.

"We were leaving. I was shot. I..."

Ben didn't want to think about it. "How are we remembering things we technically haven't lived through?"

A tap on the door had them wiping their tears and straightening. It would be Clint.

"Come in," Amanda called out.

Clint narrowed his eyes. Ben waited him out. He didn't want to argue.

"What is it?" Amanda said something first.

"I need to know what Casey said to you guys. And why you were sleeping in your own beds, not being held against your will. Is there something you need to tell me about her?" Clint pinched his nose as blood poured into his hand.

He swayed, bouncing off the doorframe, and took off toward his room.

Ben tugged Amanda's hand and pulled her along, supporting her until her legs caught up with the rest of her. "Come on, we need to go see Doc."

"What are you doing?" Amanda didn't try to pull her hand away.

"Doc?" Ben called out before they got to his office.

"Ben?" Doc looked at Amanda. "What's going on?"

"It's Clint. Ever since he got back from being held, he gets nosebleeds and hasn't been acting right." Ben held his breath.

"He's also had headaches and now is the proud owner of a small scar above his left ear." Amanda frowned. "I can't recall the importance of the placement of the scar, but this niggling feeling is out of reach why."

"No. Oh, why didn't I notice when I looked him over. He insisted he was fine so I just did the basics of taking his blood pressure and listening to his lungs. You know, the usual." Doc started shuffling across his room, shoving things around on his desk.

"What's going on?" Ben's stomach lurched.

"I need to call Chloe's uncle, but I would say they implanted a chip in his head. It's a new technology to turn their enemies instead of taking them out. If they can sway them to their cause, they ship them back home where they take out the rivals, so the Monarchs don't have to lift a finger. The scar is a telltale sign of the procedure. If only I had noticed sooner." Doc held up his phone and dialed before it sank in what he said.

Ben couldn't believe they did something like that to Clint, but it made sense.

"Are we going to be able to help him here, or do we need a hospital so they can remove it?" Amanda, on the verge of crying again, gritted her teeth and held her head high.

Doc's hushed brief conversation ended; his shoulders slumped. "There's nothing we can do. Chloe's uncle informed me he started to have his suspicions when he picked up Chloe and found a drug in her system to erase the previous two hours. He was already doing research to confirm Chloe's suspicions at her request before he accused Clint of being compromised. The chip we're talking about is one of the newer ones. Clint has no ability to reign in his urges of what the Monarchs want him to do. There aren't any checks and balances going on in his mind." Doc tapped his fingers on the desk.

"You mean like killing Casey?" Finally answers to his questions explained Clint's rationale to Ben.

"Yes."

"Doc, can't you take it out?"

"That is serious brain surgery way outside of my wheelhouse of expertise." Doc plopped down on the corner of his desk.

"Can Casey remove it with the healing relic?" Amanda clung to hope, and he couldn't blame her.

"You know, it might work if we knew where she was." Doc missed her as much as they did.

"We may know where she is, but we'll need help getting Clint there." They couldn't get close enough to try and sedate him. Clint would be on guard after bringing them back and both of them adamant they trusted Casey.

"One thing her uncle did say, was that if they implanted the newest one, they built in a failsafe. If oxygen hits it after it's been implanted it will immediately release a toxin into the air. The bioweapon will take out not only the patient but also everyone else in the room." Doc covered his face.

"No. Oh no, Ben. How do we find out?"

"I don't know, sis." Ben stood, not sure where to go next. Clint was literally a ticking time bomb.

Twenty-Eight

"Okay, let's do this. I miss the side of Clint who protected the key. I have an idea that may work on the chip if it's the newest tech. He has to be in the frame of mind before the Monarchs nabbed him. That way, he'll let Casey remove it." Amanda crossed her legs as she sat on the table in Ben's room.

"Get off my table. Sheesh. We were raised to sit in chairs, not on tables." Ben kicked one out on the other side from where he sat.

"Ugh, why do you have to be rude? It's not like you were using this part of the table," Amanda huffed and crossed her arms but sat in the seat.

"Mom would have smacked the back of your head if she saw you sitting like that." Ben chuckled.

"Can we use the sphere to find Clint and have him talk to himself?" Amanda suggested.

"I don't know. What if it started to turn us again? Are we being selfish? If it thinks we are, I don't want to go back to where we were." Ben relived every memory of what the sphere stole, making him not care about anything or anyone. All he had wanted was vengeance even though it wasn't his to grab.

"What if we let the sphere turn on and see what it suggests? Clint never gave it a choice to display a timeline.

He manipulated it to his choosing each time." Amanda's voice lowered as footsteps sounded outside the room.

"Do you have it here or is it still locked away?"

Amanda hopped off the chair. "It's in the lab."

"I'll get it. If Clint comes back, stall him." Ben turned to the door.

"How am I supposed to do that?" Amanda scoffed.

"Rail about Casey; it should keep him occupied." Ben wrinkled his nose before he checked the hall and departed.

He jogged as fast as he dared without raising suspicions if someone saw him. He pulled the drawer open on the cabinet they hid everything in and about ripped it out of the tracks. The drawer held one case, the sphere. Casey only took the relics, but they still had the cases. Now they were missing.

Amanda practically bounced on her feet. "Any problems?"

"Didn't see anyone." Ben slid the sphere's case to the middle of the table.

"You found it in the storeroom?" Why did she question where they always kept the relics?

"Right where we kept it. Why do you have a weird look on your face?"

"For a second I had a sense of déjà vu the sphere was missing." Amanda shook her head. "Never mind. As quickly as the impression was there, it's gone again."

"Chloe's uncle said a serum wiped her mind of the altercation. Did Clint do that to you, too?" Ben tried to control his breathing at the image of Clint doing that to his sister.

"With how he has been, I wouldn't put it past him."

"The sphere may have been there, but the relic cases aren't." Ben didn't know where Clint would have taken them.

"Clint told me Casey took them when he told me Chloe had been attacked. At least the relics weren't in them." Amanda opened the lid of the sphere.

Ben's hands shook as he held hers and bowed his head. Oh, how he missed this. "Father, I know we have no right to ask for Your guidance in anything we do. We need Your help. Do we bring Clint here? Is that the only way to persuade him? Have him tell himself this is wrong? Show us which way to go. In Jesus' name, Amen."

"Amen," Amanda gasped.

The sphere hovered above the box, highlighting a scene starring Clint. Amanda ran to lock the door. Clint junior paced the roof in the shimmer when he patrolled one night. It was their Clint because he didn't have a relic weapon in his hand, and he wore an earwig. He kept pushing it farther in his ear as if he was listening to someone.

"I think this is where we need to go. I'll do it. Don't let anyone in the room."

Ben's hand around her elbow stopped Amanda. "I should go."

"Oh, and if someone wants to get into this room, I'm expected to throw my massively strong body at the door to stop them?" Amanda crossed her eyes and stuck out her tongue at him.

"At least you admit I'm massive and strong." Ben flexed his bicep.

"I also think you're an idiot." Amanda flipped a pen at him.

"Fine. Go, before it disappears." Ben motioned with his hand.

Amanda jumped through and Ben watched her point to him through the portal. Clint nodded as Amanda motioned with her hands.

Clint junior surged into the room and bent over at the waist, propping himself up with his hands on his legs. "I think someone needs to explain this to me one more time, because I hate jumping."

Amanda and Ben went through everything that happened since Senior showed up, to them being taken, to Casey disappearing, and to the mess they were in now by abusing the sphere's powers to manipulate it to change the past the way they wanted it—and her labels of senior and junior.

"Seriously? You went against the relics and God? What is wrong with you?" Junior bellowed.

"Quiet!" Amanda hissed.

"How long did the Monarchs have Clint senior? This is weird asking about myself." Junior sat on the edge of the table.

Amanda pointed at him while smirking at Ben. She kept her mouth shut and didn't mention her big brother scolded her for doing the same thing.

"A few months. When he came from the future, he was already different. Now we can barely talk about Casey without him almost losing control over his anger. He said she killed you and he saw it on a vidcast. There is a darkness in him." Ben wanted him to have the answer to fix all of this.

"Casey would never do that. Anyone who spends five minutes with that woman knows she is incapable of violence against people, much less us. The Monarchs have something the military is hearing rumors about; they can—" The doorknob rattled.

"Hey, let me in," Senior called out from the hallway.

Amanda unlocked the door but kept it from swinging open all the way. "Hey."

"Where's Ben?" Clint senior's voice was strained.

"Here," Ben called out.

Clint's eyes narrowed as he stared at Junior. "Casey killed you."

"I'm not that Clint. Well, I am but from a different time," Junior told him.

"You used the sphere without telling me? What, you think I don't know Casey twisted up your heads so you wouldn't see her as the monster she is? You can't trust her." Senior slammed the door, blocking their way out of the room. Blood dripped over his lip. He swiped the back of his sleeve across it to sop it up.

"That isn't what this is. We are asking for help. For you to understand something happened to you. The Monarchs muddled with your brain." Senior didn't let Ben finish before he pulled a gun from his waistband.

"Oh, they did do something. They opened my eyes to the truth! How can you take her side over mine? We talked about this before." Senior motioned with the barrel for them to move to the other side of the room.

"Clint, I know what they did to you. There have been talks about this new gadget they have. It can mess with..." Junior flinched when he became the center of his own attention.

"You think I don't know what this is. They are trying to replace me with a naive version of myself. All you are going to do is get yourselves killed. Why won't you listen to me? I can't stop someone who is walking into a fire covered in gasoline any more than I can stop you, apparently."

"We tried talking to you, but you won't hear us out. You will only consider your version of events," Amanda tried to argue.

Senior sneered. "My version. How can what I saw be a version of anything but fact?"

"God can help you sort this out. Let me guess. You haven't spoken to Him in a long time."

"No! I refuse to discuss this. You don't know. You weren't there. You didn't hear yourself scream, the sound cut off at being tortured to death." Senior wavered.

"I know using the sphere for personal gain is wrong. How dare you put these people who are in your charge to protect in danger? This is not an honorable thing to do. This isn't your hate or anger. It is the Monarchs' warped method, twisting you into someone you're not, because I don't hate Casey. She is like a sister to me. Someone I love and am willing to die for. Inside you is the real me. Take a good hard look at yourself in the mirror, buddy, because there is no one who can fix you except you. Fight this. You have to let go of the hate they warped your mind with. What did God say about hate? It is the same as murder. The Monarchs murder people. You don't! He also said not to let the sun set on your anger." Clint junior picked up the Bible. "This is where you let your anger and hate go. To God! He can take it from you if you let Him. He is stronger than this trial you are going through. He sent His son to die for you, and all you have to do is accept it in your heart. You were already redeemed before the Monarchs stole your mind, but you have to accept His forgiveness and follow Him."

"I know. I'm the same as you, remember?" Senior slouched and lowered his gun hand to his side.

"You can fix this. I know there's a part of you deep down who wants to, but you're stopping yourself. You are the key's protector. It's what you were born for. Trained for. All the military discipline made you the perfect candidate to carry out God's plan. Do you want to deny yourself the honor He hand-picked you out of all the people in this world for?" Junior put a hand on his shoulder.

Devastation morphed over him. The junior version finally got through to him. He lowered his voice and continued to talk to him, and they both bowed their heads.

A few minutes later, the sphere lit up, highlighting the rooftop Junior had patrolled before he came through. "I've got to go. You know I have to take turns protecting the believers in our group."

He smiled at Ben and Amanda and then stepped through. The sphere disengaged and settled into the box.

No one said anything for a while until Clint senior put his gun away and turned to leave.

"Do you want to talk it out?" Ben wasn't sure if Clint should be by himself.

"No, I'll be back." Clint left without a backward glance.

"What do you think Clint was going to tell us about the Monarchs before Senior walked in?" Amanda twisted her fingers together. "My guess is it's about the chip."

"How are they getting such advanced tech?" Ben struggled to keep his voice low.

Amanda and Ben discussed how the Monarchs' chip hijacked his limbic system, meaning he couldn't govern his actions on that side of his brain.

"What are our plans if their little heart-to-heart doesn't give us our Clint back?"

"I'll ask Doc for a sedative, and we'll take him to Casey. Maybe she can purge the filth from his heart like she did for us." Ben put the sphere in the case.

"That won't work." Amanda seemed nervous.

"She did it for us."

"Yeah, but I don't think we had as much going on in our heads as Clint does." Ben knew Amanda's feelings for Clint still played an important role in how she wanted to handle everything.

"Of course he does; he's smarter than both of us put together." Amanda snorted and Ben smiled, trying to lighten the mood.

Both were somber as they went to grab dinner. The lights flickered.

"I don't like this." Ben linked their hands and ran for the workroom.

Clint wasn't there.

"Where is he?" Amanda rubbed her hands up and down her arms.

"No clue, but if the Monarchs found us, no one's safe." Ben turned and Clint leaned against the doorframe.

"Normal Monarch scare tactics, small bursts to disrupt our electronics, but nothing too serious to concern ourselves with. The generators will last, but we will need to work on moving everyone." Clint pushed past Ben.

"Are we going to talk about what happened in my room?" Amanda darted her eyes to Ben.

"Nothing to talk about. Nice gesture, hoping I believed the lies my other self told me, but it wasn't enough to make me fall for Casey's tricks." Clint's lifeless eyes tracked Amanda as she backed away from him.

"You can't be serious. I have never wanted to hit someone as much as I do you. There's no reasoning with you, is there? The Monarchs have already won. They turned you into someone you're not." Ben prepared to pull back his fist and let it fly.

He thought he had seen a change in him earlier. He prayed he saw what his actions did to their group, to the chosen ones. The longer they had to contend with him, leaving Casey, the easier a target she became for the Monarchs to come back and end everything.

"You are either with me or against me. And if you choose the latter, well, you won't like what I'll be forced to do. Since you depleted the sphere's charge to try a stupid stunt, now we have to wait again until we can destroy Casey once and for all. If you aren't going to contribute, leave with the rest of them. I can manage this on my own." Clint's jaw clenched.

Ben shook his head at Amanda to let it go. They would have to try another way.

"Fine, whatever." Amanda sassed but didn't move to leave.

"What now?" Ben's only option was to act like he would go along.

Clint would never fall for it but if they distracted him long enough, hopefully Ben could come up with a plan. Clint's military training put him at a clear advantage against Ben and his sister. As he was a skilled fighter they didn't stand a chance against him. He and Amanda would have to meet in private, or paranoia would cloud Clint's already fractured mind. Not a particular side of Clint he wanted to deal with.

"Which one of you wants to tell me what Casey is up to and whose idea it was to use the sphere without all three agreeing to it?" Clint squared up to them.

Ben and Amanda shared a look as Amanda swallowed hard.

Twenty-Nine

Snowflakes large enough to knock out a small child fell from the gray, overcast sky. The day started chilly, and before Casey knew it, the winds howled their discontent and let her know their potential. A large tree fell in the backyard, narrowly missing the coop.

Thank goodness she deployed a shield deflecting it as the wind kicked up and sent it spinning in the other direction. The load of firewood out of it would last at least a number of months. That morning, she pulled in the last bundle from the left side where she stored the logs, so it gave her plenty of room to season the new stacks before use.

Casey sighed as she realized she would need to trudge out and pour hot water in the bucket for the chickens, who were scratching through the fallen flakes, looking for something to forage. Their feathers were fluffed to their fullest, creating a layer of heat to keep the worst of the chill from their bodies. Months passed since Amanda and Ben rejoined Clint. She hadn't seen anything from them since. A heavy weight sat on her with the idea she lost all the progress she made with them.

Daisy pawed at the back door to go out.

"Come on girl I'll go with you." Casey filled the largest pitcher and stomped her feet into her boots but didn't bother lacing them up.

The chickens ran around her, anticipating a pail of corn. "Sorry ladies, not until tonight."

Ice already formed around the edges of the water in the bucket she strung up from one of the beams. She upgraded their enclosure and put in a quarter-inch layer of plastic flaps as a buffer from the weather at the top of the ramp.

The hot water steamed as the frigid breeze glanced off the surface. The ice didn't stand a chance against the newly added liquid. When the chickens realized she didn't have any scratch for them, they clucked their disapproval and waddled through the flaps to forage for something to peck at.

Daisy growled at the corner of the barn.

Casey had added more lights since last year and cleaned it up. There weren't any good hiding places, but the hair stood up on the back of her neck all the same.

A hissing spit escaped from a small fluff ball of a kitten. "Where did you come from?"

Its thin matted fur didn't do anything to protect it from the elements. Daisy dropped to her belly and crawled forward, whining a little, her tail furiously in motion.

The kitten hunched its back and tried to fluff out its tail as it spit again, hissing as an afterthought.

"You are too small to keep all the mice away that should have wreaked havoc by now. Where's your momma? Is she responsible? I haven't had a run-in with any of those mice trying to eat my chicken feed." Casey thought she would have seen a lot more when she tried to figure out the best way to store grains and corn.

Another set of eyes peered over the straw in the corner. They were bright blue and the cat was a gorgeous seal point.

"You're a beautiful momma. Let me see what I have to fatten you up since you are such good little mousers." Casey tried to have Daisy follow her, but she refused.

She got an old bowl of water and some ground chicken she normally fed the dog and added bone broth to give the smaller one some nutrients since it looked old enough to be weaned.

She almost tripped over the little spitfire, who now danced around, trying to attack Daisy's tail that flicked side to side. Casey sat the bowls on the ground and stepped back. As long as the cats gobbled up the meal fast enough, she wouldn't have to worry about the broth freezing.

Momma hesitated but soon couldn't deny her hungry stomach. The kitten ran up and started lapping at the broth surrounding the ground meat. Tiny mewling fuzz balls bolted past the two, and Casey counted four more babies. She wouldn't complain. With all the extra meat she stored due to so many chicks being born, the room in the freezer slimmed almost to nothing. She removed the rooster a month ago.

The chicken wire kept the cats away from the new flock. Daisy inched toward the food.

She would let the cats stay. They would eat their weight in little rodents, and she wouldn't have to worry about their droppings carrying diseases or contaminating the grains.

Casey whistled. "Come on, girl. Let's feed you so you can come back and play."

The dog didn't waste time following her to the house, and Casey made sure she would have a full belly before she went back out to visit her new friends.

Casey remembered Ben telling her all the dogs perished with the viruses the Monarchs developed, but there were some somewhere for Daisy to be here, and those kittens told her life found a way around the devastation released by terrorists.

The lights flickered as the wind picked up. Casey added a few more logs on the fire. They crackled and popped, sending minuscule sparks into the air. She tucked the quilt around her as she settled back against the cushions in the chair and drifted off to the snow blanketing them in a winter wonderland.

Howling woke her and she stumbled to her feet, almost falling on her face as she tried to unwrap her legs from the blanket.

She forgot Daisy outside.

Casey scarcely got the back door open when Daisy and all the cats bolted into the house. "What the..."

Daisy stood at the door growling. The hair along her back bristled. She'd never heard such a noise from her before. The shield reacted to Casey without thought.

The rumble of a helicopter sounded far way. Too far for her to be able to normally hear. Her sharp hearing kicked in.

She ran around, turning off all the lights. She couldn't do anything about the fireplace. If she tried to put the flames out, it would only make more smoke. If she lucked out, they wouldn't be able to distinguish the smoke from the snow at a distance. She lit up her fingers with the sparks of the relics.

If the Monarchs were finally making another stand against her, she would be ready. She had only grown stronger in her powers since the last time. They were still out there and were no match for Casey.

Another low growl left Daisy. The dog sounded like something she didn't want to tangle with if it turned on her. The dog herded her from the living room, moving backward and pushing her toward the front door. She nudged her with her nose until Casey's back hit the solid wood and still continued to inch into her, making Casey think she wanted her to go outside.

In a soothing voice, she kept her volume low. "Good girl. It's okay. You never did this when we were outside, silly girl. Why the fuss now? We'll be quiet and they will fly right by. They won't notice us."

Casey couldn't convince herself of the half-truth she told the dog. She ran her hand down her fur. The dog immediately settled but never took her eyes from the back door. Momma cat curled around her babies as she tried to clean them. Casey would attempt baths tomorrow.

The chopper swooped low. Casey held her breath. She couldn't gage how far off they were because she couldn't tell if her hearing picked up the sound normally or if her enhanced hearing made them sound closer than they were.

"It's too dangerous to stay out here. We won't be able to find her. I'm sorry, Chloe, but I won't put your life in danger by trying to find Casey and Clint." A man's voice sounded above the spinning rotors.

"Just a little more," Chloe's urgent voice pleaded.

Casey ran out of the house waving her arms. The helicopter banked right, heading away.

"Alright, I'll come back on my own. Clint gave us the location, but with the pulse that knocked down the grids in the surrounding states, we can't access those coordinates. We'll start the search up again as soon as there's clear weather. This is the only chopper not affected by the attack so when it is slotted for emergency evacuations they take precedence," a man's voice soothed Chloe.

"Sweetie, we won't stop looking. If they're out here, we'll find them if it's the last thing we do. Gretchen's dad is also trying to find records and property deeds. We still haven't recovered from the EMP. Going through county records stored in old boxes in some dank basement is putting a wrench in our plans to find them fast. But right now, we need to head back. We're low on fuel. We won't do them any good if we don't live through this."

They were looking for her!

She almost cried knowing how close she came to seeing her friend again, only for it to be ripped away.

Hope sprung like wildflowers in March. Blooming in various colors, filling her with a warmth she refused to let herself rely on. Losing her passion for life after being knocked down every turn this harsh world threw at her, slowly dimmed her internal light just a bit. Casey didn't want to become the shell of who she was deep down, the part of her who still fought for what she wanted. Ben, Amanda, and yes, Clint. They were who she had left, and she'd fight for them if they weren't able to themselves.

Her cheeks burned from the huge smile pasted on her face. Daisy wagged her tail, pouncing in the white drifts, only to reappear with a pile of snow on her snout.

The past few years were hard, but it helped knowing her friends never gave up. If she hadn't hidden from the search going on in her own backyard, imagine everything she would have had access to. Why didn't she hear their conversations before now?

"My beautiful little lady, they are going to love you. Wait until we tell them dogs do exist and were able to live through the pathogens the Monarchs released." If a dog's immune system found a way to wipe it out, maybe it wasn't too much to assume human's complex systems doing the same.

Thirty

Ben turned the sphere off when he heard Clint stomping their way. By the sound of his boots, Clint's mood would keep Ben on his toes and watch what they said around him today. Clint's situation put him past the point of redemption. They couldn't reason with him or make him see his actions were wrong. The Monarchs had done too much damage. Draining the sphere was an ingenious option they came up with to keep Clint from using it.

Amanda stayed up all night reorganizing her notes on the prophecy.

"Here he comes. Try and curb your temper. It will only tip him off, and we'll have to take him on. You know we can't beat him. With his training and years of service, he is better at hand-to-hand than I am. I can hold my own against the pathetic excuses of troops like the Monarchs, but to a professional soldier, I'm nothing." Ben hovered over Amanda.

She glanced up at him. "He struck our friend and knocked me out! That is the only explanation for the gap in my memory. Chloe at least had the advantage with the hospital having the serum to reverse what Clint did."

"Shh, hold onto your anger. We'll tap into it when we need to, but for now, for the sake of Casey's life, we need to keep it under wraps. You are the best at keeping secrets, so let this one be worth more than anything else you have ever done in your life." Ben pressed a kiss to the side of her head before making his way into the storage room.

"Anything worthwhile?" Clint pushed them hard to come up with a solution for the sphere needing to re-energize between portals.

Amanda didn't look at him. "Nah, nothing has changed. You said the parchment seemed to continue writing our legacy as times changed, but I don't see any added script than when Chloe and I originally translated it."

"Is it because the relics are separated?" Ben offered.

"No, you and Amanda were gone when an entire new section lit up and appeared out of thin air." Clint pulled out his go bag and started checking everything again.

They were in a holding pattern since Clint brought the two of them back. Ben had a hard time originally coaxing any information out of Clint to where he trusted him again. Convincing him Casey hadn't twisted his mind, making him the enemy in his eyes, was hard enough. Now they walked on eggshells. Not knowing what would throw his friend into a rant wore on both him and Amanda.

Clint stormed out of the room without looking back.

"Where did he go now? I don't know how much more of this I can take," Amanda finally spoke after hearing Clint's steps fade away.

"I know, sis. We will fix this. There has to be something we aren't thinking of."

"I miss the old Clint. The one who joked with us and protected us in his macho he-man type of thinking. I miss the soldier. This vigilante junk he is spewing is not him. I could ring the Monarchs' necks for what they did to him." Amanda's thick voice told him she slid past an icy lake surface of upset and right onto the verge of breaking down.

Ben didn't want to see that. He already witnessed so much. It broke his heart when he couldn't fix things for his baby sister. He didn't care how old they got. She would always be the little sister he felt the need to protect and keep safe.

"You know." Amanda shook her head and smiled.

"Oh no, I know that look. You are thinking of something crazy or stupid. Which one is it this time?" Ben propped his feet up on the table as he took a seat on the stool next to her.

"How about we do both? Crazy and stupid!"

Ben groaned. "Why do I have to be related to you? Do I want to know what you have planned?"

"We're going to swap Clints." Amanda bit her lip.

"Yeah, and how are we going to do that? It's not like we can just pick one up and drop the other one off. Clint said Junior was dead. He watched it happen." Ben didn't want to know what his sister cooked up.

"We go to the farmhouse with the sphere to the time before Clint comes here. Before Casey is deserted on the island of critters and the gathering of her own groceries. Did you see all of those scrumptious salad fixings ripe for the picking?" Amanda chuckled.

"How can we pull it off? Clint's all over the sphere, watching for any indication it's ready for another foray into our future." Ben didn't like it.

He didn't want to attempt something behind his back so soon after Clint's conversation with himself when they'd used the sphere without his knowledge. He didn't trust Ben. Amanda maintained the ruse she never sided with Ben, so Clint ignored her, much to her chagrin. She still looked at him like she did in school, following him around like a little lost puppy waiting for those few precious seconds he would acknowledge her.

Ben hated that for her but also for Clint. He was mortified he'd wounded her so deeply when he told Clint about her diary. She forgave him, yet he still beat himself up about it.

"Because there is new text on the parchment." Amanda beamed.

"You lied?" Ben dropped his boots to the floor.

"In school, I did take every theater subject." Amanda blew on her fingernails before buffing them against her shirt.

"Yeah, yeah. What have you got?"

"Like you can read it. Back up a little. You're breathing gross brother air on my neck." She shooed him back with her hand flopping around like a dead fish.

Ben held his hands up and took an exaggerated three steps back.

"Hardy har har. Anyway, it says to save one you have to let go of the other."

"And how do we know it's talking about Clint?" It didn't make sense to Ben.

Amanda pointed to a symbol he recognized.

"Weapon," Ben answered before her.

"Very good." Amanda seemed impressed.

Ben scowled. "Don't act surprised. I know about five different words, or symbols. They match the ones on the exterior of the cases for the relics. The latch clicks into a large circle."

"Yeah, to keep them locked. I've seen them but there isn't a symbol there."

Ben brought the crystal case for the sphere out. When he opened the lid, Amanda gasped.

"Has that been there this whole time?" She ran her hand over the metal embossed with a hieroglyph that matched the parchment.

"You and Chloe dissected the parchment. Me and Clint the relics themselves. I know these cases in and out. Oh, my gosh!" Ben placed the case on the table.

"What?" Amanda backed up, hearing the panic in his voice.

"I think there is something else here. Look."

Amanda peered around him to the small cluster of symbols in the back left corner of the chest. She pointed to the right bottom corner. Sure enough, another cluster embossed that spot.

"Let me grab my pen." Amanda snagged the pad of paper off the table.

Ben stood back and wondered what other potential strengths these cases secretly held in their inner depths. Amanda whistled as she scribbled faster than he read, so he held himself back and let her work uninterrupted.

Instead, he pulled the old photo out of the filing cabinet of the three of them as kids at Clint's aunt's and uncle's. One of the best days he had as a kid.

"Ben?" Amanda called out to him.

They didn't argue once. They were down by the river, digging in the mud.

"Ben?"

They chased and captured frogs, only to let them go, watching them hop away.

"Ben!" A wadded-up piece of paper hit him in the back of the head.

"Yeah, what did you find?" Ben shook himself and tucked the image into his back pocket.

"Are you okay? I called your name three times." Amanda's pencil cracked from gripping it too tight.

Ben flashed her the picture. "Running down memory lane."

Amanda pilfered it from his hand before he blinked. "Oh my gosh, I remember this day. I have the same picture in my Bible. His aunt died right after that, didn't she?"

"Yeah. Clint and I got caught pasting stars on his ceiling after we fell and broke his bookcase." Ben chuckled. "So, you gonna tell me what the cases' hidden secrets are?"

"They have power sources. Or at least the sphere does. I won't know about the others until I can look at them." Amanda pushed on the two corners at the same time.

The sphere lit up and hovered above the crystal enclosure. Soon a timeline ran across the screen. Casey and Clint hacked up a large tree. Littered trees in a distinctive path around the land hinted at storm damage in the background.

Amanda sighed as she watched Clint laugh while he and Casey split everything from the largest to the smallest pieces. The sloppy stacked wood grew bigger the more they watched.

"He never laughs. Ben, I haven't heard him laugh in a long time. The Monarchs broke his ability to smile." Tears dripped down her cheeks.

"Come here." Ben swallowed her up in a hug as she clung desperately to him.

"I miss him so much." A choked sob tore through his sister.

"I do too. He's been my best friend for so long. When the Monarchs took him, it shredded me. I never got all the pieces back." Ben rocked back and forth as he soothed not only his sister but his own jagged grief.

She stiffened in his arms.

"What?"

"In all the stealthy searches of you and Clint's room, I never thought of something. Where is one place we would never think to look for something?" She raised her eyebrows.

"In my stuff." Ben admitted it was ingenious.

"I'll be right back. I think I know where to look." Amanda rushed toward his room.

She was back in less than a minute with a slip of paper.

"Where did you find that?" Ben snatched it out of her hand.

"In the middle of Psalms 119." She swallowed hard as he read the page written by the Clint locked as a prisoner in his own body.

They were right to be suspicious of their friend. "We could have used this information before now."

"How did you get the sphere to work?" Clint's voice startled them from behind.

When they faced the man of the hour, Amanda clutched the back of Ben's shirt and slid the page from his hand, tucking it into her back pocket.

"It...um...did." Amanda stumbled over her words as she wiped the streaks off her face.

"I don't believe you." Clint stopped mid-step to watch the scene unfold through the phased-out field.

Casey manipulated the shield to move a large chunk of tree in front of Clint, who went to work on it with a chainsaw. He threw his head back and laughed as Casey flexed her arms as if she lifted it by herself.

No one said anything as they watched the scene play out.

"I remember that day." The whisper was almost too quiet to hear.

Clint grabbed his head and screamed as he collapsed to the floor.

"Go grab Doc!" Ben yelled.

Amanda flew out the door as Ben kneeled by his friend.

"Clint? Can you hear me? I'm right here with you, buddy." Ben gently shook his shoulder.

He didn't see anything hinting at an injury, so he wasn't sure what to make of what happened. Sounds of people running in the hall ended as Doc, Chloe, and Amanda entered the room.

"Chloe?" Ben thought she'd gone back to her uncle.

"I brought this." She held up a small neuro scanner. "Amanda, did you fill him in on our conversation about the Monarchs doing something to Clint?"

"We didn't talk about that. I woke up in Clint's room on Ben's bed, and he said you were injured and in the hospital. He said Casey stole the relics and knocked you out. I didn't learn about the chip until Doc told us after talking to your uncle when we expressed our concerns with Clint's behavior and bloody noses." Confusion clouded Amanda's features. "Doc talked to your uncle and learned you had been drugged."

"Oh right, they immediately administered the antidote to counteract the drug he gave me to erase hours of our memory when it showed up in my bloodstream. Clint hit me, so it would be my guess he took the relic's cases. Casey was never here. When you started to leave in the escape tunnel with the sphere to keep it from Clint, he came into the room. I clamped my arms around his neck and applied pressure to restrict blood flow to his brain, knocking him out, but it only lasted about fifteen seconds. Then he struck, laying me out with one punch. Then I guess he went off to grab you." Chloe placed the small device against Clint's head on the left side.

Lights displayed in a frantic pattern, flashing back and forth.

"It's too late for him. The logic circuit they embedded is more advanced than we imagined. We can't fix this." Chloe covered her mouth with her hand.

They quickly restrained Clint and transported him to the infirmary. Padded restraints were used to keep him from hurting himself.

How did you tell your best friend terrorists commandeered his brain and he was no longer himself?

When Casey removed the venom strands from Ben, it opened his eyes that they were in the wrong.

"Amanda, I think we need to show Chloe what we found today. I have an idea about where he hid the relic cases. I'll meet you here." Ben took off for his and Clint's room.

A faint memory of a sliding sound one morning before he got up danced in his mind. But Clint was asleep when Ben got out of bed, so he thought it was a dream. A secret compartment must be in their room.

Ben kneeled and tapped on the floor. He covered every inch, tapping away like a crazy person. He tipped their beds upside down, exposing the springs under the mattresses but nothing else. Next, he tried the closet.

Tap.

Tap.

Tap.

Was he wrong? Ben found nothing in the closet.

Tap.

Tap.

Thunk.

Ben stopped halfway behind Clint's bed by a small, almost unnoticeable, depression. If he wasn't right next to it, anyone would have missed it.

He pressed on all four corners. It didn't move. Next, he tried to glide his hands against the wall to slide it out of place. He would use a hammer if he had to and demolish the cover to get in. He tilted his head a certain way; along the bottom of the door, he saw small symbols. He pressed them and the panel lifted up and out of the way.

Those words were something he and Clint created when they were young. It was their cipher code from when they wrote letters back and forth in their secret spy phase as kids. Only he and Clint knew about it. Maybe the real Clint still lingered in there somewhere.

Ben lugged out the relics bag and did a quick inventory to make sure everything was there.

Yep.

He jogged back and heard Chloe's ohs and ahs at what Amanda explained to her.

"Found them." He dumped everything on the table and quickly spread out the chests and opened all the lids.

They all backed away. Every single relic chest sported additional markings inside the cover. They were different than the markings on the sphere. But that wasn't what made them speechless. There were relics in each and every case.

"Ben, did you take these from Casey?" Amanda leaned forward.

"No, I pilfered these out of a hole in the wall Clint stashed them in." Ben had no words for the fact his best friend kept so much from them. "Can you guys decode the symbols, so we know what we have to work with?"

Amanda and Chloe were already busy writing. He backed up and let them talk through everything.

Chloe looked up. "Doc did another scan of the chip embedded in Clint's head. It also has a trigger switch. They can push a button and he will be...before he hits the ground."

Their news explained why they both looked like they'd been crying. His friend was a walking time bomb. Not only was the chip rigged to stop it from being removed, but there was a secondary system to stop any deserters.

He thought a possibility they could salvage his friend would present itself, but he was already dead before they went in to rescue him from the Monarchs. He served his purpose, so it made sense why he easily escaped. They were ready to release him to do their bidding.

Ben sauntered down to the cafeteria, his gut twisted up in knots. He loaded up three plates of sandwiches, remembering everyone's favorites. Chips overflowed from the plates while he set drinks in three of the corners of the tray he balanced on one hand. They needed to eat but it would sit like lead in his stomach.

He backed up to the door to open it when Mark ran over and held it for him. "Thanks."

"Sure," Mark looked around and lowered his voice. "Is there something we need to know about?"

"What do you mean?" Ben didn't want to give anything away.

"I saw Clint in the infirmary. Is there a reason we have him restrained?"

"You know about the Monarchs taking him captive?" Ben knew everyone did.

"Of course. We were all so happy to see him come back." Mark straightened.

"They implanted something in his brain. They are messing with his mind." Ben shifted the tray, so he could hold onto it with both hands.

"Is that why he has been *off* since he's been back?" Of course, Mark and the others had noticed.

Ben nodded. They wanted to keep the information that the Monarchs were breathing down their necks quiet for the time being since they hadn't attacked yet, and they didn't want to panic everyone. "We aren't broadcasting that information yet. Only you, Doc, Chloe, and us three know."

"So, what do you need us to do to help him?" Ben appreciated Mark's optimism.

"Nothing we can do. The technology is advanced years beyond anything we have available to remove it. It's only a matter of time; we need to leave him behind. He's fighting it but I don't think our Clint exists anymore. He is a danger to us all. We're going to send you guys ahead of us to the new houses we have ready. We will care for Clint, so the Monarchs won't know where we went." Ben hated to be the bearer of bad news.

"So, we're going to the underground houses?"

"No, Clint knows about them and may have compromised their location to the Monarchs. Chloe said her uncle has another idea: the houses in the grove no one thought were still standing. We'll go after Doc does what he can to make Clint comfortable. The Monarchs put a kill switch in his head. It is only a matter of time before they push the button once they know he is compromised." Ben tried to keep his voice steady.

Mark sucked in air. "No."

"Please don't share information with anyone yet. We'll tell them once he is gone. No need to start a panic and have people running around, alerting the Monarchs to where we are." Ben couldn't express enough how panicked people did stupid things and got innocent people killed.

"Let me know what we can do, and I'll make it happen. I'm sorry, Ben." Mark placed his hand on his arm before going back in to eat.

Ben gave each of ladies a plate he'd put together for them. They murmured between themselves and pushed off to the side three of the five cases.

As they finished their potato chips, they pushed the fifth one over to join the four.

"Lay it on me." Ben sat back.

"First off, I'm sorry we never saw the markings to decipher them," Chloe started.

Ben held up his hand. "We all missed them. No need to take the blame on this one all on your own."

Chloe clinched her jaw. "The sphere. I agree with Amanda it has its own recharging system. The healing stone removes the healing ability when the person it's absorbed into stands directly in front of it and presses the same two corners as on the sphere's case."

Would Casey ever be able to forgive them for not figuring out how to send her home to her family all those years ago?

Amanda picked up where Chloe stopped. "The ring, it's a weapon."

"Really?" Ben hopped to his feet pacing several steps.

Finally, something he could contribute. Wait, hazy weird flashes of Casey activating it in the years he lived with her and Clint popped into his head. They were more of a dream than a vivid memory. He remembered the rays decimated the tree trunks. Now they didn't need Casey to trigger them on this side.

"Yes, the key or the case can call up their powers."

"Clint's weapon?" Ben prepared for the next stage to reunite the chosen.

"We're getting to that. Slow your horses." Amanda held up her bracelet. "The shield can be expended against the chosen but only in a protective way. Since Casey is still true in heart to what needs to be done and being a child of God, she can use them to separate us and keep us from hurting her or from being a target."

"Makes sense." He believed Clint when Casey first projected them through the time loop using the relics on her end.

"The weapon, however, can choose who it annihilates. It can be used in conjunction with the sphere, so it is one large dome of destruction. It scares me that it might technically cause the end of mankind." Chloe shivered.

"Here's an interesting tidbit." Amanda waited until he looked at her. "Do you recall the statement Casey said about the other versions controlling the winds with the ring? They can control the elements."

"No, they can't. It's not in the parchment." Ben sighed.

"You're right, it isn't in the parchment or the symbols of earth, fire, and wind. If you press the symbols in order, it turns on the nature portion. It doesn't need the key to activate them, which explains why the three of us in the other version didn't know Casey and only used the element function." Amanda shoved away her empty plate.

Pounding boots had them all on their feet blocking the relics from view.

"Clint's awake," Mark announced.

Thirty-One

Clint moaned as the pounding in his skull reached a whole new level. He remembered Chloe came back and her words froze him to his core. He was going to die.

He never thought too deeply about death as a soldier or when the Monarchs invaded America. Inevitably, his time would come fighting the good fight. Clint came to terms with that, but to have someone able to push a button and end his entire existence scared him on a whole new level.

In the back of his mind, Ben and Amanda, his closest confidants, helped him through the dark days when he wasn't conscious of his actions. His mind gave him a glimpse of the changed man their contraption made him. He screamed when he had no control over his body.

He wanted to claw his way out and let them know he was alive. Somewhere in this hijacked body, the old Clint lurked. He had very few moments of clarity. But when he did, he held onto them with an iron grip. No matter how loud he tried to scream to get their attention, the chip-controlled side muted him. He feared what he did while unconscious.

Now hearing Doc talk to someone on the phone about his *condition* let him know his fate of never leaving this place alive. The evil possessed by the Monarchs reminded him why God gave them the relics as a counterbalance. The implanted chip separated the two sides of every person. The good side from the bad. Kind of like heads and tails on a coin. Two identities yet one. It shut down the emotions that made them human. Once in place, it consigned the noble side for higher reasoning, telling them not to do something bad, into a dormant phase by locking it away. The other, darker personality most people kept in check was now released to the forefront. The perfect soldiers for the Monarchs to wield. A killing machine with no conscience to counterbalance the evil. They followed directions with no questions asked.

Could they short-circuit his brain? Give himself a jolt? He remembered doing that to Gretchen in the motel as they waited for her to be reunited with her family. He would need the relic, but could he use it on himself? He concentrated on trying to recall his time with the Monarchs, but there were only missing chunks.

If Casey healed herself, why couldn't the reverse be true with him if he used the weapon to undo what the Monarchs did?

He endangered everyone if he stayed while the Monarchs controlled his mind. He was relieved his right mind was awake. Maybe the pain when he thought of Casey collapsed the circuit and let his true side out for a bit. The vision slammed into him, making him groan as a dull ache swamped the left side of his head.

Clint tried to open his eyes. The brightness ripped through his skull as he groaned and closed them again.

"Go tell them he's awake," Doc's soft voice requested.

"Doc?" Clint wanted to stay in charge, but it was only a matter of time before he ended up back in his cage.

"Clint, son, how are you doing?"

"It hurts. I can't stay long. I can already feel the circuits turning back on. Don't let me hurt anyone else. You have to shut it down." Clint fought for every word he spoke as he felt himself slipping.

"Clint?" Ben gripped his hand.

"Use the relic. Fry this chip they stuck in me. They're trying to take over again. I can't let them win. I think you're right, Amanda. Find the old Clint. Go while you still can." Clint's vacant eyes stared into nothing, his voice thick.

"No. You're here now. Doc, can we keep it from switching back on?" Amanda cried.

"Amanda it is something we have never seen before. It will implode if we try to take it out. A failsafe in the older models sends out an electrical impulse that fries anything and everything it touches. When oxygen hits it, this upgraded one sends out a toxic gas. He will be brain-dead in a matter of seconds." Doc explained what Clint heard him telling someone on the phone. "I know body parts and how they work. This circuit mumbo jumbo needs more expertise than my training allows."

"Let me go, guys. Restore the world. Technically, I'll still be with you, but not the broken man I've become." Clint felt the other side taking over. It was too late. "Go find the good side of me. The man you can be proud of. Not this version where I disappointed all of you."

Clint tugged on the restraints hard enough the material started to rip. He was going to end this now. How dare they try and take this away from him.

Ben, Amanda, and Chloe tried to back away from Clint.

"You are more trouble than you're worth, little girl." Chloe gasped as he spit his venom at her.

"Mark, get everyone out of here." Ben hurried out of the room with him.

Good, one less person to deal with while he tried to work his way off this bed. He gave another good tug, flexing his muscles and straining against the fabric.

Another bit of tearing rent the air.

"Here, give this to him." Doc tossed a syringe on the bed as he hobbled away on the cane he leaned on for as long as Clint had known him.

Amanda pulled the cap off with her teeth as she moved back, eyeing his wrists. She plunged the needle into his skin without a second thought.

Clint surrendered himself to the liquid flowing through his veins. How dare they attack him like this? Doc's cane clunked against the floor as he shuffled back in with a device he placed against the side of his head.

A weird hum vibrated in his skull. Soon, darkness overloaded his system.

CLINT ROUSED TO WHISPERS. "Hello."

"He's awake."

"Nothing like stating the obvious. What happened?" Clint tried to raise his hands, but they stopped about an inch off the bed.

"Which Clint do you think he is?" Amanda mock whispered.

"Which Clint?" It took a second before it dawned on him.

Ben leaned in. "Clint, are you in there?"

"Something's in my head. You have to leave. Go to Casey before I transport back here. You need to leave me behind. Nothing can stop the Monarchs from seizing my mind again. It's asleep right now." Presently lucid, it wouldn't be long before he became a spectator to his life again.

"I'm not leaving you," Amanda bit out.

"Ben, look at me. I'm not the man you knew growing up. You can't trust me. This thing can't be removed. I heard Doc talking about the repercussions if they try. I can't live like this. Please." Clint saw the moment Ben agreed with him.

"Can you keep from divulging information and telling the Monarchs where we went?" Ben had a valid point.

"Probably not. I've been trying to keep our secrets, and for some reason, I have control over the relics and the farm, but anything else I let go because I can only manipulate so many things before it's too much. They know we're here. They extracted our location while I was under again." Clint shuddered.

"We already got everyone out. They're gone." Ben nodded at Amanda, who slung the pack over her shoulder.

Amanda kissed him on the forehead. "I wish—"

"No, there's nothing anyone can do for me. At least you can pass on the information about their mind control. Get it into the right hands to do something about it. I haven't been in charge of my body for a long time. I'm afraid I can't come back this time. If it is my last action on this side to give myself for my best friends, so be it. I'll go out with a bang." Clint tried to lighten the mood.

"Don't joke about this!" Amanda turned her back to him.

"Now you know what I felt when I watched you shot in the other time. It ripped me apart. Amanda, I never told you how much you mean to me. That side is still in here. He's hanging on. You are making me hang on, making me a stronger person than I've ever been before. If only we explored what could have been between us. Don't let Junior friend-zone you. He loves you as much as I do." Clint laid it all on the line. "Pass the word to my military contacts. They can retrieve my body and find a way around this thing."

Amanda choked on a sob but held back like the strong woman he fell in love with. "Now you want to tell me this?"

"I was a coward not telling you my feelings. I'll do what I can to keep them out of my head, but I know Casey didn't kill me. They twisted my mind to see what they wanted me to see. But this is the real me, for a little while. And I don't want you to leave without letting you know you are such a beautiful brave woman. Any man would be proud to have you on their arm." Clint wanted to wrap her up and console her, but it would never happen.

"Shut up." Amanda's eyes reddened as she bit her lip and turned away.

"I get where you're coming from, but know you devastated her." Ben sat at the end of the bed.

Clint wouldn't take back his words. "I know. I wish I was strong enough to have told her sooner. I was scared. I've never let anyone have my heart like I did her, and she didn't know she had it. This whole time and I stood on the sidelines like a chump."

"Well, you are a chump." Ben shrugged.

"I can't take back what this evil side of me did. All I can do is ask for your forgiveness. Tell Casey I failed her."

"You didn't fail anyone. The Monarchs stole your conscience, making you a monster not of your own actions. There is nothing to forgive, and Casey would feel the same way."

"Stay with me until I'm not me again. Because once they know you are all gone, they'll push the button. I don't want you to go yet." Clint tried to put on a brave front for Amanda.

"I'm not going anywhere until it's time. You're my best friend and brother in every sense of the word. We have been through too much for me to abandon you." Ben sniffled but kept his voice steady.

Clint's eyes stung while he swallowed hard. "I'm afraid. For the first time in my life, I'm scared for myself. How selfish am I?"

"Not selfish. It's called being human." Amanda slowly walked toward them.

Over the next hour, they told stories from their childhood, laughing and relishing their last moments together. Clint knew the Clint with Casey they would be joining would acquire his rush of visions from his last day and hoped he'd make him proud. He sacrificed himself to keep everyone else safe.

At least God knew his true heart, not the black one overflowing with anger and hate. He regretted not being strong enough to take over. This stupid thing in his head counted down to an implosion. What information did the Monarchs squeeze out of him? How many people did he put in danger with the knowledge they were able to extract? Would his sacrifice give them the time they needed to end this once and for all?

Clint felt when the other side started to wake up. "It's time."

"No, can't Casey try to heal him? You can't tell me she can't deliver some sort of micro-healing bubble from the shield to make it inert." Amanda pointed to his head.

Clint struggled. "It's too late."

"Ben?" Amanda rested her head on Ben's chest.

"Take care of her." Clint gave a chin lift toward Amanda.

Ben nodded as a tear escaped down his cheek. "I always will."

"She doesn't need to see this; I only have a few seconds left. Yo squirt. I love you and I think I always have..." Clint faded to the back.

"You are all dead!" Clint's toxic words rushed out.

Clint saw them take out the sphere and turn their backs to him, dialing up a time he couldn't see. At least he had the other relics hidden in the compartment in the wall. They would reward him for securing those weapons.

Ben peered over his shoulder. "Love you, brother."

A sob tore free of Amanda. She wrapped her arm around her brother's waist as Ben pulled her closer, and they surged through the shimmer, leaving Clint alone with no one around to free him.

Clint yelled. Someone better let him loose soon, or they would pay.

Several hours later, Clint finally broke the buckle on the restraint and pulled free his other limbs. He stormed down the hall. Night had fallen and none of the lights came on. The silence was eerie. Where was everyone? He flipped switches every so often, but nothing happened. Chloe's uncle must have turned everything off. He would include them in his retribution list. They would regret ever crossing him.

Muscle memory took him to his room. A flashlight illuminated the space with a circle on the ceiling when he pulled it out of the nightstand. He flicked the beam over his side of the room.

He gaped at the wall and the cover that lay on his bed. They took everything. Every last relic. His scream of frustration warped into a scream of agony as his body doubled over twitching. Electric charges fried the cells in his brain around the implant. The Monarchs were telling him he was no longer of any use to them. After all he'd done for them, they were going to end it like this?

Thirty-Two

Casey and Clint were laughing as he tossed the last log onto the stack of firewood that would last them two seasons. She still missed Amanda and especially Ben. Only a day on the farm and she was ready to spend the rest of her life mapping out a garden and planting fruit trees like they had in the grove.

"Easy way to stock up on logs. However, let's not go through another tornado. I can do without the stress of not knowing if we're to be swept away in the wild crazy winds." Clint clapped her on the shoulder as a shimmer appeared in front of them.

Clint shoved Casey behind him as she enveloped them in a large shield. She peeked over her shoulder at the window where the den sat and wondered how a portal opened when the sphere was still in pieces in its case.

Ben and Amanda casually walked out and stood as the portal dissolved.

"Amanda?" Clint's hoarse whisper barely left his lips.

Ben smiled but rubbed his hand over the back of his neck. They'd lived through something that scarred them.

Casey sank to her knees as she wailed. She'd missed him so much; she still hadn't gotten over their loss.

Ben strolled through the shield and crouched in front of her, his forearms on his legs, his hands hanging between his thighs. "Hey, sweetheart."

Casey launched herself into his arms. Sobs tore through her and racked her body. Ben stood with his arms wrapped so tightly around her, her feet dangled free and didn't touch the ground.

"Hey, big brother. You going to put my best friend down so I can give her a hug?" Amanda's voice sounded right next to them.

Casey laughed but only gripped Ben tighter.

"Sorry sis, she won't let go." Ben kissed her cheek and whispered to her. "I've got you. I'm never letting you go."

Several minutes later, she finally loosened her hold to see Clint and Amanda exchange a look between them.

Amanda tugged her in for a hug. Casey realized she'd changed from the woman she first met. Casey pushed her back and took her in. Shadows bruised the skin under her eyes. Her friend looked as if laughing and joking would be a foreign concept to her.

"We've been through a lot." Amanda spun around so she faced Clint.

He crushed Amanda in a hug. "Missed you." His voice hitched, losing the calm, soothing timbre she loved hearing from him.

Amanda's sobs soon added to Casey's as she clung to Clint.

Ben pulled her to him. "I've got you. I'm so sorry. I won't ever be able to say it enough, but maybe I can show you through my actions and love over the next, say what, fifty years?"

Casey snorted. "For what? It wasn't your fault the sniper took you out. It's not like you can stop a speeding bullet."

Casey buckled but Ben held her up as flashes of events over the last four years overloaded her in the possible timeline she hadn't yet lived. Casey shook her head. Were these truly the friends she'd known all those years ago? The ones ready to die for her? Their attempts to break her were fresh in her mind though it hadn't happened yet.

Clint dropped to his knees with Amanda hanging on for dear life. His eyes met Casey's, a sadness she'd never seen before reflected in him. Not even at the loss of Amanda and Ben. He cupped Amanda's face, swiping his thumbs over her cheeks. "Oh, sweetheart. Yes, I do love you. I always have in one way or another."

Ben pulled her toward the house. "We need to have a conversation to catch everyone up on all the events to make sure our sides mesh with what we faced."

"Wait, how are you here?" Casey stumbled over her feet when she tried to look over her shoulder to see if Amanda and Clint were following.

"I'm starved and with all the wood chopping, I'd say you probably are also." Ben nudged her through the door.

"And someone needs a shower. Gosh, you stink." Amanda playfully pushed Clint toward the stairs.

"I'll be right back." Clint disappeared.

Casey used the shower on the main floor and opened the door a sliver when Amanda said she had some clothes for her.

Casey snaked her hand out to grab them. She dressed faster than normal.

Clint still toweled his wet hair when she sat at the kitchen table. She pulled hers back into a dripping wet braid to keep it out of her face. It would dry with a wave to the strands, but she didn't care.

"Okay, do we have a tale to tell you." Ben met her eyes. "To make sure we are all on the same page, did you two get a rush of memories outside?"

Clint and Casey nodded.

Clint folded his hands in front of him. "It started when I went back for Amanda and Ben. You were stuck here by yourself for three years."

"Try four." Casey didn't think she would survive alone, but she thrived.

Ben started in when Clint appeared, and they had two Clints for a while until the Monarchs captured them. Clint picked up where Ben left off and told of his months of torture before escaping after watching what he thought was her murdering him.

Amanda added bits and pieces to it as more memories flooded Casey of fighting them and trying to survive the winter months of her first year.

Ben hung his head when Clint recounted his moments before the Monarchs fried his brain as he gave his life to keep her safe.

Casey couldn't talk. The air seemed to leak out of her, and she couldn't refill her lungs. Each of them experienced death except her. All three of them. Why hadn't she suffered like her friends?

"Stop it. Don't go there. It was my choice. I never intentionally told them about the relics or this place." Clint stretched across the table and took her hand.

"They know because they came here a few times over the years." Casey told them what happened before they reappeared in the picture and defended herself against them.

"How did the shield encompass that large of an area?" Ben interrupted her.

Casey shook her head. "I have no clue. All I know is God told me I would have rest for a while on all sides. It was a bit before your alter ego selves showed up."

"You didn't call for help? Why not ask Chloe to set you up with a food drop?" Clint growled.

Casey laughed so hard she hoped it didn't turn into relieved tears. "You had the phone. I looked everywhere for it when I realized you put it in your pocket before jumping back."

"No!" The horror on Amanda's face almost had her cackling again.

"I saw a garden during the times we jumped. How did you do that with no seed?" Clint asked.

"The ravens." His face made Casey laugh again.

"You told me about that when you kidnapped me. Turnabout's fair play. Well done, my dear." Ben winked at her.

"What? You never told me about any ravens." Amanda raised her hands.

Ben draped his hand over the back of her chair. "Like God fed Elijah in the desert, he used ravens to do the same here."

"Oh my gosh, you ate ravens?" Amanda shrieked. "Eww. I'm going to be sick."

Clint held his stomach as he laughed.

"No," Ben finally got through explaining between fits of laughter.

"I was going to say." Amanda gave a dramatic shiver with her abnormal fear of birds.

"No, but deer...pretty delicious," Casey claimed with a straight face.

Amanda's jaw dropped. "But..."

Clint also sputtered. "You know how to hunt?"

"I didn't, but I tried. Or at least I will. But the knowledge is already with me."

Soon, they were eating a feast and filling in the blanks talking about the events hurdled them into another tailspin over the last four years. Between all the visits from the Monarchs and the chosen that hadn't happened yet, Casey wondered where that would leave them.

"So does this mean we now have to face the Monarchs sending troops here?" Amanda licked BBQ sauce off her fingers.

Casey turned to Clint. "They were here literally hours after you left. They congregated for about three days before they attacked."

"How did you keep the shield up so long?" Amanda smiled and Ben returned it.

They knew something she didn't.

"Where are the relics?" Ben stood.

Panic flashed through her. Were they the real Ben and Amanda?

"I don't think we need those out right now, do we?" Clint agreed. At least she wasn't the only one who thought it was a bad idea to pretty much hand over their only line of defense.

"It's okay, you big lug." Amanda raised an eyebrow at Casey. "Could we walk through your shields while we were separated?"

Casey knew she asked about when she captured them and sent them back. "No."

"Did we go through the shield now?" Amanda smiled.

"Clint, the shield would have stopped them if they weren't on our side. Through all the times you ported to me, never once were you able to skirt my defense." Casey smirked at Amanda.

"We want to show you something we discovered before Clint." Amanda's lips trembled and pressed together.

Clint pulled her into his arms. "I'm right here. And I'm still me. The Monarchs never got their hands on me to implant that chip."

Amanda nodded against his chest as she inhaled a deep breath. "Don't leave me again."

"Never." He pulled her along to the den.

With all the relics out on the desktop, they opened all the lids.

Amanda pointed to the four corners. "Symbols."

"What?" Casey checked the healing relic. Sure enough, small innocuous-looking symbols adorned the top two corners.

"If you put your fingers on the top on both sides at the same time, the healing relic will be pulled from you, encased back in the stone, for the next generation." Amanda sounded almost dejected.

"I could have gone home," Casey muttered.

"It's my fault we didn't know this. Clint and I researched the boxes while Amanda and Chloe deciphered the parchment. We never put two and two together that all the cases hid powers and needed to be activated." Ben held up his.

Casey pulled out the parchment. "I think you need to read the new additions."

Amanda turned her wrist over. "What's this?"

The markings on her skin glowed and flickered as Amanda ran her hand over them. "They are the ancient writings from the prophecy."

"I figured as much." Casey lowered her sleeve.

"When did these come out?" Amanda moved the relics to the side and unrolled the scroll.

"After you died." Casey didn't want to remember the dark day she couldn't heal her friend.

Ben updated them about the extra powers on the cases while Amanda read the new passages.

"Sounds about right. Casey activated all of those. The only one that seems to be new is that the healing stone can retract its powers from the host and the sphere is rechargeable. What about repairing itself?"

"Not possible." Amanda kept her head down.

"We saw it happen." Clint sat on the window seat behind the desk.

"The pieces glowed and snapped back together. This happened over several weeks. Clint went to you guys on the final night. It showed the room where Ben and Amanda were talking the night before she died. Since God healed the sphere, we agreed it was a sign to fulfill the prophecy and unite the four chosen ones. Only when Clint went through, it blinked out and fell apart again. His relic absorbed into me, and I realized my worst nightmare truly happened." Casey felt the fear grip her at what they would face when the Monarchs charged forward with their plans in the coming week.

"We're here now." Ben pulled her to his side.

"Well, I've technically never been alone. God was with me every step of the way. I never realized how much I needed to lean on Him to survive in life. And I'm not talking about how you pulled me into the future and I now combat terrorists. Back home, I never leaned on Him enough to let Him handle small things that stressed me out, making them too much for me to process on my own. If we give our all to Him with our whole hearts, it is then we can see His works in the smallest things." Casey wished she would have realized that so much sooner.

"No mention of elemental use either." Amanda ran her finger over the words as she continued.

"Wait, the first visit by the terminator-variety chosen ones. Ben, your ring engineered the winds and put out a prairie fire." Casey couldn't wrap her head around the bonus relic news.

The room quieted as they each contemplated mastering the next-level relics.

"You guys, it says something about transferring powers to children." Amanda's face went deathly white.

Clint rushed to her. "What does it say?"

"We can." Amanda's finger led to a newly filled section that had not been there before she and Ben came back.

"This wasn't here this morning." Casey's hands shook. "We can never let these fall into the Monarchs' hands. They would destroy all people on this planet who didn't agree with them."

"Trials and tribulations." Ben sighed.

Casey zoned out as they discussed their next course of action. She imagined a child with Ben's blue eyes laughing and swinging on the tire swing out back. His little cheeks were red from the chill in the air as autumn winds gusted across the fields. Ben with him on his shoulders, talking about how great God is. Yellow static arched through his little chubby child hands as he made the swing float back and forth by itself.

Amanda caught Clint looking at her and blushed. Arms swaying in conjunction with each other, the little girl's feet leaving the ground as they walked. Giggles filled the air bringing smiles to her parents' faces. The child holding onto both of their hands had the color of Amanda's hair along with Clint's dimple.

Casey came back to the present. No way would she let the Monarchs stop their children from living a life free from insurgents.

"We stop them now. It's time we take this war to them. Instead of always being on the defensive, we go on the offensive. They will be here in a couple of weeks. They sent so many squadrons, I couldn't count the number of soldiers. I say we ambush their ambush." Casey smirked at her joke.

"I'm not sure this is such a good idea." Clint glanced alternately at Amanda and Casey.

"I think it's a great idea. They won't see it coming." Ben twisted the ring on his finger.

It was still just a ring.

"I know how to activate the new levels of each relic." Amanda gestured to their storage containers.

"Before we do, we need to take into consideration, since I was the one they planted the chip in, in the past, I may have conveyed some sort of message telling them all of this. I don't know if I can be trusted." Clint didn't know how wrong he was.

Casey trusted him explicitly. "You don't have the chip because you never went back into the past to grab Amanda and Ben. Let me know if I have this right. From when we left the warehouse to now has been almost two years. You two coming forward kept Clint from returning for you so the last four years never happened after we got here."

"Sounds right to me," Amanda agreed.

"I say we prepare for the invasion that will happen in the next few weeks. We need to practice with the weapons and build up the defenses around here. I remember where their point of attack started and how far the shield stopped. If I practice now holding up the shield as long as I can, I should be able to extend not only the scope of the shield's defenses but the capacity of its borders. The shield stayed up when I fell asleep, but not from anything I did. Explosions on the east side of the property woke me when they finally attacked." Casey tried to remember as much detail as possible.

"Perfect. You and I will work on counterattacks from their actions when you defended yourself and took out all the surrounding states with a massive EM pulse. The Monarchs took advantage of the situation and went in and wiped out entire cities and left nothing but rubble. They informed me when they held me, you intentionally laid waste to everything single-handedly and the pulse is what killed everyone not the Monarchs. They played video after video of the destruction. It was very compelling. The chip in my head provoking me didn't take much to turn me against us. They staged a false illusion of you pulling the trigger." Clint took a second.

No one said anything, knowing he needed a minute to compose himself of some of the worst things to ever happen to someone.

"Let's activate the relics, and while they practice, you and I can talk strategy." Casey had two of the cases in her hands and started for the kitchen door.

They all stood in a line as Casey deployed the shield, blocking out prying eyes if they had any unwanted visitors.

"Ben, your ring has massive destructive power so no pointing it at anything you don't want to splinter into smithereens until you have command over it." Clint nodded to Amanda, who pressed the corners of the box.

Yellow sparks flew and swirled around Ben, lifting him off the ground. Casey's chest swelled with hope for the first time in a long time. Could they accomplish this?

Even though they hadn't lived the tragedy of the last four years, all the memories of the alternative timelines clogged their minds, still making the experiences feel real.

Ben's eyes flecked with the yellow matching his ring. Soon, he lowered himself to the ground and stretched out his neck on each side. "Let's do this."

He held out his arm and concentrated on the dead oak on the other side of the field. A yellow beam burst out and blasted the trunk in half, raining the field with splinters they would be mowing around for years to come.

Amanda whooped as she danced in place.

Casey laughed as Clint shook his head.

"Okay, your turn, Amanda." Casey lifted the case and pressed two corners.

Opalescent swirls lifted up from her wrist and floated around her body, expanding and increasing in size until she encompassed the entire place in her shield along with Casey's.

"Amanda, you can change the density of the shield and shove objects out of the way. When the Monarchs' took down the shield and I redeployed it after they shot me, it dug into the ground as it surged out from me like a bulldozer."

Ben brushed his fingers over her elbow. "You were shot?"

"Well, not yet technically since it hasn't happened yet. And yes, more than once." Casey turned to Clint. "A device the Monarchs invented made the shield drop. They circled the dome and at the same time put these small discs against it evenly across the field, and that short-circuited it or something. Once down, several slugs hit me. I concentrated on the shield to reactivate enough to cover me and shove the Monarchs away. I may have released more power than necessary, but I panicked. I didn't know what else to do."

Ben pulled her to him, kissing her head and holding his lips there for several seconds.

"You never have to deal with them by yourself again." His rumbly voice soothed her.

Soon, another hand landed on her back while Amanda squeezed her hand.

"Here you were, trying to survive, and we added to your distress." Amanda's voice quivered.

"This time they won't know what hit them." Clint started to withdraw when a magnetic force pulled them back together.

"Amanda." Casey didn't contain her excitement. "I can heal the shield if they use those devices, I think. God told me to heal the shield during one of my many skirmishes."

Swirls of static surrounded them.

"Casey, are you doing this?" Clint still couldn't withdraw his hand from her back.

"No, it's not me," she answered.

"Now that my chosen are back together, you will be an unstoppable force for justice."

Their hearts glowed with coordinating colors of their powers. Soon the magnetic band holding them together snapped, sending them sprawling across the grass.

"Let's do this." Clint smiled.

Thirty-Three

The reunited chosen ones stood about three feet apart, looking at the horizon. It had been four weeks since Ben and Amanda rejoined them. The shadowy line said a storm was coming. Whether by nature or man was yet to be seen.

A rumble of an engine moving closer told her it was man knocking on their doorstep. They were here. The sun rising behind them blocked out their numbers.

"It's time." Clint's calm rushed out to all of them.

He more than proved he was still the man they all loved over the last couple of weeks. He took twice the number of watches and never let the others down.

They trained every day with their appointed relics and prayed this wouldn't end with the Monarchs taking over the world. Clint heard from his military contacts they didn't recover his body when Amanda and Ben left him behind. The warehouse was torched, leaving no evidence. They didn't have the manpower to sift through the debris looking for him.

They voted unanimously, if it came down to it, they would die fighting instead of being taken. It wasn't worth the lives around them and in the world to hand over the uniquely absorbed weapons in each of them. The Monarchs would tear them from their bodies using the serum or torture them like they did Clint. So, the option to surrender never made it to the table.

The prophecy was finally fully written. They woke up to find the parchment's extra space removed. It only unrolled to the last line they read, saying it passed on to the next generations. And to raise their offspring in God's ways or evil would befall the world, bent on eradicating every believer left.

The ground vibrated under their feet as the first row of vehicles breached the boundary of their property.

With no thoughts to herself, Amanda deployed the shield. They discussed if Casey couldn't heal it like she did before, that she would deploy hers and switch back and forth with Amanda.

Amanda's skills used a secondary shield as a giant medieval armor flinging things out of their way. Hay bales sat in ruins. A long single blow from a horn cut through the morning. All of the vehicles stopped in a perfect line.

Men and mantises rushed at the shield.

"What the heck?" Amanda retreated.

"Those are what we were telling you about. They are mechanical and the EM pulse can take them out. Make sure you strengthen the shield, or their barbed legs can cut through. I'm not sure if they will take it down like they did before, but if they do, I'll be ready with mine. Pray they only have one crack at erasing our protection. It seemed the last couple of times they tried, they only had enough juice in their little baubles for one attempt. When I put the shield back up, they didn't try to take it down again." Casey nodded at Amanda, trying to sound confident when, in fact, her nerves were a frayed mess inside.

Everything was in God's hands. She may only be human, and with all her flaws, she tried her best to show a strong front.

The suited man stepped forward. "Ah, Casey brought friends out to play."

Clint matched his forward movement and smiled. The man tilted his head as his shiny eyes flickered. He didn't have reasoning like humans do such as fear and worry, but she swore he tried to figure out how Clint fought on their side.

His eyes changed again, turning a dark gray and then back to shiny.

Clint chuckled. "Trying to figure out why you can't fry my brain? Sorry, not an option on this model. You should understand that phrase."

Casey tried to keep the bark of laughter from bursting forth. It came out as a snort.

"Clint!" Ben scolded him but couldn't keep the smile from his lips.

"We came to speak with Casey. If you leave now, we will let you go." Android man shifted back to his professional, inhuman speech.

"Oh well, if you promise, that means you have to keep your word. You promise not to assassinate me? I mean, that's a fantastically excellent offer, isn't it?" Amanda challenged.

"Yes, we will let you go. After you denounce your God."

Laughter belched from them, stopping him in his assurance they wouldn't go after them.

"Okay, that will never happen, and I'm going to say you need to work on your sarcasm side of development. This guy is a joke." Amanda flicked her thumb toward the leader.

"Yes, sarcasm. To make a mocking remark usually in exaggeration of what is meant. I will adapt those skills in my next version."

"Oh, stop." Clint's red pulse followed by a beam from Ben raced toward the machine. Addressing Casey, he said, "Does he always sound so annoying when he talks?"

Casey raised her shoulders to her ears. "Pretty much."

The leader sidestepped but not soon enough as Ben concentrated and sped up his pulse, so it beat Clint's to him. He jerked and shuddered as his body took the full impact of Ben's ring.

A large hole, from molten microelectronics, opened up on his chest. He swiped at it with his hand but only managed to transfer the liquifying solvent.

"Kill them all!" were the cyborg's last words.

"Ready, Amanda?" Casey would wait until she couldn't hold the shield anymore before she jumped in with the healing power.

"Already there." Amanda steadied her hands after shaking them out, getting ready to move.

Her head tilted from side to side as she bounced on the balls of her feet.

"Hey sis, you ain't in a boxing ring," Ben joked.

He tried to lighten the mood because if Casey saw the fear in Amanda's eyes, her brother did too.

At least fifteen shield-penetrating orbs were pressed to the outside of their safety net.

"Ben, leave her be. She knows what she's doing." Clint whispered in Amanda's ear for several seconds.

The effect he had on her self-confidence was clear when she stood stock still and waited for the Monarchs' next play.

The gadgets switched on and static skated over the surface to Amanda. She screamed as she fell. Clint ran to her, but she held up her hand to stop him.

"Amanda, I'll be there in a second. Be...prepared. We talked about waiting to heal the shield until the last minute." Casey's hieroglyphs lit in a frantic pattern, too fast for her to comprehend.

Amanda sucked in air, trying to counteract the pain coursing through her veins.

"Casey, your arms." Amanda forced her wrist over, trying to read the wild pattern.

"Now!" Blue flowed through Casey to the shield instead of to Amanda like God instructed her to do before.

Amanda's met Casey's eyes as the last static discharge dissipated. The Monarchs stood around, unsure of what happened. She never had backup before when dealing with their nuisance. The shield held for the time being.

They looked at the puddle of their leader and soon pulled another set of discs from behind their backs. Smirks that the chosen wouldn't be ready for two sets gave them overinflated egos, believing they would be victorious.

Amanda opened her mouth in a silent scream as the mantises crawled all over the outside. Their barbed legs, now equipped with red laser beams, cut into the shield. Casey healed Amanda, shoring up her reserves as she continued to supplement the shield. Amanda held on with Casey healing the surges it delivered through the contraptions.

Casey concentrated but couldn't release the shield. "I can't get my shield up."

"These must be different than what you encountered before." Ben stood in front of Casey to cover her.

"I can't control it much longer." Amanda started to retract the shield.

Clint and Ben held up their hands as a large mantis crawled out of the earth behind the front lines and crushed some of the Monarchs who didn't get out of its way fast enough.

"Too bad we couldn't let that thing take them out for us." Amanda let the shield drop.

No one moved.

The mantises who fell when the shield collapsed, also frozen, seemed to wait to take their cue from the Monarchs. If it hadn't been a life-and-death situation, Casey would have laughed at the indecision by their enemy.

A well-dressed man picked an imaginary piece of lint off his suit and stood next to the large mantis.

"You can still walk away. Denounce your God and give us Casey. It's as simple as that." The Android bartered as if negotiating points in a contract.

"Are you kidding me?" Clint sighed before sending a red pulse at the man. "Is that answer enough for you?"

The man sidestepped and issued a command. The large mantis moved first, jolting the rest of them into action.

Casey ducked as a leg swiped at the four of them. Clint distracted it with his weapon, and at the same time, Ben rolled and came up under its belly and shot a beam from his ring into the abdomen.

Its shrieks made Casey's ears ring, but she tried to ignore it and moved to avoid the first punch thrown at her, raising her hands as yellow sparks flew from her left hand and red sparks from her right. Shots were fired as she and Amanda conformed shields around each of their bodies.

"Come now. This is unnecessary." The cyborg tutted at them. "You may not be the one we can control, but this one is."

Clint senior, as Amanda called him, stepped out from behind a row of Monarchs.

Amanda took a step in his direction. "Clint?"

"This is awkward," Clint stated beside Casey.

Ben put his arm around Amanda's shoulders. "We watched that chip destroy you. How are you still here?"

"You left me alone to die, but they came for me and I had no choice but to join them. They feel I'm more important to them alive than dead so they saved me. She has corrupted all of you." Senior kept in pace with the leader, who slowly approached.

"No, I haven't. I know they hijacked your mind with that chip. Why didn't you kill me? You had so many opportunities." Casey implored him to listen. "I think you are still in there. My personal guard, my safety net. Deep down you are still in control. You can't kill me any more than you can kill yourself."

"Enough of this. Him being here is your answer to whose side he is on." The android nodded at Clint to finish the job they gave him.

A faltering step forward and he clenched his fists. Another move and his shoulders shook. She was right; he was fighting it.

Amanda covered their Clint while Casey guarded Ben, putting them in the Kevlar protection the shield offered. A white light engulfed Amanda and dropped her to the ground when she tried to run. The shield continued to shrink and threatened to constrict Amanda.

"Amanda!" Senior—chipped—Clint pulled a gun from behind his back and shot at the operator of the light, shattering it to pieces. The man behind it screamed as the internal components delivered numerous beams, hitting several Monarchs and melting their flesh from their bones.

"Don't let the light touch you!" Ben helped Amanda up as a bullet tore through his arm.

Casey flashed to the day he was shot as they buried their friend and her daughter. She couldn't heal Ben in the past, but she would save her friends today.

Senior Clint lay in tortured misery, clutching his palms to the sides of his head.

Casey spiraled the red and yellow static together in a long staff. She threw it at a line of Monarchs. It impaled several together. They landed hard and did not move again.

"Ben!" Clint tapped into his relic, sending fire that torched the ground and everything in its path.

Ben let a rolling wind out of him and corralled the flames, sending the Monarchs to the east, running for their lives.

"Concentrate on the woman. The others are collateral damage. Take them out!" The other non-human walked through the back of the enemy toward the front, kicking Clint as he passed.

"How many are there of him?" Ben fought with everything he had.

Amanda held her hands out, creating an opaque wall, and propelled it toward a line of men who were trying to work their way around to flank them.

The shield crushed them against the house.

Casey didn't see a Monarch flip a disc in the air until it was too late, and it stuck to the side of her personal shield. More shots sounded as static shorted out her armor and short-circuited her powers.

The sun dimmed.

"The eclipse will help us to be victorious today!" the next android yelled, riling up the men's spirits, so they renewed their efforts.

"And now there is an eclipse?" Ben protested; another thing hampering their victory.

Casey hardly registered Amanda's shield drop when she screamed. A large man flipped Amanda over his shoulder. She squirmed against him but was no match for his size.

"Come with us and we won't take your friends. They can stay here and live out a happy farmer life," the giant jeered and pulled out a large knife.

"I don't think so." Clint senior stalked forward from behind enemy lines, his face blanched and sweating as he struggled to aim his gun. The shot rang out, stopping several Monarchs around him.

Amanda fell from his shoulder, and he landed on her. Her yelp had Ben and Clint rip him off her and toss him to the side as if he didn't weigh anything. She sat up with her brother's help. A large slice crossed from her cheek to her hairline. Blood poured through the slash.

Casey recalled her first encounter with the different version of the chosen. They didn't know her, and their relics performed differently than now. The cut across Amanda's was face in the exact place as the other one.

She peered at the sky. The moon continued to overshadow the sun.

The Monarchs outnumbered them by at least twenty to one. They all stood with their backs to each other, so they all faced a different bunch of angry, hate-twisted faces. Fury and rage poured from them.

The leader charged at senior Clint, who never took his eyes from Casey. "You're right, I was always in here. I fought them. I'm sorry it took me so long to find my way back."

A quick swipe with his mechanical arm severed Clint's head from his body.

Amanda screamed.

A shot rang and the other Clint grunted. He stayed on his feet next to her, so she wasn't sure where they hit him. The android inspected his cuticles as he sauntered over to face Casey. He finally seemed interested enough to put his manicure second to the situation after the brutal deadly blow he just dealt to Clint senior.

"I tried to tell you. If you would have come with us, we wouldn't have to do this." He nodded and Casey twisted her neck around to look at Ben when a gun discharged.

"No!" Casey held her hands up.

The Monarchs pulled night vision eyewear from their packs.

The final phase of the eclipse plummeted the land into night although the sun rode high in the sky. She strained to make out who stood in front of her.

Unable to block the blow to her stomach, it knocked the wind from her. Amanda grunted along with Clint. She hadn't seen or heard anything from Ben since the sound of the gunshot. Casey shot her foot out and kicked someone and smirked when they yelped.

Red tentacles wrapped around her throat. It was the same weapon Clint used against her before. The ground under her feet shook.

"Ben." Casey tossed out a shield.

Small yellow orbs orbited around them, lining the inside of the dome as Ben shook from the effort to give them an advantage. Blood soaked his shirt.

Militant Monarchs advanced. The sound of their marching feet increased the terror inside her. Anticipation hung thick in the humid air. Another tremor in the soil opened a chasm, and several of the enemy tumbled into the abyss. One wrong step and her friends would plunge to their deaths.

Amanda threw the shield, knocking back five Monarchs. One reached her and flipped her up and over him. Her arm dangled limp from her side as she staggered to her feet.

Casey turned her head as far as she could while in the weapon's grip. Clint grappled on his back, holding a different man with a large knife at bay as the blade continued down into his stomach.

They couldn't fight like this. Ben shoved a couple back with another gust of wind. A fireball erupted from Clint's weapon, propelling the giant off him into a burning pile of human remains.

"Father, be our guiding light to oppose your enemies." Everything slowed down around them.

"You already have a part of Me in you the day you chose My Son and accepted Him as your personal savior into your hearts. My holy spirit living in each of you is also My light."

The symbols glimmered and flared as every one of them lit up like a Christmas tree on her arms. The Monarchs squinted. A bullet slowed to a stop in midair halfway between the barrel of the gun and Ben's forehead.

Three of them ducked and the bullet continued to travel in the same trajectory, disappearing into the trees.

Mr. Leader, perplexed at the scene that unfolded, tilted his head to the side. His circuits were unable to understand or put together how she did what she did. He started to jerk as if having a seizure, releasing her from the weapon's grip. She dropped to her hands and knees, taking in gulps of air.

Ben clutched her right hand while he grabbed Amanda's left. Amanda linked with Clint's while he finished the circle by grabbing Casey's left. They had their backs to each other, facing away from the relics and merged as one ultimate force. Pure white light flowed from the chosen.

Several Monarchs took off and ran away from their comrades, who stood against them. Some of the Monarchs didn't appreciate being deserted and shot them in the back. A good fifteen of their enemy fell without the chosen raising a hand.

She refused to take her eyes off the enemy, who stood in front of her to see what the relics were doing. A bullet slammed into her chest. She dropped and found the other three had also been hit. She sent the healing to her friends first.

It was a little awkward, but they stood and still held hands.

Casey closed her eyes as a warmth rushed over her. She opened her mouth, the words of "Amazing Grace" pouring from her in heartfelt awe and wonder what God could do for someone like her not worthy of His sacrifice and love.

Amanda joined her with Clint and Ben's deep baritone voices filling the silence.

Several more Monarchs fled and met the same fate as their fellow soldiers. The remaining, faithful to the terror they instilled in others, aimed their weapons at them. Cartridges flew through the air, ejected by the firing of the guns.

The ground shook, opening the gap wider and taking a few more with it. Amanda's eyes shone as she manipulated the ground through the elemental side of her relic.

Blood congealed at their feet while Casey healed them, and they sang.

When the smoke cleared, the Monarchs faced their enemy, who still stood firm.

The colors of the relics twisted around them and arced out, hitting several of the Monarchs, and tossing them away as if they were nothing. The shield glowed and shot out from her and Amanda, making the two combine into a thick molten wall that flew in every direction, bypassing everyone still fighting. The Monarchs' lights and weapons sputtered and flicked off.

The Monarchs tossed their guns and turned to run. Thirty feet away, they stopped and put their hands up.

"Are you seeing this?" Ben called out.

Casey looked over her shoulder, and Ben's eyes were alight with the purest light she'd ever seen. She couldn't wipe the smile from her lips.

"You mean the Monarchs' little minions with their hands in the air surrendering? Yep." Clint still hadn't released her hand.

A flash of blinding supreme light had them closing their eyes and ducking their heads to the side.

When nothing else happened, Casey peeked. Two angels of the Lord stood in front of them. They must have been the reason the Monarchs stopped. They were now all dead. The angels approached and the one on the left bowed his head in acknowledgment to her.

In awe of the power they exuded, she wanted to kneel but she had long ago decided to never kneel for anyone but her Heavenly Father.

"You never lost hope, even when you were afraid and kept getting knocked down. God the Father sent us to destroy what shouldn't have been. You are free to live your life, but know this. When the call goes out, He expects you to answer. You and your generations to come will be the keepers of the Relics. You'll be in charge of wielding great power. Don't abuse it, or we will hold you accountable for the charges God deems worthy for whatever actions need to be taken. Take heed to follow Him always and not walk in the sin of man who is of the world. Access the earth's resources and build yourselves a valley, a small paradise of Eden." They nodded at Amanda and vaporized in front of their eyes in a dazzling flash of light.

Amanda held her hands over the ground. Opaque pearl beads, the same color as the shield, dripped from her fingers and circled around them. With each added drop, the circle expanded. Soon, the chasm closed and a mile in each direction, rows and rows of mountains surged to the surface, growing higher and higher, creating a valley. A waterfall sent a mist into the sky as it crested and fell into a large lake to the west. The minuscule water drops, reflecting the sun, created a rainbow.

When they turned to take each other in and catalog the damages, they saw what the relics had created. Hovering a foot off the ground, a cross was lit with the colors of the relics.

The sun peeked out from behind the moon.

The Monarchs didn't exist. There were no signs they had ever been on the land surrounding them.

Peace wrapped around them.

With their arms around each other, they stood in front of the cross. It was a marker established by God to be a witness of the battle won today on His behalf. Mountains surrounded them on all sides, shutting out the world. A clean source of water flowed, giving them a much-needed supply to irrigate and grow their crops.

"Look." Amanda pointed to the south.

More fruit trees than she had ever seen dotted the landscape. Clint chuckled. Casey turned to see a cow and her calf padding along the gravel road.

"Talk about homesteading. This takes self-sufficient to a whole new level." Ben's smile widened.

"Is it finally over?" Casey cringed as she asked, hoping she didn't jinx it.

"It's over...for now."

Epilogue

"Mommy, I want to use the swing!" Casey smiled at her son's blue, pleading eyes—like his father's—imploring her to make his cousin shorten her time on the tire swing suspended from the large oak in the front yard.

"Matty, you need to give her the same amount of time you got. It's only fair." She couldn't believe her son was already four.

When they named their son, they decided to combine her mother's name, Maddie, and her brother's name, Matt. It had been Ben's idea, and she loved it as soon as he suggested it.

"But I don't want to wait." Her son kicked at a tuft of grass.

"You talk nice to your mom, or it will be a timeout for you, young man. You always treat her with the utmost respect." Ben wrapped his arms around her, placing his hands on her rounded belly.

"Yes, daddy." Matty wrapped his arms around her legs.

Casey, due any day now, couldn't wait to welcome the newest member of her family.

Ben and Casey didn't want to move away so while Clint and Amanda married and moved into his uncle's house, she and Ben built on the other side of the fields their own cozy little cottage.

The shield from her and Amanda reverted the world to a time before computers, internet, and satellites. Thousands of people ended their lives refusing to live in an archaic world.

The mountains protected them from the chaos. Chloe's uncle confirmed the mountains put off a weird magnetic field that erased their little paradise from the earth's surface unless you were physically there. It kept anyone from stumbling into their lives.

"Casey, how are you doing?" Amanda waddled over to her, and Casey couldn't help but laugh at the size of Amanda's stomach.

They were having twin boys. Ben's ring of truth could determine the gender of the unborn babies. Clint was over the moon, while Amanda looked miserable. Their daughter, Tilly, who still occupied the swing, would be a big sister about the same time Casey's son became a big brother.

The years had been good to them. They were contained in their private paradise and what she learned in her gardening skills, during her alone years, came in handy, and she taught Clint a thing or two. They talked about the crops to grow each year and rotated them, so they produced more.

"Love you, my Casey." Ben leaned down and kissed her cheek as Clint lifted Matty onto the tire swing with his daughter Tilly, so they sat facing each other. Their legs draped into the center of the tire held up by four lengths of chains.

Their giggles floated in the breeze.

Matty laughed as he made small yellow orbs dance around them, and Tilly sent red static coursing over the small orbs.

"Thank you, Father."

"You are welcome, my darling daughter."

Storm clouds brewed on the horizon. Casey gripped her husband's hand. He squeezed back as Clint and Amanda joined them. They were ready.

About the Author

K.A. Moore, born and raised in Kansas, is a retired 911 police dispatcher with over thirteen years of service and will be the first to tell you dispatchers are a special breed all their own. Her real passion is writing and putting her imagination into works of fiction. Faith-based Christian suspense is her preferred writing theme, with wild, crazy dreams as the backdrop to many scenes that seem to come alive in her writing. As she writes, her Chihuahua scampers for the coveted position of curling up in her lap while creating her stories.

www.ingramcontent.com/pod-product-compliance
Lightning Source LLC
La Vergne TN
LVHW040825090826
845145LV00001BA/202

9781957223155